SMALL TOWN TROUBLE

Trouble Cat Mysteries #5

LAURA BENEDICT

KaliOka Press

For Procter Benedict, a prince among cats. He left us too early but lives forever in our hearts.

CHAPTER ONE

*T*here's nothing like an overenthusiastic canine to ruin a stakeout. I have my eye on a blue sedan parked across the street from the Walsh estate where I'm visiting, but it's deuced difficult to concentrate with an obnoxious Jack Russell terrier barking up at me from the driveway. All of the other cars belonging to the guests of the massive party going on at the house behind me are parked in a nearby field, but the men who directed the parking are long gone. The dark-haired woman in the sedan is a latecomer, and she stares unmoving at the Walshes' posh house, her eyes hidden by sunglasses. With no small degree of nonchalance, I stretch across the top of the deliciously warm brick pedestal at the edge of the drive and squint down at Jocko, the offending white and tan, perky-eared creature. Who has ever heard of such an idiotic moniker? Jocko, indeed.

I know for a fact that Sherlock Holmes never had to deal with such an annoying canine—not counting that Baskerville brute, of course. Sherlock, who is my role model and personal hero, made good use of an intelligent chap named Toby that was half-spaniel, but these Jack Russell types are thoroughly mad. They dash about the countryside *yapping constantly, chasing down rodents (an occupation much more suited to accomplished cats such as I), and bothering horses.*

I warn Jocko to calm down with a low growl. In return he whines and pants and waggles that ridiculous curled tail. What a hopeless wretch he is.

At home in Wetumpka, Alabama, my human, Tammy Lynn, would never have such a beast hanging about. But she and I came to western Kentucky to visit Erin Walsh, whose late mother was Tammy's childhood babysitter. Unfortunately Tammy was called to Milan, Italy, to authenticate a priceless book that some monks found in their library. The Italian antiquities bureaucracy would only make it available for a few days, and she had to leave me behind with Erin.

It's true. I don't sound like I'm from Alabama. I spent much of the first of my nine lives studying that excellent Cumberbatch actor's Sherlock Holmes films, and acquired a bit of an English accent. Of course only other cats like my brilliant detective father, Familiar, can hear it. But I have no problem motivating the humans around me when I engage in traditional feline vocalizations.

The woman in the car is staying put. I consider popping across the street or chasing the hapless Jocko her way to get some movement from her—angry-looking people who stare at houses usually mean danger— but the foolish dog would no doubt be run over by a passing tractor or pickup truck. One somehow feels responsible for the Jockos of the world.

Instead I leap onto the impeccably paved driveway, inches from Jocko's head, making him jump back a mile. Anyone who says cats can't smile has never seen me after I've played a clever trick.

The party has been in full swing since my third nap of the day. Most of the guests—employees and their families from Bruce Walsh's (Erin's father) car dealership—are swimming or fishing or careening about on noisy Jet Skis on the Cedar Grove Lake cove that meets the Walsh property. The Walshes have even set up a few picturesque changing cabanas near the property's strip of manmade beach. The less adventurous guests are in the swimming pool or eating. But I've done the rounds back there and want to avoid further contact with the youngsters and their sticky hands, so I enter through the carelessly open front door with Jocko panting behind me.

Hearing angry voices I continue to the library door, which is open a few inches, and slip neatly inside. Hapless Jocko, who doesn't seem to understand that he could push the door open a bit further to enter as well, sits down in the hall and whimpers pathetically. But Jocko's not my concern right now.

Erin, a sweet, strawberry blonde co-ed who's home for the summer from the University of Kentucky, leans forward, her hands balled into fists at her side. Her face is pink beneath her freckles, a sign that she's angry and frustrated. I've seen that look on Tammy Lynn's face a time or two. But when I see the other woman, who wears a canny, unpleasant grin, I understand why Erin is frustrated. The woman is her stepmother, Shelby Rae, who's only a dozen years older than Erin. Shelby Rae is also Jocko's human, and believes it's her job to meddle in Erin's business.

Neither of them glance at me as I stroll to one of the many tall windows overlooking the front garden and settle on the back of an enormous couch with stripes like a cafe awning. From there I can find out what's wrong between Erin and Shelby Rae and observe the car out front. What does the woman in the car want? Is she dangerous? I intend to find out.

"WHAT IN THE world were you thinking, child? Your daddy's going to be so upset. You know we think tattoos are trashy on women."

If she hadn't been so angry, Erin Walsh would've laughed out loud at her stepmother. Shelby Rae, with her bottom-grazing miniskirts and heavy makeup, had the market cornered on trashy. Her family wasn't much better and seemed to have no visible means of support aside from the *little helper checks* (Shelby Rae's words) Erin knew she'd been writing for years. But it was her condescending *child* that made Erin want to wipe the Corral Me Coral lipstick off Shelby Rae's collagen-injected lips. She didn't believe in the stereotype of an Irish temper, but she could swear she felt the anger in her bones.

"I'm not your *child,* Shelby Rae, and I won't be talked to that way by you or anybody else. Daddy has asked you, and I've told you a thousand times, to stay out of my business."

Seven years ago, just after Erin's mother died, Shelby Rae, who worked as the receptionist at the dealership, had taken Erin under her twenty-something wing and become like a big sister to her. They went shopping together in Louisville, and traveled down to Nashville to see a Taylor Swift concert. They did cosmic bowling and Shelby Rae even helped her buy a bra that was more substantial than her training bra. It was Shelby Rae who drove her to the drugstore to pick out sanitary pads after Erin called her whispering, "Shelby Rae, I *started.*"

But two years later, Erin's father asked her to come into the library—the very room in which they now stood—and with a beaming Shelby Rae at his side said, "We have wonderful news to tell you, honey."

If only her father had instead taken her out alone on a walk on the lake trail, or driven her in the boat to dinner at *The Captain's Table* on the other side of the lake to tell her. Or he could've asked her how she felt about Shelby Rae and if she thought it was a good idea for him to marry her. She might have understood. She might even have been glad to have her suspicions confirmed. She wasn't blind or stupid. Her father sometimes stayed out late, and he and Shelby Rae shared *significant* looks when she came to pick up Erin. If only...

That's not what happened, though, and here they were.

"Oh, come on. Did you forget you have a tattoo on your backside?" Erin pointed at Shelby Rae's ample left hip. "You have a *snake* back there. What kind of person has a snake on their butt?"

Shelby Rae pursed her lips and stuck her recently-altered nose in the air. "It's an asp. Like Cleopatra. And it's gold and blue. It's *art*."

Erin scowled. "I'm nineteen. It's perfectly legal if I want to tattoo my whole face." She pointed to her lightly freckled forehead. "I could get a freaking butterfly parade all across here."

In fact she'd completely forgotten about the new tattoo when she'd taken her shorts off by the pool. Seeing the tattoo, Shelby Rae had pulled Erin away from her best friend, MacKenzie Clay, and hurried her all the way into the library. Erin only just now wondered why Shelby Rae had been watching her in the first place.

"You're being silly." Shelby Rae shook her head. "Only criminals have tattoos on their faces."

"Oh, so I guess it would be okay if your Uncle Travis, who's out back drinking Daddy's beer and about to eat the biggest steak from the outdoor fridge, gets a tattoo on *his* face?"

Shelby Rae crossed her arms across her breasts. Erin knew she hadn't had to have *those* fixed like she'd had her nose done. She'd once overheard one of the salesmen at the dealership comment on Shelby Rae's *enormous assets*.

"Why are you so hateful, Erin? I've never done one single thing except be nice to you. This is a *very* stressful time, with the lawsuit just over with. You haven't been here. You don't know what it's been like. That woman from the lawsuit has been hanging around, and I've hardly even seen your father for months." Her high voice stretched into a familiar whine.

The lawsuit. Erin's father had brushed it off whenever she called him from Lexington. A woman named Tionna Owens was killed when her car's brakes failed just minutes after she'd left the dealership's service department. She'd dropped in to ask them to take a quick look at the brakes because she thought there was something wrong. According to Earl Potts, the service manager, he'd told her they were very busy and she could make an appointment for another day. He said she'd grown angry and declared she would take her business elsewhere. The county didn't find grounds to prosecute, but her family brought a civil suit against the dealership declaring that they it had a record of the car's brake problems and a duty of care to examine it immediately. But the case had been dismissed.

"He doesn't even listen to me," Shelby Rae continued. "Nobody listens to me!"

"That's because you're a drama queen. Nobody needs your drama, and I'm sick and tired of it. Stay out of my business." Erin knew she was being as dramatic as Shelby Rae, but she was beginning to wish she had kept her apartment in Lexington and had picked up a part-time job there for the summer, or just volunteered at a rescue shelter. Bumming around New Belford and hanging around the house—even if she was often with MacKenzie—was turning out to be a bad idea.

Shelby Rae huffed out of the library. When she pushed open the door Jocko barked up at her with frantic joy. Erin saw the startled faces of two women she didn't recognize over Shelby Rae's shoulder. Great. Now everyone would know they'd been arguing. How long would it be before her father was asking her why Shelby Rae was so upset?

Erin walked over to the window. The library had always been one of her favorite rooms. She put a hand on the end of the high-backed sofa and Trouble, the clever black cat Tammy Lynn had asked her to look after, nudged her hand with his velvety nose.

"Sorry about that," she said, scratching the cat behind the ears. "I don't really hate her. She just gets to me sometimes."

The cat purred. Tammy Lynn had told her that Trouble was good at solving mysteries and had saved her more than once.

"Don't worry. I can't promise you any mysteries, but we'll find something to do that gets us away from here."

Erin gazed out the window as she stroked the soft fur on Trouble's back. She could see a blue sedan parked across the road with a woman inside who appeared to be staring the house. A shiver went up Erin's spine. She knew the woman: she was Bryn Owens , Tionna Owens' wife.

Bryn and Tionna Owens had owned New Belford's Two Hearts bakery together; and while Erin and MacKenzie were in high school, they often met there for coffee. Tionna had a special fondness for MacKenzie who, like Tionna, had a mother who was black and a father who was white. Erin's eyes were opened wide when Tionna told them about times in the city when she and her parents were ignored in restaurants or cursed at on the street. Erin knew there were a few people in and around New Belford who felt the same way, but she never thought of it as affecting MacKenzie. To Erin, MacKenzie had always been just MacKenzie, her best friend since kinder-garten, and MacKenzie's parents were Mr. and Mrs. Clay. Now, she knew better.

After Tionna died in the wreck, Bryn put a *closed* sign in the bakery window. The sign was still there. Erin was familiar with grief. The pain in her gut had lessened considerably in the seven years since her mother had been killed, but it never really went away.

Trouble snapped to attention, slipping from beneath her hand to stand on his back legs and put his front paws against the window. The cat never missed a thing.

A rumbling motorcycle pulled up behind Bryn's sedan and stopped. Erin wondered if this was someone she was supposed to know.

A guy wearing blue jeans and a slim black T-shirt whose sleeves took on the taut muscular shape of his upper arms and shoulders, put down the motorcycle's kickstand and took off his helmet. When he pushed his sun-streaked brown hair from his face, she recognized his profile. His look was different—a little more relaxed and, frankly, sexier—than she remembered.

Noah Daly had been two years ahead of her in school, and he'd been a loner. A bit geeky, but still a loner. A lot of girls thought he was cute, but their mothers made sure they didn't get too close because Noah's father, Jeb Daly, was known to be bad news. When Noah was about to enter high school, Jeb did the unthinkable—he used a gun to rob the New Belford branch of the Kentucky Patriot Bank.

At the time of the robbery, Erin's mother, Rita, was in the building to drop off a dozen of her special mocha and cranberry cupcakes as a birthday surprise for a friend. But it wasn't Jeb Daly who killed Rita. Zach Wilkins, the deputy who responded to the silent alarm, shot her accidentally.

A few years later Erin's father hired Noah Daly to work in the dealership's service department. What had he been thinking? And what was Noah Daly doing talking to Bryn Owens?

· · ·

"HERE, MOM." Noah handed his mother, Annette, an insulated tumbler of sweet iced tea. She took the tea and smiled up at him from her chair at one of the umbrella tables by the pool. Only eighteen when he was born, she was younger than the mothers of most of the guys he knew, but her beauty had faded quickly. She'd long ago started dyeing her auburn hair to hide the gray that showed up before she turned thirty. And because she worked long hours managing a big convenience store near the interstate, she didn't get much exercise, and so carried a little extra weight. But the thing Noah noticed most about her was that her eyes didn't sparkle as they had seemed to when he was little. Still, unlike most guys he knew, he'd never once been ashamed to be seen with his own mother.

"Why aren't you out on the lake, honey? The Jet Skis look like so much fun. Didn't you bring swim trunks?"

Noah glanced around him. The women near the pool wore sundresses or shorts or bathing suits, and the kids were either in the pool, or dripping water as they played close by. Most of the men he worked with were in swim trunks and T-shirts in or near the lake. All of their girlfriends wore bikinis.

"Not going in the water today, Mom. Not in the mood. I just didn't want you to stay at the house today."

She leaned close to him, whispering. "*You* have nothing to be ashamed of, Noah."

"I don't want to talk about it, okay? We're here, and that's what's important."

A tall man wearing relaxed khaki shorts and a comfortably faded polo shirt ducked his head beneath the umbrella and laid one of his large hands on Annette's shoulder. The hair at his temples was gray, but the rest was what Noah had heard his mother call strawberry blond. With his friendly green eyes,

Bruce Walsh always looked like he was about to share good news.

"So glad you could make it, Annette. I told Noah I hoped he'd bring you to the party this year." He nodded to Noah. "Even if young Noah here decides to bring along a sweetheart, you're always welcome to come, too."

"Mr. Walsh—"

He didn't let her finish. "Please, Annette. Call me Bruce, and don't get up. We get to be the grownups here, right?"

"It's a wonderful party," she said, settling back down in her chair. "Look at all these fancy decorations! Even these pretty tumblers are red, white, and blue. I'm so happy all these children are having a good time." As they watched, a small girl shrieked with delight as she started down the pool slide, her arms waving above her head. When she splashed into the water, then quickly popped to the surface, even Bruce laughed.

"Shelby Rae and I feel a deep sense of gratitude to the people who make Walsh Motors successful. It's a family, and I like to take care of that family." He held out a freshly-opened bottle of Budweiser to Noah. "Something cold? Hot day to be out on that Yamaha of yours. You know, the invitation is still open for you and the boys in the department to fish off our docks any time."

"Thanks, Mr. Walsh." Noah took the beer with a nod. "I've come out here early a few mornings this spring and summer. But I park over on the access road and fish off the far dock so I don't disturb you all. The yellow perch and bass are running big this year."

"Oh, that bass," his mother said. "That's something special."

Bruce agreed.

To Noah, the most impressive thing about Bruce Walsh

was his sincerity. Sometimes he sounded like a politician, but Noah knew that Bruce always kept his word. When he hired Noah on, he said he didn't expect any more or any less from him than any other employee, but that it would be a great favor to him if Noah would keep his father, Jeb, from coming around after he got out of prison. Keeping the man who was ultimately responsible for his boss's first wife's death away from his place of business was a promise Noah had been happy to make. Especially because *he* didn't want to have anything to do with his loser father either. He was glad Bruce didn't know that promise might soon be tested.

Shelby Rae, who had married Bruce long before Noah started at the dealership, was more of a mystery. When she visited, she certainly didn't hang around the service department. A few of the guys called her a *gold digger* and others referred to her as a *nice piece of ass*. Right now she was a dozen feet away, among a tight group of men surrounding Junior, the hired cook. The men were all older and a couple of them were checking out the plunging neckline of Shelby Rae's short white sundress as though they wanted to fall in. One of the less obvious guys put a hand on her back, and she whipped her head around so that her long, curled ponytail nearly hit the man on the other side of her.

"Quit it, Uncle Travis!"

Noah smiled. The guy deserved it, but he merely chuckled and pushed his thin black hair away from his forehead, unfazed.

A couple of the other men, including Earl Potts, the service manager, dropped back, embarrassed. It could have been one of them instead of the intrepid Travis. He was her uncle? Talk about awkward.

Bruce and his mother were still talking. Noah wasn't sure

what he'd missed, but the conversation had turned back to the expensive tumblers used for the party's drinks.

"Shelby Rae went a little crazy on making sure everything matched. I think she planned on about a thousand guests instead of a hundred and fifty. Everyone gets to take one home, but let's get you a couple extra boxes, too."

Noah's mother laughed. "Oh, I couldn't let you do that. They're so expensive. I'm sure your wife will want to return the rest." But Noah could tell from the way she was looking at the tumbler on the table that the idea excited her. They had so few nice things at home. She insisted that Noah put half his paycheck in the bank "for college, maybe, or a house of your own someday." He hated that she worked so hard but couldn't afford nicer things, even if they were just thick plastic drink glasses.

"You'd be doing me a favor." Bruce gave her a wide smile, and his eyes were kind.

She blushed.

"Erin, honey?" Bruce called to his daughter, who was sitting beside MacKenzie Clay at the opposite side of the pool. "Can I get you to come here for a minute?"

Erin Walsh said something Noah couldn't hear to MacKenzie, who had been in an economics class with him senior year. Then she gave her father a small smile and lifted her long legs from the pool to stand. She removed her reflective gold aviators from the top of her head and put them on so that her strawberry blond hair swung free. Unlike her stepmother, she was dressed down, wearing cream-colored shorts that rested softly on her narrow hips. Her purple Allman Brothers Band T-shirt was tied into a knot, revealing a triangle of pale, flat stomach. The glimpse of her skin put a different kind of knot in Noah's stomach, and he glanced away.

He and Erin had never been friends, but they were always aware of each other. Neither of them had been allowed to attend his father's trial because they were too young. He saw more of her when she started at the consolidated high school as a quiet freshman. People referred to her as "Erin Walsh, that girl whose mother got killed." But Noah thought of her as something more: the girl whose life his father had ruined. It didn't matter that Jeb Daly had been bluffing with an empty gun during the robbery, and that it was Deputy Zachary Wilkins who actually shot Rita Walsh. His father was still responsible.

It wasn't until last Christmas that Noah started to think of her in a much different way. She'd come into the dealership with Shelby Rae to be surprised with a spanking new Challenger that her father had bought her for Christmas. Its 700 horsepower engine only had 42 miles on it, but Noah had put twelve miles more on it himself after Earl told him to take it out to make sure it ran perfectly before Erin arrived. The sleek black car was a beauty, with sports suspension and paddle shifters on the wheel that meant the driver could switch to manual without even touching the stick.

Driving that car on the highway and on a couple of backroads he knew well had been among the sweetest fifteen minutes of Noah's life up to that point.

But the day only improved when Bruce Walsh later called back to the department to ask that the car be brought around. Almost everyone was gone for the day, so Noah started the Challenger with the special red fob that engaged the full 700 horsepower (instead of the black fob that gave you only 500), and drove it around to the front of the dealership.

Erin stood on the sidewalk, her hair tucked into a knitted cashmere beret, her mittened hands covering her eyes like a little kid. Her father's arm was around her shoulders. When she uncovered her eyes, Noah saw a look of pure delight. She turned and hugged her father. When she finally pulled away, a lock of her hair fell from her beret and brushed her lightly freckled cheek. It was in that moment Noah knew, given half a chance, he could fall in love with her.

CHAPTER TWO

*a*s Erin sorted through boxes looking for an unopened package of tumblers, she was aware of Trouble watching from a nearby counter. Trouble wasn't the only one watching. Noah Daly stood in the doorway, his hands in the front pockets of his jeans. To tell the truth, he looked a little embarrassed, and she felt kind of bad for him. Her father was always giving away things. Once he'd given away a Renoir lithograph of a little girl to her cousin, Janine, because every time she came to the house she would stand in front of it, twirling her hair trying to look like the girl.

"It's really nice of your dad," Noah said.

His voice was deeper than Erin remembered. A lot about him was different, and it made her a bit uncomfortable. Ever since she could remember she'd thought of him as someone she should hold a grudge against, even though she wasn't usually the sort of person to hold grudges. But she should be entitled to this one, right?

She shrugged. "He likes to gift people things. Drives Shelby Rae nuts."

"My mom loves decorating for holidays. You should see our house on the Fourth of July. She's already got that bunting stuff all over the front porch and flags all over the flowerpots. She'll probably invite our next door neighbor over just so she can use the glasses."

Erin smiled. Her mother had loved to decorate, too. There were still boxes and boxes from every holiday from Easter to Christmas and Valentine's Day up in the attic. Shelby Rae used a big florist from Louisville for special occasions instead of putting up decorations herself. They were okay, but they were taken down after every holiday, and then replaced with different ones the next year. Erin swore that she would have a home of her own and use her mother's decorations, so she could have her memories back.

"Hey, look out!" she said.

Without warning, Trouble had leapt from one counter to the one nearest Noah, and knocked his beer over. The foaming liquid streamed onto the floor, and Noah and Erin froze, staring at the mess. Trouble sat licking his paw as though nothing had happened.

"Let me," Noah said. "Paper towels?" He looked flustered, as though the spill had been his fault and not the cat's.

Erin handed him a dishtowel and she grabbed the roll of paper towels. "Um, the bottle? Could you set it up so it doesn't spill anymore?"

Red-faced, Noah righted the bottle, though it was nearly empty.

They set to work together. As they wiped up the mess, Noah's T-shirt sleeves rode up his biceps, exposing colorful tattoo work. Unthinking, she touched the edge of one sleeve, lifting it the slightest. Noah startled and tipped back.

"Oh, God. I'm sorry," Erin said. "I don't know why I did that. How embarrassing."

Now a leg of Noah's jeans was wet as well. She was surprised when the corners of his mouth lifted with amusement. "I guess you skipped that part of the high school handbook that said it's not okay to touch somebody unless you get their permission first."

"Seriously, I'm sorry." Erin quickly pulled another length of paper towels off the roll and pushed them at him. "Maybe this will help. You know, he's not even my cat. He's just visiting, and he's not usually so obnoxious." She gave Trouble an irritated look, but he was busily grooming his ears, ignoring her.

"Hey, it's really no problem, Erin. Really." Noah pressed the paper towels against his jeans as she finished sopping up the floor. His smile was a little crooked, but it only made him more real, more interesting.

She was about to ask him more about the tattoos, but shadows appeared in the doorway, drawing her attention.

"What happened here?" Erin looked up to see her father and Sheriff Bowen, side by side. Sheriff Abel Bowen had been a friend of the Walsh family since long before she was born.

"We had a little spill," she said.

Noah scrambled to his feet.

"Bruce, remember that time out at your folks' cabin when somebody decided it would be fun to flood the floor with beer and dance in it?" Sheriff Bowen's face had been serious when he entered the house, but now he smiled.

"I do," her father said. But he was distracted, unsmiling. "I believe that *somebody* was you, Abel. Wasn't it?" He touched Erin on the shoulder as he walked past her. "Let's get this over with."

Erin didn't like the look on her father's face. "Something's wrong, Dad. What is it?"

"We'll be back in a few minutes," he said over his shoulder as several others entered the room.

"What's going on?" There was panic in Erin's voice. Trouble rubbed his head against her arm, but she barely noticed.

"Oh, Erin! That woman was watching the house again." Julie Berry, who'd been her mother's best friend, stood close to Erin, looking as though she were about to cry. Her deeply-tanned face was freckled like Erin's, but it was mostly from years of playing tennis and gardening. Her blond hair was that silver-ashy shade preferred by country club matrons, and her only makeup was coral lipstick that was oddly similar to Shelby Rae's. Her bright blue eyes and athletic arms and legs were her best features. Erin loved Julie out of habit. Although they no longer spent much time together, Julie still called her occasionally and made a fuss over her on her birthday. Until Erin graduated high school, they drove down to Memphis for an overnight at the Peabody every year to see the ducks and play tourist.

"I thought that was Bryn Owens out there," Erin said. "She just sits there, staring. It's creepy, but she hasn't come to the house or anything."

"You saw her out there? How can you not worry?" Julie touched Erin's arm. "Sometimes you're just too trusting, sweetie. What about the notes? I heard your father and the sheriff talking about some notes she left on your cars. Chief Deputy Wilkins chased her off. I think he was keeping an eye out and when he saw her he called to alert the sheriff. I don't know why your poor father's even going out there now. There's nothing to see."

Erin glanced at Noah. Was he going to say anything about talking to Bryn? He looked past Erin as though he were trying to see beyond her father and the sheriff. Then his eyes came back to hers. No guilt. Maybe just mild curiosity. She remembered who his father was. Remembered that she probably shouldn't trust him.

"What did you say about notes?" Erin asked. "I don't know what you mean, Julie."

"You didn't know? They were on the windshields of your father's and Shelby Rae's cars."

"What did they say?"

"Were they threatening?" Noah was interested now.

Of course he's interested now. Is he involved with Bryn?

Julie shook her head. "I can't know everything. You know how I detest gossip. I just thought you already knew. I love you like you're my own daughter, honey."

She enveloped Erin in a tight hug, and Erin could smell her lemony verbena scent, which she always wore in summer. The hug was unnecessary, yet comforting. Erin closed her eyes.

Just a few minutes earlier she had been having thoughts about getting close to Noah. Now she knew her whole family might be in danger. She opened her eyes to see Noah scratching an appreciative Trouble behind the ear as he watched her. Maybe there was danger there, too.

NOAH HELD his mother's elbow as he walked her to her car in the field adjoining the Walshes' manicured front yard. She wasn't old or the least bit infirm, but still she leaned on him a little. He wasn't sure if she was feeling unsteady on the uneven pasture, or simply reluctant to go home. Above them, a pink and purple sunset bled slowly through the sky. He was concerned about his mother, but he half-wished he were sitting on one of the Walshes' docks watching the sunset with Erin next to him. After the scene with that witch Julie Berry in the kitchen, Erin had avoided him, and he wasn't sure why.

"Or I could just get on a unicorn and fly home. Doesn't look like it's going to rain fairy dust anytime soon."

"Sorry, Mom. What?" Noah realized he had no idea his mother had been speaking. "Here, be careful." He guided her around a mud-filled depression.

She pushed him away playfully. "What's got you bothered, honey? Bruce Walsh's pretty daughter, or Bruce Walsh himself? He's a little condescending, but he's a good man. He's older, of course. Must be forty-nine or fifty. Your..." She didn't finish, but Noah knew she almost said, "your father's age."

They were both quiet for a moment.

"Do you want me to follow you home?" Noah was grateful she didn't bring up Erin again.

"Stay for the fireworks. You love fireworks, and I have to get up early. It's been a long week, and tomorrow I've got an early shift." They stopped at her small Toyota. "I've really appreciated you being home as much as you have. It's been a big adjustment, but we're doing okay, aren't we?"

"What is it Grandma used to say?" Noah rolled his eyes. "Everything's peaches and cream."

"Ha! Maybe it *is* the girl then. At least she's taken your mind off other things."

"Goodnight, Mom." He handed her the box containing the tumblers, then leaned down to kiss her cheek. "Text me when you get inside the house. I'll head home after the fireworks."

Why the hell am I going back to the party? There's nothing for me there.

As usual, his mother seemed to read his mind. "There's

nobody who's too good for you, Noah. It doesn't matter who your father is. You did *nothing*. You hear me? We don't have to apologize for him. Not ever."

His old anger at his father surfaced. "How many times did you tell me you were going to divorce him? Now you're acting like you've changed your mind. Which is it? I don't understand."

"Let's not go through this again. Not here." She pointed to a family walking across the field of parked cars, the father carrying a sleeping child. "We had such a nice day. Please don't spoil it."

"I'm not a kid. Don't talk to me that way."

"You need to stop making my life hard over this." His mother's voice dropped to a whisper. "Don't carry your anger onto that motorcycle. I don't want anything to happen to you."

Noah was pissed off, and he turned to go back to the party, the discussion unfinished. As he walked away, he hunched his shoulders. Sooner or later he would have to go home, and his father would be there, and there was nothing he could do about it. He kept his eyes mostly on the ground and gave only a terse nod to the approaching family. The woman worked part-time in the dealership's inventory department, and she offered Noah a faint smile. But the man carrying the child gave Noah a warning look.

Great. Just what I need. Everyone thinking, "That's Jeb Daly's son. Stay out of his way."

Back at the party he grabbed a beer and took it out to the far dock, which was empty of people. Over the next twenty minutes, the emerging stars and deepening sky worked their magic and he relaxed. As the dock filled with his co-workers come to get a better look at the fireworks that were about to be set off from the lake's swimming platform, he looked among them for Erin. He thought about leaving, but there was no guarantee he'd even see her again this summer. The thought made him feel oddly lonely. Besides, he knew what was waiting for him at home, and he wasn't in any rush to get there. She didn't show up on the dock.

BY TEN O'CLOCK all the families had gathered up their beach towels and swim goggles and toys and loaded them into their cars with their tired children to go home. Only the singles and a few couples remained. The caterers had also gone, but left the outdoor kitchen island set with cookies and brownies and lemon bars, along with pitchers of iced coffee and bottles of flavoring syrup. At Bruce's urging someone had lighted a small bonfire on a sandy bank overlooking the lake. The fire was small enough that it wasn't too hot for the temperate evening, and Noah sat near it on a low camp chair, drinking coffee and talking to Saul, who detailed the cars to ready them for delivery. A faint aroma of gunpowder drifted in from the lake.

Noah looked up at the starry sky. "Man, I could fall asleep right here, listening to the water lap, and the owls talking."

"Tell me about it." Saul took a swig of beer. "Fiancée's out of town. Another brew and I'd rack for sure."

Noah put his head back, but something landed on his lap, and he sat straight up. The black cat—what was his name? Bubbles? No, *Trouble*—swished his tail along the underside of Noah's chin.

Saul laughed. "Probably a barn cat or something. Just pitch it down."

Noah knew Trouble wasn't a barn cat. Barn cats didn't jump in your lap and start rubbing against you like you were their new best friend. At least he didn't have to worry about fleas. Trouble was sleek and well-groomed.

"Dude, what are you doing outside? The coyotes would hunt you down for fun." Noah scratched Trouble behind the ears.

"Friend of yours?" Saul gave Noah a curious look.

"He's probably not supposed to be out. I think Erin—" Noah stopped at the sound of Erin's name, surprising himself. "The Walshes are cat sitting him or something."

"Keep 'em outside with a bowl of food, is what my family always did. If they wanted to eat, they either caught mice or fought to keep the raccoons off the porch."

Holding the placid cat in one arm, Noah walked down the bank toward the house. There were still plenty of lights on inside, but he couldn't see anyone. How late was it, anyway? He would go home as soon as he put Trouble inside. But when he touched the door handle, the door suddenly opened and he was face to face with a startled Erin. Now she wore a loose V-neck sweater that almost covered the legs of her shorts. Her hair was pulled back, too, in a low ponytail. She looked good.

He held out Trouble to her. "He was out by the bonfire. I thought maybe he needed to come in since he's not from around here. Coyotes and stuff?"

Erin took the cat but didn't seem exactly engaged.

"Is something wrong?" Noah asked.

Erin shook her head. "I don't think so. It's just that Dad can't find Shelby Rae, and he's kind of freaking out. She does this all the time, goes out and grabs a drink in town with a girl-friend. But she's not answering her phone and her car's here."

"I could help you look for her."

The Jack Russell terrier Noah had seen earlier, once in

Shelby Rae's arms, scrabbled at Erin's feet, desperate to get outside.

"Jocko, get back. Now!"

The dog kept trying, so she pushed him back gently with one foot until he finally got the message.

Erin smiled. "Sorry. Listen, you're so nice. But that's Shelby Rae. She loooooooves to be unpredictable. She'll turn up. Thanks for bringing Trouble back. Bye."

Noah told her, "Good night." Then she closed the door.

He watched her through the glass as she walked through the kitchen, and dropped the cat gently to the floor. The little dog hurried ahead of them both.

He'd wanted to ask, "When can I see you again?" Except the words hadn't come.

CHAPTER THREE

*H*umans can be so stubborn. You'd have to be a brainless pet like Jocko not to have noticed the attraction between Erin and that Noah Daly. I picked up on it as she observed him from the window talking to that bothersome woman in the blue car. At least I've learned who the watcher is now. I was alert to Erin's hesitation and mixed emotions. Before we left Wetumpka, Tammy Lynn told a close friend about Rita Walsh's death and the role Noah's father played in it. But as soon as I met Noah, I knew he was a decent chap and that he was perfect for Erin. He's smitten with her, too.

Have I mentioned yet that matchmaking is another of my prodigious skills? These two are proving to be on the difficult side. Erin and her father are worried about Jocko's human, Shelby Rae, and I knew that Noah would be just the person to help her calm down and focus on making sure all is well in that quarter. Believe me, it was not a proud moment when I threw myself in that young man's lap. The lengths I must go to in order to point out the obvious to these humans are *absurd*. The fact that Erin practically shut the door in his face after delivering me was mortifying. I take some solace in knowing that perhaps the stress of the situation is clouding her judgment.

. . .

NIGHTTIME IS MY TIME. *When Erin tells her father she's going to turn on all the outside lights and take a lantern with her to see if Shelby Rae is still on the property, he says he'll be out to help look after making a couple more calls. Erin gives me a questioning look.* "Do you want to help, Trouble? Don't run off, okay?"

I jump off the table and follow Erin and Jocko into the empty backyard.

Jocko runs aimlessly around like the fool that he is. Jack Russells aren't exactly tracking hounds, though they are respectably good at finding vermin. (Not that I'm implying that the vivacious Shelby Rae is vermin, mind you)

Erin and I go head toward the lake. The fishing is quite respectable here, and even though I'm not all that fond of water, I caught some nice little minnow snacks before Tammy left. Tasty, but they would have been super in a butter cream sauce. But now is not the time for snacks. Erin is worried, and I can't help but remember how upset everyone was about the woman watching the house.

Shelby Rae's scent is everywhere on the beach. She spent the morning supervising the caterers and the people setting up the charming striped beach cabanas. Her shoes were most inappropriate, with short heels that sank into the sand and dirt. She directed everyone with one hand because in her other she carried her ever-present tumbler of half lemonade and half sweet tea.

I peek beneath the overturned canoes and the pile of inflated inner tubes. No one is under either of the docks, though there is a shocking amount of debris. I'm appalled that guests would be so uncivilized.

The cabanas are more interesting. There's nothing of note in the first one except a pair of child's swim goggles that look small enough to fit the irrepressible Jocko. But Shelby Rae's scent is strongest in the second cabana. The cord that's supposed to be stretched across the inside for hanging things dangles to one side. There's a scarf, too, that I recognize. Shelby Rae is very fond of scarves, and the last time I saw her she was wearing this one in her hair. But more telling is the heeled sandal and the half-filled tumbler partially buried in the sand. The lid is askew and I can smell lemons, but something stronger too. Gin, perhaps? Shelby Rae was definitely here. But is this the last place she was before she disappeared? Had she gone for a late swim?

Even more interesting is the long slit in the canvas at the back of the tent.

I have to let Erin know what I found.

No sooner do I start to leave the cabana than I hear Jocko's sad whimper outside the tent's flap door. He hasn't figured out how to get inside, and after a moment, his black proboscis is right there in front of me, underneath the canvas, looking like some unpleasant, wet bug.

I know it's a defect in my nature, but I can't help myself. Quicker than a flash, I extend one claw and give his snout a quick swipe. Not a serious swipe, really.

Jocko's yelps produce the desired effect. A few moments later, Erin comes running to see what the disturbance is about. Jocko isn't so useless to me after all. I emerge, a silent wraith, from between the cabana's flaps. Erin shines the blinding flashlight on me, and I slip back inside so she'll follow.

"What's this?" The flashlight's silver glow fills the interior of the cabana.

She picks up the tumbler gingerly with two fingers, then drops it again and takes a small step back. I'm glad she realizes it might be evidence. In case she hasn't seen it, I raise up and push the slit at the back with my front paws. She sweeps the light over the slit, the shoe, and the scarf, as well. Her breath quickens, and I can tell she's in distress. To comfort her, I come back and rub against her leg to let her know everything will be all right. In return I receive an absent-minded stroke down my back.

"This doesn't look good. We have to tell Dad."

WITH TROUBLE and Jocko following behind, Erin went back up to the house to find her father. She wasn't sure what to think about Shelby Rae's things she'd found in the cabana. It didn't seem out of the question that Shelby Rae had simply forgotten her scarf and shoe there, but Erin didn't remember seeing her in either the lake or the pool. Shelby Rae didn't like swimming in the lake and was terrified of the Jet Skis. Since she and Bruce had gotten married, she'd only been out on the lake in a boat a few times that Erin could remember. That was just fine with Erin. Both she and her father loved to go fishing together, and he would often take her out in the cabin cruiser with MacKenzie and some other friends if she asked. When Shelby Rae was around, she made sure everything was about Shelby Rae. That's why Erin had been surprised to hear in the middle of their argument that she was unhappy, and that her father wasn't spending more of his free time with her.

It was true that he wasn't around much. If he wasn't at the dealership, he was golfing or involved in some civic project. Could it be that he had also finally tired of Shelby Rae's neediness, her childishness?

When Erin discovered him a few minutes later in his office, his face drained of color, she knew that wasn't the case.

A piece of creased paper lay open on the desk in front of him. Her strong, determined father looked as though he might faint.

Erin rushed to his side. "Dad! What's wrong? What is it?"

As he picked the paper up to hand it to her, a ring clattered onto the desk. Shelby Rae's diamond and platinum wedding band. Erin took the note and read.

We got your pretty wife. If you call police we will know and she will die. She is safe for now. Put 50 thousand dollars cash in a bag and leave it on the blue drum in the barn on the old Stratton Farm. Don't bring anyone with you. If its not there before noon tomorrow you will get your wife back dead.

"Is this some kind of joke?" Erin looked at her father's stunned face. He shook his head slowly.

She laid the paper on the desk. "Who would do this? We have to call the sheriff, Daddy. Right away. They can't have gotten too far." But talking to her father was like talking to a statue. He stared, watching her face as though hoping she didn't see the same threatening words on the page that he'd just read. Leaning over the desk, she studied the crude, carefully worded statement. Ransom notes only showed up in movies and books, yet here was one right in front of her. And it was talking about Shelby Rae. A dead Shelby Rae.

The wedding band glittered in the lamplight. It was puzzling that the kidnappers had sent it instead of an earring or shoe or piece of clothing or lock of Shelby Rae's hair. The ring was easily worth a few thousand dollars—not a fifth of what Shelby Rae's flawless two-carat diamond was worth, but plenty. Would they really kill her if they didn't get the money?

"Even if you pay them, you don't know that they'll bring her back. We can't handle this on our own."

"Why would someone take her and not me? I don't get it."

"We'll get her back, but we need help. The police might already have an idea of who would do such a thing."

"It could be anybody," her father said. "Someone who has a grudge against me. Or against Shelby Rae." His handsome face was rueful as he looked at Erin. She knew she wasn't going to like what he was about to say. "I know you two have your differences, but she really does care about you. She's tried to be good to you."

It wasn't the time to get into it with her father about how Shelby Rae had changed their relationship in recent years. He'd never been a hands-on father, or an attentive husband, for that matter. Her mother, Rita, had been Erin's best friend, the person she most wanted to spend time with, and only later did she realize how little her father had been around while he was trying to grow the dealership. After her mother's death, they'd gotten closer—at least until Shelby Rae started hanging around. It had almost been like he'd wanted Shelby Rae to mother her, before he and Shelby Rae had gotten together. There was a dark, half-buried thought in the back of her head that perhaps he and Shelby Rae had begun a relationship even before Shelby Rae had decided Erin needed a friend. Maybe even before her mother's death.

No, I won't think about that.

"I really think we need to call the sheriff. Maybe we don't even have to make it official. He can just give us some advice."

"Abel Bowen is a friend, but it would be unethical for me to hide the fact that there's been a crime. I'm going to pay the ransom. That's the end of it."

Erin was stubborn, and she knew whose genes had made her that way. There was no use arguing with him.

"They said noon tomorrow, right?" Erin picked up the paper, which seemed old, and smelled a little musty. If the police *did* get involved, they would find the paper covered with her and her father's fingerprints, which wouldn't be helpful at all. "You're not going to take the money out there tonight, are you? I want to go with you if you are. They could be waiting, Daddy. They could hurt you, too."

"I've got the cash. If I do it tonight, maybe they'd get her back before morning." He sighed. "God only knows where they're holding her."

As though he knew they were talking about Shelby Rae, Jocko, who'd been watching them, gave a sharp bark.

Her father leaned down and scooped the small dog into his arms. Jocko immediately wiggled against him and started licking his face excitedly. "I know, buddy. I know. We'll get her back soon."

The reality of the situation washed over Erin, and she suddenly felt very sorry for her father. Shelby Rae could be dead already, and the kidnappers would get their money whether she were alive or dead. They'd kept the more expensive ring, and now would have another fifty thousand dollars.

"They said she's safe, Daddy. We don't have any choice but to believe them. When we get her back..." She tried her best to sound positive. "Maybe we should call the police then. Because what if they decide to do it again? They might take you, next time."

"Or you," he said, finishing her thought. "When the dealership took off, your mother was worried that someone might try to kidnap you, and I didn't take her seriously. If something happened to you, too, I couldn't bear it."

Moved, and a little shaken by the emotion on his face, Erin put her arms around her father. He hugged her more tightly than she could ever remember him hugging her before.

ERIN MADE COFFEE and they sat at the kitchen table discussing all her father's ideas about who might have taken Shelby Rae and why.

He was focused on business associates—a transmission specialist he'd had to fire the previous month, and even the owner of the other big car dealership in the county. There were rumors that he was financed by some shady people from out East, who were also in the local marijuana trade. Erin mentioned Bryn Owens, but her father rejected that idea.

"She's hurt and still grieving. I don't think she's dangerous." The look in his eyes reminded her that he also knew a lot about grief.

Erin didn't mention Noah Daly, but the idea that Noah might be involved nagged at her. Given who his father was, it wasn't impossible.

By the time her father made her go to bed at three a.m. they were no closer to an answer.

ERIN WOKE EARLY after only a few hours sleep, anxious to know if anything further had happened with Shelby Rae. Trouble sat in an open bedroom window looking outside at the gloomy morning, his tail swishing languidly. She vaguely remembered a tussle at the foot of her bed in the night. A lonesome Jocko had wandered from his bed on the floor in her father's and Shelby Rae's empty bedroom to jump onto her duvet. But Trouble was already settled in the place he'd claimed after Tammy Lynn left for Italy, and he'd hissed at Jocko. Erin had been too tired to referee, but had heard the cat's paws thump lightly on the floor as he jumped off the bed. The swish of his tail this morning told her he was still irritated.

Jocko was now curled on the bed, nose to tail. Shelby Rae rarely went anywhere without him. Had he been in the house when she was kidnapped? It made sense that he wouldn't have wanted to be outside during the fireworks.

After she showered and made her bed, Erin put her damp hair in a ponytail, dressed in shorts, a T-shirt, and light hikers, and went downstairs. The house was quiet. Any other day her father would be in the workout room on the treadmill, but when she walked past the high-ceilinged family room, she spied him splayed awkwardly across the couch. He was dead asleep, a half-empty bottle of single malt and a glass of the amber liquid on the coffee table in front of him. He wasn't much of a drinker, and seemed to Erin like the last person in the world who would turn to booze in a stressful situation. Maybe his life with Shelby Rae had changed in some way since Erin was last home at Christmas.

When Jocko came running down the stairs headed for the family room, Erin grabbed him and whispered that he needed to stay with her and come eat breakfast.

In the kitchen, she gave him the lamb and rice mixture Shelby Rae cooked up every few days and kept in the fridge. Trouble got wet cat food that he sniffed at and ignored. When she substituted a generous helping of steak left over from the party, he contentedly began to eat. The cat definitely had a refined palate. She put on a fresh pot of coffee, knowing its smell would eventually wake her father. While it was brewing, she ate a protein bar and some blueberries and strawberries the caterers had left behind.

Where was Shelby Rae being held and who had her? The whole situation felt strange. Well, stranger than she thought a kidnapping might feel. That the kidnappers had referred to the "old Stratton Farm" was a huge clue that it was someone local. A stranger would have no idea that the land with the abandoned, burned out double-wide would be called "the old Stratton Farm." There were no signs, and the last Stratton had died off five years earlier.

Seeing how upset her father was had struck at Erin's heart. Maybe there was some jealousy there, but she knew that was not the better part of her. It hurt her to see him so unhappy, and she wanted to do everything she could to fix it. It helped that she had plenty of time on her hands and a natural curiosity that MacKenzie teased her was closer to nosiness. She had a few hours until he delivered the ransom. How much could she do?

"Let's go guys." After screwing the lid onto a travel tumbler of black coffee, Erin went out the kitchen door, Jocko and Trouble following behind.

CHAPTER FOUR

*a*s soon as we're on the path to the lake, I trot ahead to the brush behind the cabana where I discovered Shelby Rae's shoe and scarf. I dislike leaving humans behind, but sometimes they're simply too slow. One should forgive them for not being quite as smart as a cat I suppose, but mysteries could be solved with greater alacrity if they paid better attention to what I observe.

Erin continues down the beach, walking toward the far dock, obviously gripped with the notion that Shelby Rae was taken away in that direction. But it doesn't make sense. Whoever took Shelby Rae must have gotten away on foot, to a car parked nearby. The partygoers would've noticed a boat, and none arrived during the day. Shelby Rae, for all her extravagant femininity, is not at all petite like that darling British waif, Emma Watson. And she's taller and more zaftig than Erin. This is all to say that it must have been a person of some strength who carried her away.

Fortunately, that dreadful canine is following after Erin. It was an act of pure pity on my part to let him onto the bed last night. There I was, in the middle of a satisfying grooming of my magnificent tail, and he appeared out of nowhere. Plonk! There went my concentration.

I'm not heartless. One senses that such creatures are driven by pure emotion, unlike me, who is nearly all intellect, except for my careful affection for certain humans. Jocko is miserable with missing his human. Having spent time with the noisy woman, I have no idea why, but I am familiar with missing my own human, Tammy.

I slip into the brush behind the cabana. I like the solitude of these Kentucky woods. They're pleasantly cool in the morning in the way the woods are only on fall and spring mornings in Wetumpka. As I make my way through the flora, my sleek fur mostly repels the burrs and briers that bother other creatures. All about there are broken twigs and crushed wildflowers, signs that someone else, someone larger than I, has recently been this way. But whether it was a human or a deer or a large canine, I can't say.

In the distance, Erin calls my name. If I'm going to do my job of finding out who took Shelby Rae, there's work I'll need to do on my own. If there hadn't been so many people around yesterday, I might have noticed Shelby Rae's abduction.

Thirty feet or so into the trees, a path opens up. Just shy of the opening, I spy something incongruously large and white lying in a pile on the ground. It's formless but not large enough to be a person. My whiskers shimmy with anticipation, and my stuttered vocalization is involuntary. Getting closer, I see it's a swath of gauzy white fabric littered with dirt and irregular red-brown splotches. I give the fabric a careful sniff and recoil. Human blood.

When I lean in again, something crashes through the brush behind me, and I leap to safety. I'm not one to be pounced upon, and I have a good idea what or who it might be.

Jocko springs into the clearing and lands on the bloody fabric. Given that it smells strongly of both Shelby Rae and blood, he no doubt sussed it out from a distance. From my perch on a birch tree stump, I find myself rather admiring the scamp. That is until he drags the clothing back into the woods, catching and tearing it on everything in his wake.

Canines have no respect for the chain of evidence. Idiots.

A minute later the fool adds insult to injury by dropping the thing at Erin's feet, and receiving all the praise and accolades that should have come to me. Traitorous wretch! I can see I'm going to have to stop going so easy on him if I want credit for my sleuthing.

"DADDY!"

Erin opened the kitchen door, anxious to show her father Shelby Rae's swim cover-up that Jocko had dragged out of the woods. She called for him again.

"We're in here, Erin."

It wasn't her father that answered, but it was a voice she recognized. What was Julie Berry doing at the house at 8:15 in the morning, the day after Shelby Rae's kidnapping?

Julie stood grinning over Erin's father holding a tray containing a mug of coffee, a small glass of tomato juice, and an egg on toast. Was it Erin's imagination, or had the vodka bottle been moved from the liquor cart to the side table? Was the tomato juice actually a Bloody Mary? Her father sat on the edge of the sofa and looked up from his hands, bleary-eyed.

His eyes widened when he noticed Erin. "Dammit, what time is it?"

"Quarter after eight." Julie and Erin spoke at once. Julie gave a self-conscious laugh.

"I rang and rang the bell, but no one answered, so I let myself in the kitchen door. I hope that's all right." Julie gave Erin an innocent, pleading look. "Your daddy looked like he'd had such a rough night. I made him just what my daddy taught me to fix up for the morning after one of his nights out with the boys. Good protein, some caffeine, and just a lick of the hair of the dog."

Julie gave her a mischievous wink. So there was, indeed, vodka in that drink.

"I'm grateful for the breakfast, Julie." Bruce didn't really sound grateful. "But why are you here? How did you find out?"

Julie put the tray down in front of him and all but tucked a big cloth napkin in his shirt—the one he'd been wearing the day before and had obviously slept in. "You are such a silly, Bruce. It's our quarterly meeting for the Rita's Friends charity. Breakfast here before you go into the office? Third Monday of the month?"

Erin interrupted. "This isn't a good time."

"There's no need to be unpleasant, Erin." It was hard to miss the scolding tone in her voice.

"No, it's *really* a bad time. I think you should go. I'll see you out."

"Bruce, what's going on here? Did Shelby Rae say something? I know she doesn't like that you've kept me on as director—"

"For God's sake." Bruce put his face back in his hands.

"What did I say? Will someone *please* tell me what's going on?"

Jocko got up on his back feet and put his paws on Bruce's knee to lick his hand. Bruce scratched him behind the ears. "Good boy," he whispered. "We think Shelby Rae went out somewhere last night. She didn't take her phone, and she hasn't come home."

Erin caught a flash of pleasure in Julie's eyes before her face took on a look of dismay. "She ran off—" Her voice trailed off, but both Erin and her father heard her say, "with someone?"

Bruce stood up so quickly that he nearly upset the table.

All the dishes rattled and the Bloody Mary sloshed out of the glass, reminding Erin of the bloodied shirt in her hand. She would wait until Julie was gone to mention it.

"Get out of this house!" Bruce pointed to the door. Erin saw how his extended hand trembled.

Julie turned to her. "I don't wish Shelby Rae any ill. You know that, Erin. She and I get on better than the two of you. In fact I heard you arguing yesterday. Maybe you upset her."

"It's not any of your goddamn business!" Bruce canted forward, his face close to Julie's startled one. "Get out, and stay away from us. Rita would be ashamed to hear you right now."

Erin took a step toward Julie to get her moving. She'd never seen father so angry and was afraid of what he might do. She almost felt sorry for Julie. *Almost.* Taking the woman's arm to get her out of the family room, she heard her father breathing heavily behind them.

"Did you have a purse or anything?" Erin kept her voice a whisper

Julie started to shake her head, then said, "It's in the kitchen with the papers. I didn't mean anything. I only wanted to help. I thought you and Shelby Rae were sleeping in, and I know she doesn't cook much anyway. I really did just want to help." In the kitchen she gathered her things and tried to hug Erin, but Erin stepped away.

"I'm not angry with you, but leave dad alone right now. He's angry with you because he loves Shelby Rae and is worried about her."

When Julie opened her mouth to speak, Erin raised her hand. "Stop. With any luck she'll come back today and Dad will be fine."

"Shouldn't you call the police? What if she's been

kidnapped? I know I might have been out of line when I asked if she'd run away with someone, but there's a reason I said it. A valid reason. It wasn't because I'm..." She faltered and took a breath. "I care very deeply about you and your father. I don't want to see either of you hurt."

Erin got Julie out of the house without going into further detail about Shelby Rae's disappearance, and extracted a promise that she wouldn't tell anyone Shelby Rae was missing. She had a good idea of exactly how much Julie cared for her father. Julie Berry was not a subtle woman.

With the shirt still under her arm, Erin returned to the family room only to find it empty. Trouble was sitting on the couch, washing his face and behind his ear with one black paw. Seeing that the yolk was broken on the egg, she smiled. No one else was going to eat the thing, so the animals might as well have it. Though she reminded herself to make sure her father did eat something. She took the dishes to the kitchen, set the shirt on a stool, and made her father fresh coffee and a bowl of cereal with fruit.

When her father came downstairs fifteen minutes later, followed by Jocko, he carried a red, white, and blue canvas bag he'd gotten at an auto dealers' convention. It wasn't bulging, but she suspected it contained the fifty thousand in cash from his personal safe. The safe in which he also stored the jewelry her mother had left her, as well as Shelby Rae's more valuable pieces. What did Shelby Rae think about Rita's jewelry being in the safe? Did it bother her? She'd never said, and Rita had been gone long enough that her name didn't come up often when she and Erin were together. The house had even been substantially redecorated two years after Shelby Rae moved in, and, with Bruce's blessing, she'd slowly gotten rid of many of the pieces that Rita had loved. Erin considered it dumb luck that Shelby Rae had hired a Nashville decorator with excellent taste to make most of the changes.

"Daddy, you need to eat something."

"Is that woman gone? Maybe I was too hard on her, but she had some nerve coming in the house and making breakfast. What in the hell was she thinking?"

"Sit down. There's cereal and fresh coffee."

"I'm nervous as a cat." He set the duffel on the island. Noticing the dirty garment on the stool, he picked it up by one loose edge. At first he looked puzzled, but when he saw it was spotted with blood, his eyes clouded with concern.

"I didn't want Julie to see it. Jocko brought it out of the woods this morning. I don't know where he found it. You think it's blood, too, don't you?"

"Jesus." Bruce held the shirt to his face and breathed in Shelby Rae's scent, his eyes closed.

"There's not very much. Maybe it's not hers." Erin tried to sound hopeful, but her heart wasn't in it. The shirt was definitely Shelby Rae's. She looked away, discomfited to once again witness the deep emotion on her father's face.

"The sooner I get this money to them, the sooner we'll get her back."

"About what Julie said. You know I would never do anything to hurt Shelby Rae, right? What we argued about was really dumb. I don't know why I got so angry."

Bruce raised a hand, interrupting her. "I'm not blind. We both know Julie's wanted to take your mother's place for years. She's a sad woman, and I used to feel sorry for her. But the last thing I'll put up with is her trying to get between you and me."

To hear him say that took away some of the guilt weighing on her heart. What remained was the guilt over her childish hope that Shelby Rae would get bored and leave, or her father would decide he didn't love his second wife after all.

"Then let me go with you to drop off the money. Please."

"I want you to stay here in case she comes back. There's a chance. Somebody could be watching the house."

"Like Bryn Owens? She's not out there now."

"She wouldn't be if she kidnapped Shelby Rae. But there could be someone else. Someone who's being paid to watch. You know where the Mossberg is. Use it if you need to. I'm not going to mess around with these people. I told you I want you safe."

Erin didn't have to ask him if he was carrying. His shirt hung loose, and that meant his Sig Sauer P238 was tucked into the waistband of his khakis.

He took a long drink of the cooled coffee and put the mug back down on the counter.

"I'll text you when it's done. If nothing happens while I'm there, I'll go to work as usual. I don't want anyone to start asking questions, and I don't trust Julie to keep her mouth shut. Look out for Shelby Rae. For anything."

ERIN USUALLY DID what her father asked her to do, not just out of respect, but because in most things—except when it came to Shelby Rae—he was right. But this *did* have something to do with Shelby Rae and he wasn't thinking straight. If Shelby Rae returned to find the house locked up, she could get in using the code on the garage door. And Jocko would be there to greet her. That wasn't so bad, was it?

She waited until her father had been gone for five minutes before she grabbed her phone, keys, and the Mossberg and headed for her own car. Trouble and Jocko stood at the door leading to the garage as though they knew where she was going.

"No. I don't need any help, guys. I put the TV in the family room on Animal Planet. Go watch cheetahs or something." Jocko's ears lowered and she could've sworn Trouble was scowling at her. "I'll be back. I promise."

THERE WERE TWO WAYS she could get to the Strattons' abandoned dairy farm, and Erin took the fastest, steering the Challenger carefully even as she hurtled along the oil and chip backroads. The Mossberg sat securely in a case in her car's trunk. Not the most practical place, but it was there if she needed it. She couldn't get the idea that her father might be in danger out of her head. A part of her wanted to call the sheriff right that minute. Up to this point, she'd gone along with her father's wishes (mostly), but now he was alone, putting himself at the mercy of the kidnappers.

Who could the kidnappers be? Was Bryn Owens really capable of something so vicious? All along, Erin had had the sense that Bryn's lawsuit wasn't about money, but punishment. Anyone who saw Bryn and Tionna together could tell that they loved each other deeply. And the bakery was their labor of love. Bryn Owens was not a big woman, and probably couldn't have manhandled Shelby Rae, who was taller. But she could've taken her at gunpoint, or she might have had help.

The previous night, Erin had wondered about Noah, too. He certainly had reason to hate her family. But even though she'd seen him walking away from Bryn Owens's car, he'd later been on the dock watching the fireworks. She and her father agreed that Shelby Rae had probably disappeared while they were going on. Erin had wanted to join Noah on the dock, but it felt too awkward. He'd also stuck around long after the bonfire was lit, and she didn't like to think how disappointed he'd looked when she shut the door after taking Trouble from him. He probably thought she hated him. She found herself wanting to make it up to him.

There was another possibility that bothered her. What if Shelby Rae had cooperated with someone in her family to get the fifty thousand dollars? That Uncle Travis was certainly creepy. Erin didn't know him well, but he'd been busted for check forgery at least once. He might be small time enough to settle for fifty thousand easy dollars. Or what if he—or someone else—was blackmailing Shelby Rae about something?

Erin shook her head to try to stop her mind from generating such crazy ideas.

She remembered how, when she and MacKenzie were eleven, MacKenzie's Sheltie dog, Mikey Cyrus (formerly "Miley" but *she* turned out to be a *he*), had gone missing. They'd put up fliers all over town and hung out at the shelter for hours on end, waiting to see if anyone showed up with him. When a week went by, Erin and MacKenzie became convinced that Mikey Cyrus had been kidnapped. It didn't matter that their parents had told them the little dog might have just wandered off. They researched dognappings online and became convinced that Mikey Cyrus had been captured either by someone who wanted to resell him because he was so cute, or by people who wanted to test cosmetics on him. Erin's mother had discovered them on the computer, looking for the email addresses of the people in the science department at the Bluegrass Junior College. Never mind that no one did any kind of scientific research at the junior college, let alone animal testing. Erin sulked for two days. Finally, at the end of the second day, someone called MacKenzie's house from a town about ten miles away to say they had the dog. They'd found him going through a spilled garbage bag near their apartment dumpster, and when they approached him he practically leapt into their arms. Fortunately he was still wearing his collar and tag engraved with the Clays' address and phone number.

So it hadn't been Erin's nascent detective skills that had brought the dog home, and maybe she was a little paranoid. But paranoia wasn't necessarily a bad thing. Perhaps she was being a little hard on Shelby Rae, too. It wasn't like Shelby Rae had ever been a criminal.

Erin drove the Challenger down an overgrown, once-graveled road leading to the abandoned farmhouse next to Stratton's dairy farm. When she got out, she was careful to lock the car without making the alarm beep. By the time she made her way to the treeline nearest the barn where her father was to leave the money, she saw him already heading back to his truck, his head bowed. He wasn't messing around. This was no game to him. She knew he would do anything to get Shelby Rae back alive.

Once in the truck, he sat for a few minutes, staring at the barn. Erin hated that he was alone. Why hadn't he let her come with him? She felt a little guilty that she hadn't stayed back at the house, as he'd asked her to. But, *dammit,* if he wouldn't call the sheriff, *somebody* needed to make sure he was okay. Like some kind of superhuman sheepdog, her father was always taking care of people. But who was there to look after the sheepdogs of the world?

She startled at the sound of her text alert, and quickly silenced it. She hadn't meant to leave her phone on. Ironically, the text was from her father.

Dad: It's done. Is she back?

Did he imagine that kidnappers worked that way—so
quickly?

Erin: No nothing yet. Is everything okay?
Dad: Going into the office. Call me when she shows *up.*
Erin: I will.

Hearing her father's truck start, Erin looked up. She was so
hidden in the trees that he would have had a hard time spotting her. Also, he wouldn't be looking for *her.*

After he was gone, she stayed put. Thirty minutes later she
was hot, bored, and scratching her bare legs non-stop because
of the bugs and long grass. A few cars and pick up trucks
passed by, but otherwise nothing was happening. How did
actual police deal with being on stakeouts? At least on television they had doughnuts or coffee or deli sandwiches. She
wanted to kick herself because she hadn't even remembered to
bring a bottle of water.

She thought of hiding in the barn itself. It was more
dangerous, but it was the only way she could know for certain
who was picking up the ransom money. Tucking her phone
into her shorts pocket, she parted the whip-like branches in
front of her, but froze when she heard the whining engine of a
four-wheeler cruising through the woods to her left. She
shrank back, worried she'd been seen. The four-wheeler didn't
hesitate as it burst into the old pasture headed for the barn.

The vehicle was far enough away that she couldn't get a
good look at the driver, but she was sure it was a man. He must
have been watching for her father to know that he'd already
left the ransom.

The driver wore amber-colored work pants, boots, and a
black hoodie that hid his hair and the edges of his face, which

was fully covered by a black morphsuit-like mask. The eyeless mask made him look sinister and dangerous. Before Erin thought to get out her phone to take a picture, he disappeared behind the barn, and she cursed.

One thing was certain. Shelby Rae wasn't inside the barn, or her father would've seen her. And if the person picking up the ransom was the kidnapper, Shelby Rae was hidden away somewhere else. Either she was locked up, or someone else was guarding her.

The four-wheeler didn't shut off. There must've been a second entrance to the barn, because after less than a minute, the four-wheeler revved and appeared again, headed back the way it came. The driver still wore his hood up, and the red, white, and blue bag was slung across his back. As the four-wheeler bounced over the pasture, Erin was able to get a couple of pictures before it disappeared into the woods. She weighed the idea of following it, but there was no clear path or road the way it went. Plus, it was long gone.

She knew she should've felt like she'd accomplished something by getting the pictures, but it didn't feel like enough. No matter how she zoomed in on the man on her phone, she couldn't see enough detail, and the four-wheeler had no license plate. Checking to make sure no one else was coming, she stepped over the busted fence and hurried to the barn.

ERIN LOOKED UP at the sound of movement in the barn's rafters. A half-dozen ragged holes revealed the perfect blue of the sky and sunlight that bathed the interior in mellow light. The air smelled of rotted hay, dirt, and old cow dung. She was careful where she walked because someone had busted up the stalls, leaving splintered wood and rusting nails all over the ground. A red-winged blackbird cried out from the edge of one of the holes above her, and she jumped, laughing nervously.

The note had told her father to leave the money on a blue steel drum. She found the drum easily, as it was the only industrial item left in the barn. Grasping the drum's edge, she tried to rock it. But it was immovable. She shivered to think what might be inside. A weighted-down body? What if it was Shelby Rae?

She pulled her hand back, afraid, and glanced around the barn. The idea was too macabre. *Impossible.* Yet not impossible.

Determined, Erin made herself look more closely at the drum. Scraping away the rust and grime from the edge with her house key, it looked like the drum had never been unsealed. Squatting in front of it, she could just make out a dusty printed label: Grade 80 Steel Chain. She sighed with relief. That would explain why the drum was so heavy. A search of the barn turned up nothing, and she decided to leave.

No one seemed to be following her, so she drove home more slowly than she had on the way to the barn. True to his word, her father wasn't at the house. She'd expected him to change his mind and come home to wait. It surely had to be hell for him going through the motions of his day, only being able to think about Shelby Rae.

Erin let Jocko out, then nervously checked the house phone's voicemail to see if the kidnappers had called. It was a thought that hadn't occurred to her before she'd decided to follow her father. Fortunately the only messages were from a pest control company wanting to set up an appointment, and a long, pitiful message from Julie that was part apology and part suggestion that she could come over and help in any way she could—to make dinner or clean up after the party or just offer moral support.

Moral support. Right. Erin rolled her eyes. The woman just wouldn't give up. What if her father *had* married Julie? She imagined Julie fawning over her father, trying to pretend to honor Erin's mother's memory, while at the same time relishing her relationship with Erin's father. At least Shelby Rae didn't pretend much. Shelby Rae cared about Shelby Rae. Everyone but her father was clear on that.

Uncertain about what to do next, she spent the next couple hours cleaning up from the party, and wondering if they would ever see Shelby Rae again.

"Noah Daly, please come to the service desk."

Noah looked up from the computer that was diagnosing the shimmying Ford Focus he was working on. Nothing was coming up, which happened sometimes. He would have to get the car up on the lift to take a look.

The page was disconcerting because no one ever came to see him at work. He took his phone out of his coveralls. No worrying messages or texts. His mother always texted if she needed to be in touch. Leaving the computer to finish its work, he walked to the gray steel door leading to the service desk. The door's head-high, square window revealed the man waiting at the desk. Noah sighed.

At the sound of the door opening, the man gave Noah an overenthusiastic smile. "There you are!"

"What are you doing here, Dad?" He knew he sounded like a sullen teenager whose father had shown up at a party looking for him. That's about how he felt.

"Can't a man visit his hardworking boy? It's lunchtime, right? Let's go eat."

Jeb Daly was nearly six feet tall, but he hunched his shoulders like a man who wanted to be invisible. It was as though he were afraid of being caught doing something he wasn't supposed to. Which, of course, was too often true. He and Noah shared the same brown eyes and chiseled, cleft chin, but Jeb's face was long, his jaw as delicate as a woman's. In the week since he'd been released from jail he'd started a beard that, to Noah's surprise, was growing in with patches of gray. He hadn't worn a beard in prison because, as he said, "You don't want to give people something to grab onto."

Behind the service desk, Earl busied himself at his computer, but Noah could tell he was listening. Everyone at the dealership knew Jeb Daly was the person responsible for Rita Walsh's death. Noah hoped Bruce Walsh would remain in his office until they were out of the building. He had promised to keep his father away.

It was ten minutes till noon, and Noah wasn't usually one to ask for special privileges, but he guessed Earl would be okay with him leaving early.

"Mind if I take my lunch now? That Ford won't need more than another thirty minutes, and I'll get it done as soon as I get back."

Earl raised a wooly eyebrow above his smudged glasses and shifted a glance from his computer screen to Jeb and back. Some of the guys called Earl a Hobbit behind his back, but he was one of the sharpest minds at the dealership. He could make parts appear like magic and always knew which mechanic was right for which job. It was Earl who had exposed the transmission guy as a slacker.

He nodded to Noah. "Don't forget to clock out."

"DOES MOM KNOW WHERE YOU ARE?" Noah was hungry

despite his father's unwanted company. He swiped a French fry through the puddle of ketchup on his burger wrapper. His father surprised Noah when he had used cash from a thick sheaf in his wallet to pay.

Jeb laughed. "Your mama knew where I was for almost seven years. She ain't my warden."

When Noah returned home the night before, he'd found his mother asleep and her car gone from the driveway. While it was a relief not to see his father on the couch, Jeb's being gone meant that Noah had to get up at five-thirty to drive his mother to work. He'd tried to go back to sleep for an hour, but the sleep hadn't come. Between thoughts of his father's return from prison and the memory of Erin Walsh's calm green eyes, he lay, restless, until it was time to go to work.

"How goes working for Bruce Walsh? He give you a hard time? Seems to me he must want something from you to give you a job like that. Like he wants to stick a thumb in my eye." Jeb smiled without warmth. It was a familiar smile to Noah, one that meant he wasn't happy at all.

"What do you want, Dad?" Noah had stopped visiting his father in prison three years earlier. The distance had made him stronger, but there was still a seed of fear in his mind. He was several inches taller than when his father had gone in. But his father, unlike so many men in prison, had shrunk some, rather than bulked up. But he was still dangerous. Noah's childhood bruises were long gone, but the scars on his soul would never go away. "Cash? Isn't it part of your parole deal to get a job?"

Something hard flashed in his father's eyes, but was quickly gone. "You're a plain-speaker, boy. Just like your old man. Just like your Grandpop. I like that."

"So?"

"No worries on the job front. I'm getting on at the fish

hatchery. They call it 'habitat and custodial engineering,' but it's going to be mostly cleaning up fish shit."

Noah smirked. It wasn't the worst job his father had ever had, but it was right up there. At least it was legal. He made a ball of his empty burger wrapper and stuck it in the French fry cup.

"Yeah, go on. Laugh at your old man. That'll get you far."

"Nobody's laughing." Noah leaned forward. There was no humor in his voice. "Listen, I need to get back to work. Next time you want to buy someone lunch, take one of your drinking buddies. Better yet, toss me a five and I'll take myself out. I'm good with it if Mom wants me to sit down with both of you to eat. But you and me have got nothing to say to each other." Putting his hands on the table in front of him, he started to get up.

Jeb's hand was surprisingly strong as he squeezed Noah's wrist and held him in place. "Sit down."

Without thinking Noah did as he was told, but immediately regretted it. *Old habits.*

"Don't push me," his father said. "I'm back, and I'm living in *my* house. You're a big boy, and your mama says you can stay as long as you want because you're saving up to go to school or some bullshit. That doesn't mean I'm happy about it.

Irritated with himself that he'd responded so automatically, Noah jerked his hand away. "Just tell me what you want. Money?"

"I don't want any of your grease monkey money, son. Not a penny. I'm fine for cash. Your mama's also made it clear that what's hers is mine, too, which is the way married people should be."

"She works too hard to be giving money to you."

"Well, I guess if you don't like how we live, you can move your ass out. Or start paying rent."

Noah wasn't about to get into the family bills with his father at the concrete table in front of the Hoof 'n Whip. His paycheck paid his mother's utilities and monthly mortgage. It remained to be seen if the fish hatchery job his father mentioned would pay, or if the job even existed at all.

"I gotta go." Noah stood again.

"Hey, hey. We got off on the wrong foot here, son. It's like that with a man and his boy. I missed most of those terrible teen years. I'm sorry about that."

Noah remained silent.

"Listen. I need you to do me a big favor. I've got an eleven p.m. curfew, right?" He went on. "So *you* know I was out last night, blowing off a little steam. It's been a lot of years, and to require me to be in by eleven like some little kid is just stupid."

"What do you want me to do?"

"I went by your mama's work first thing today, and she already agreed. If anybody asks, I was sound asleep on the couch when you came home, okay? And every other night. I doubt it will come up, but I really don't want to screw up this parole. You understand. I'm a stand-up citizen, but they can't expect me to live like a friggin' five-year-old."

Noah's immediate thought was that his father wouldn't know a stand-up citizen if he walked into a church full of saints. But he also didn't want to spend any more time talking to him. "Yeah, whatever."

He left the restaurant without responding to his father's cheery, "See you at home, son!"

WHEN NOAH CLOCKED BACK IN, Earl—who never seemed to

eat, even though his round stomach strained at the buttons of his white, short-sleeved shirt with its Walsh Motors logo on the pocket—grunted in response to Noah's quiet, "Thanks, man," without looking up.

Because he'd gone to lunch early, he was alone in the garage area for a while. He threw himself right into working on the Focus to keep from thinking about his father. But it didn't work. His father got to him every time.

He'd been five years old the first time his father had demanded that he keep a secret. When the front door opened with a blast of cold air, Noah and Buzz Lightyear were under a living room table on a mission to rescue The Little Engine that Could. Noah's mother was making dinner in the kitchen. His father came inside the house and shut the door behind him with extra care. He tiptoed into the living room, which made Noah laugh because he'd never seen his father tiptoe before.

"Hey, buddy," his father whispered. "Shhhhhh." He pulled a shiny black handgun from his coat pocket. Then he took two volumes of the set of Encyclopedia Britannica that had belonged to Noah's grandmother from their shelf. Noah watched him, unblinking, as he slid the gun behind the other books and replaced the two volumes.

He squatted down in front of Noah, who was still beneath the table. Buzz Lightyear lay blinking on the worn gray carpet between them. "You ain't seen that. You don't touch it. And you don't tell your mama, or I'll spank your ass so hard, you'll wear it for a hat, hear me?"

Noah nodded. Two days later, he conveniently forgot the promise, and his mother found him aiming the gun at a front window and an imaginary boogey man masquerading as a clown. Startled by her scream, Noah dropped the gun and it went off, sending a bullet deep into the maple baseboard.

The spanking came, but not until after the fight between his parents ended with his mother escaping to her bedroom, crying and afraid. He would never forget it—the sound of her crying together with the pain of his father's leather belt against his bare skin.

THE AFTERNOON DRAGGED, and all Noah had to look forward to was going back to the house where his father would be watching TV while his mother made dinner. Maybe it was time to get his own place after all. But the idea of abandoning his mother made him sick to his stomach. Noah worried that she couldn't protect herself. Prison hadn't seemed to change his father for the better.

At least he could delay going home.

A STRIPE of rain-heavy clouds cut across the lowered sun on the lake, casting a shadow over the dock. The lake was still, except for the bugs tickling the water's surface, and the occasional fish breaking to capture them.

How to tie flies and fish was the one useful, happy thing his father had taught him. The irony of going fishing to get away from his father wasn't lost on him. Usually the first thing he would do was to tie a fly to his hook, but today he had energy to burn. Sitting reflectively, waiting for the fish to bite wasn't what he wanted to do.

Of course he was also sitting on one of the Walsh docks. That was no accident. Seeing Erin the day before had made him strangely happy. It made him want to create something. Something beautiful.

Today he had his sketchbook and pencils, so he could draw.

He was deep into it when he heard the faint jingle of dog tags. Shaking his focus from the page, he turned to the bank. He was startled to see the black cat, Trouble, sitting serenely on the dock just a few feet away from him, staring out at the lake as though he'd been there for hours. Beyond the cat, Jocko trotted down the steps to the dock. His tiny feet clicked across the boards as he approached Noah.

"Hey, guys." Noah squatted to scratch Jocko behind the ears, and the dog jumped up to lick his face. "Out for an adventure?"

Jocko ducked away from him and went to the end of the dock. He stood for a moment as though thinking. Then he dove into the water.

Alarmed, Noah stood up. Did Jack Russells swim?

A voice came from the bank. "Jocko, come!"

Noah turned to see Erin walking down the path from the direction of the house. If he'd been sitting on the other side of the dock, he would have seen her coming from far off. Spotting him, she lifted her hand in a tentative wave, and he waved back. Why was his heart beating so fast? Was it the dog? *Damn.* He'd momentarily forgotten the dog. Fortunately, the dog was paddling back to shore, all but smiling.

"Are they bothering you?" Erin called. "Trouble's figured out how to get through Jocko's dog door, and they took off."

"It's a nice day for an adventure." *Did I really say that? That sounded really dumb.*

Erin came down the steps and picked up Trouble, scolding him playfully. Her face and arms wore a hint of pink from being outside the previous day. Noah guessed that with her fair, freckled skin, she didn't so much tan as burn in the sun. Her strawberry blond hair was pulled back from her face, and she didn't seem to be wearing any makeup. He thought she was beautiful without it. Her clothes were simple: brown leather sandals, cargo shorts that hung low on her slender hips, and a gauzy, V-neck tee the pristine white of blackberry blossoms.

"Catch anything?" she asked. Trouble jumped from her arms and sniffed at the sketchbook Noah had hurriedly closed. Erin glanced at it, curious, but looked quickly away. "I'm sorry. It's none of my business."

Flustered, Noah bent to pick up the book. "Sometimes I come down to fish but end up drawing. This place is..." He hesitated. "Inspiring."

"I didn't know you were an artist." Then she tilted her head. "Wait. I remember. You did a bunch of posters for the recycling program in school. They were beautiful."

"They came out okay." In fact the art teacher had encouraged him to put together a portfolio to submit to get into college, but he'd known he was going to have to work full time to help his mother.

"Can I see?" Erin gestured to the sketchbook.

He opened it and held it out to her. They sat on the dock, their legs dangling over the edge. As she slowly paged through the book, he tried to keep his eyes on the water and the sky, but they could have been blank walls for all he noticed them. His gaze kept straying to her calm, lovely face.

"Why, they're buildings. They're beautiful. I didn't expect that." She laughed nervously. "I mean, it's not that I didn't expect them to be beautiful."

Noah smiled. "It's okay. I know what you meant."

"This one by the lake. Is that here? It looks almost like a collection of tree houses."

"It could be anywhere. The point is that they blend with their environment. Too many people live in jungles of concrete. They don't get the advantage we have. Being close to all this." He spread his arm to indicate the lake and opposite shore. As they watched a duck flew across the cove, causing the very wet Jocko to bark. "Even if people have to work near the city, they could live in nature. Suburbs that have less concrete and more dirt and grass. There'd have to be good public transportation, but the communities could be ecologically sustainable, with community gardens. Family homes, but also bigger places where people could have their own private sleeping space, but share kitchens and living spaces."

"Like a dorm?" Erin made a face. "Dorms are a nightmare."

"Way nicer. I want these to feel like homes, not people warehouses. There are places like this in San Francisco and other big cities, but nowhere that makes a priority of the surroundings. People lose touch with themselves when they can't touch nature." Wanting to take the focus off himself, he asked after her father and stepmother.

Now it was Erin's turn to look uncomfortable. "Dad's okay."

Noah read her hesitation. "You were looking for your stepmom last night. You found her all right?"

Erin shook her head. "We're expecting her any minute, if everything goes okay."

"If what goes okay?"

Erin shut the notebook. "It's complicated." When she handed it back to him their fingertips brushed, and Noah felt a pleasant hint of electricity shoot through his body.

"People say I'm a pretty good listener. I won't say anything to anybody."

Erin took a deep breath, and the words rushed out of her— the details of the ransom, Julie Berry accusing her of being involved, the bloody shirt, following her father to the barn.

Taking out her phone, she showed him the image of the man on the four-wheeler headed away from the barn.

"Can you tell who he is?" she asked. "Look at that weird morph suit mask. It's so creepy."

Noah shook his head. "I don't recognize the four-wheeler either. Everybody has them."

"Do you work on them at the dealership?"

"Not very often because your dad doesn't sell them. Some of the farm equipment places do, and there are a couple dealers around Louisville and Lexington. But without a clearer picture, it's hard to tell what kind it is." He touched the screen. "Is that the bag with the money?"

"Yeah."

"What time do you think Mrs. Walsh went missing? Any guesses?" It freaked him out that she'd probably been taken while he and so many other people were around.

"You can call her Shelby Rae. At least with me, anyway. Dad says he looked for her right before the fireworks, but it was dark, and there were so many people. He was surprised she didn't come find him. We think she was taken *during* the fireworks. I found Jocko in the kitchen afterward. The poor little guy was shaking, he was so afraid of all the noise."

Hearing his name, Jocko came over and leaned his wet body against her leg to be petted. "Somebody's going to need a bath," she said.

"Your dad won't go to the police? Why not?"

Erin shrugged. "The note said if he paid the ransom by noon today, she'd come home. I guess my dad's a trusting guy. I can't say I agree. He thought if he paid, they wouldn't kill her."

"Does he have any guess who might have done it?"

Now Erin looked steadily at him. "I think it has something to do with Bryn and Tionna Owens."

Why was she looking at him that way? What did she know?

Bryn and Tionna went to the same church his mother attended, and he knew them from around town. They often had dinner or drinks at Gerald's on the Square, the pub in town where he hung out a couple times a week. That spring, a few weeks before Tionna died, he'd been at the pub when Tionna and Bryn were eating dinner. But then Bryn had left their booth looking angry, leaving Tionna on her own. His own friends had gone, and he was finishing up a beer when Tionna caught his eye and waved him over.

God, she was beautiful, with honey-colored curls just lighter than her skin, and dark eyes that shone in the dim light of the pub. Bryn was also beautiful, but thinner and more angular. Even her voice had a sharper edge to it. In addition to running the bakery with Bryn, Tionna was a fabric artist and had the strong hands of someone who worked with them every day. She talked expressively, and they fluttered before his eyes as she talked and laughed about her peculiar wealthy clients back in New York. But mostly she let *him* talk about his job and his plans. Because she was an artist, and because she pressed him, he told her about the architectural designs that consumed much of his free time. It was the beer, he figured, that made him talk so much. Also the fact that this thirty-something, gorgeous woman was listening to him in a way that the girls he'd dated before never had.

It was after ten when they left the pub. They lived in opposite directions, but he offered to walk her home. Smiling, she accepted. What he wasn't prepared for was her taking his hand a few minutes later and pulling him into the narrow alley between the bakery and the second-hand shop next door.

Her lips were soft and wet, and she kissed him with a

surprising assurance that made him hard in seconds, though he knew he hadn't been far from it anyway, just talking with her. It was dark in the walkway. Noah's eyes were closed, and he couldn't get enough of her lips and her neck and, at last, her breasts that overflowed his hands and tasted lightly of salt and cinnamon. She moaned softly.

In seconds she had his belt and jeans undone. He worried for a moment they would fall down, exposing his butt to the night, because his hips were slender and he had a hard enough time keeping them up. But in the next moment he forgot all about his jeans.

Before he knew it she was telling him, with a smile in her voice, to button up and get the keys from her purse. Standing beside her as she unlocked the back door of the bakery, he couldn't help but notice how the security light above them made playful shadows on her breasts between the open placket of her linen shirt.

After she washed up inside she made him some coffee and settled down across the table from him with a cup of tea. His embarrassment was overwhelming, and he had little to say. He'd never been the kind of guy to have one-night stands. Though what they'd done couldn't actually be called sex, could it? Plus, she was married. To a woman. Which made him even more anxious. He had nothing against Bryn at all.

Noah was stone cold sober by the time he finished his coffee. Should he try to take her hand? Would she want to see him again? But he did nothing; and, when they were outside again, she simply kissed him on the cheek.

"Thanks. That was fun." She yawned sleepily. "Sorry. It's the chamomile, and I have to get up in four hours. I can see myself the rest of the way home." He started to protest, but she gave him a gentle push toward the walkway and started up the outside stairs by the back door.

Bryn and Tionna live above the bakery? Had Bryn seen them from a window? Heard them? Now he questioned Tionna's intentions. Maybe she had only used him to try to make Bryn jealous.

It was the last time he ever exchanged so much as a word with Tionna. The next time he saw Bryn and Tionna together at the pub they were holding hands, looking very much in love. As he passed by their table, he nodded politely. But he was sure Tionna had winked at him. Somehow it made him feel less anxious, and he stopped wondering if they would be involved again.

After Tionna's funeral, Bryn had pressured him to tell her what he knew about the work that had been done earlier on Tionna's car. He'd never worked on it himself and had nothing to tell her, though he felt badly enough that it had happened at the dealership where he worked.

It was inconceivable to him that anyone at Walshes' would've let Tionna drive off with unsafe brakes or if they believed there was any risk at all.

He met Erin's gaze. Did she think he had something to do with Tionna's death or with the kidnapping? There was no way she could have known what had happened with him and Tionna. And, anyway, why would he jeopardize his own job taking revenge on Shelby Rae because of Tionna?

"I guess you have to consider everybody," he finally said. "I wish I knew something that would help." *What if you had something to do with it, Erin? Do you dislike her so much?* Then he had a thought that truly surprised him. *I don't even think I'd care if you did.* He knew he was attracted to her in much the same way he'd been attracted to Tionna. But a relationship had been out of the question with Tionna because she obviously hadn't wanted one. Was it possible Erin might? As the daughter of the boss, Erin seemed off-limits to him. "You and your dad must really be freaked out."

"I think whoever it was took Shelby Rae out of the cabana and up the back path through the woods to the road. That's the direction Jocko came from."

Noah relaxed a little bit. At least she wasn't going to push him about Bryn.

"Did you find anything else up there besides the shirt? Let's go look again."

They gathered his gear and headed up to the back path, which was the way he'd come to the dock. Jocko and Trouble ran ahead, as though they knew where they were going.

Erin's shoulder occasionally bumped against his arm as they climbed the path, but neither of them reacted—visibly, anyway. Noah's head was full of the scent of her. He imagined the edge of her finely curved ear between his lips, his teeth, holding her tight against him...*Damn, again.* He stumbled on the path, almost falling into her.

"You okay?"

"Yep. Totally okay." *That went well.*

They were nearly to the end of the path, which opened close to the road. He could see his motorcycle on the rectangle of gravel a few dozen feet away.

Trouble stopped at a bush and bit at a curving branch.

"Hey, don't eat that, cat!" Erin reached out for the branch and started to push it away.

"Wait," Noah said. "There's something on the ground by his paw." While the sky was now clear outside the woods, where they stood was a gloomy and shadowy green. He turned on his phone flashlight and bent to pick up a small piece of jewelry. Putting it in one palm, he held it out to Erin. As she bent to look at the thing, he resisted the urge to touch her hair. *Don't be that guy.*

"That's Shelby Rae's earring. The back is missing." She picked it up and looked around. "But it doesn't help us now. She must've really been fighting."

Noah nodded. He felt bad for Erin. From what she'd told him about her argument with Shelby Rae, he guessed they didn't get along all that well. Still, she looked unhappy.

"Hey, let me give you my number. I can help you look some more." His voice trailed off, but then he continued. "Maybe she'll even be home when you get back. But text me or something. I'll help if I can."

Erin gave him a weak smile. Her eyes were clear and green.

"Yeah. That's a good idea. Thanks."

CHAPTER FIVE

$\mathcal{B}$olting awake, Erin was confused about what she heard first—the pounding on the front door, not far from her open bedroom window, or the dog barking and Trouble yowling. Whatever the order, it was chaos in her bedroom, with Jocko barking and scratching at her closed bedroom door. He jumped in circles like some mad circus dog whose tricks had gone haywire. After letting him out, she ran to the window.

"Let me in! Let me in!" Shelby Rae was hysterical, alternating between calling and pounding. If they'd lived in a neighborhood, an entire street would be awake, but her cries were lonesome as they floated over the countryside. Lonesome and terrifying.

But they finally penetrated Erin's confusion. *Shelby Rae was downstairs!*

SHELBY RAE RECLINED on one of the sofas in the family room, pillows banked behind her. Erin handed the towel-wrapped ice pack to her father who sat on the edge of the sofa. Shelby Rae's hand gripped one of his fiercely, unwilling to let go.

She looked shaken and had a blue and yellow bruise on one side of her face. The eye makeup she'd been wearing at the party was smeared dully across her cheeks, and her hair—Erin tried to make sense of her hair. Someone had chopped off hunks of it on one side without regard to shape or style, so that it resembled a Barbie doll of MacKenzie's that her little brother had vandalized when they were kids. As soon as her father had helped Shelby Rae inside and led her to the couch, Erin had hurried in with a soft blanket to wrap her in. Her bathing suit was dirty, and one strap hung, broken, down her back. She had scratches, too, on her arms, and bruises on her legs.

Bruce held her gently to him as she spoke through her tears. "I thought they were going to kill me. I thought I would never see you again."

"Baby, I would have done anything to get you back. You know that. No one is going to take you away from me again."

At that moment, Jocko, who'd been standing on the carpet, trembling with excitement, could contain himself no more, and jumped up on the couch to try to wriggle between them.

Bruce chuckled as he dodged the dog's frantic forays into Shelby Rae's blanket. "Well, this guy I don't know about. He's been missing you."

Standing a few feet away, Erin felt like she was watching something so intimate that she didn't belong there. She was an outsider in her own home. Her father, Shelby Rae, and Jocko had formed an entirely new family unit since she'd gone off to college. Shelby Rae had stopped a long time ago trying to make sure Erin didn't feel left out. Her father looked so vulnerable, and Shelby Rae, hurt and afraid. At least she was letting her husband get close enough to comfort her.

Erin knew it was a selfish thought to have at that moment, but any fantasy she had about her father divorcing Shelby Rae was gone in that moment. He was obviously deeply in love with the woman who'd replaced her mother. She'd been fighting that reality for a long, long time. But maybe he, also, had needed this near-tragedy to know what was in his own heart. Shelby Rae had complained often that Erin's father didn't spend any time with her, that she felt like he took her for granted.

"I'm so thirsty. They only gave me a little water. I don't even know where I was. And I was blindfolded the whole time. It was like a nightmare I couldn't wake up from. They wouldn't even talk to me. I don't know why they let me go."

"I'll get you some water." Erin left the room, grateful to have an escape. Trouble followed her, but Jocko stayed happily on the couch.

Erin hadn't yet told MacKenzie about the kidnapping, though God knew Julie Berry had probably already spread the word that Bruce Walsh's young wife had left him. She expected MacKenzie would probably text her before they talked, except it was now only six in the morning. And yet, she'd told Noah Daly all about the kidnapping. It had all just spilled out. Why in the world had she trusted him with that information? Technically, he should be the last person she should trust. His father had been sentenced to a six-year jail term partly because the deputy who shot her mother was aiming for him, as he fled the scene of the bank robbery.

But somehow she found herself trusting him. His brown eyes had been so sincere, like a little kid's. And he had that funny indent in his chin like someone had pressed their pinky into it when he was a baby, and it stuck. Most guys would try to hide it with a beard. Erin thought beards on young guys looked pretentious and silly. She knew she wouldn't be the first woman to trust a guy just because he was good-looking.

Did she dare text him? Something told her she should. She wanted to tell *somebody* Shelby Rae was back. He would see her message when he woke up.

> *Just wanted to tell you Shelby Rae came home a while ago. She's a little banged up but okay. She doesn't know who took her. Anyway now you know too.*

She stared at the screen, and a "delivered" line told her it had shown up on his phone. Her heart beat a little faster. Maybe he at least had the phone silenced. She busied herself getting water for Shelby Rae, trying not to look at the screen again. She would feel like a total ass if it woke him up.

Her father called from the family room.

"Coming!"

Her phone vibrated.

> Good news -- Is your dad calling cops now?

Putting the water down, she quickly replied.

> Don't know. She just got here.

> Let me know what I can do. When everything calms down you want to get some coffee or something later?

What should I answer? She already felt like kind of a jerk, texting while her injured stepmother was probably dying of thirst. Tucking the phone in her pocket, she hurried back to the family room with the water. "Sorry it took me so long."

Her father looked at her with a hint of curiosity, but he was really too concerned about Shelby Rae to pursue it.

"I'll run you a bath. Unless you want to wait for the police so they can, um, take evidence and stuff," Erin said.

Shelby Rae sat bolt upright nearly dislodging Jocko, who had finally settled down, happy. "No police. Bruce, they said *no police*. They said they'd kill me if we tell the police!" Her eyes pleaded with her husband. She didn't look at Erin.

"I know that's what they said on the note, sugarcakes. Didn't you say they didn't talk to you?"

"Of course they threatened me." Her voice was tearful. "I meant we didn't have conversations. Not after they got me to where they kept me. But they warned me before they threw me out of the van—at least I think it was a van." Her fingers strayed to the broad scrape on one forearm. Between the bruise on her face and the scrapes on her arms and knees and hands, they had treated her cruelly. What if her father hadn't paid the ransom? Erin was coming around to his conviction that they would have killed Shelby Rae if he hadn't paid. They would be equally serious, then, about not getting the police involved. All three of them could still be in danger.

"Was it two men?" Erin asked. "Did you recognize their voices?"

Shelby Rae shook her head. "Someone grabbed me from behind in the cabana and they put a scarf or something around my face so I couldn't see. All I know is that the guy was really strong." She looked at Bruce. "At first I thought he was going to strangle me. It hurt so much."

Bruce kissed her on the forehead. "I'm sorry, baby. I'm so sorry I wasn't there to stop them."

"You said *the guy*." Erin's curiosity was piqued. "You mean it wasn't necessarily two men who kidnapped you?"

Shelby Rae's brow furrowed. She looked younger and more vulnerable to Erin than she had in a long time. "I'm not sure, but one might have been a woman. The hands were strong, but I don't know, softer, maybe. Why are you asking me all this? I just want it to be over."

"Maybe now isn't the time." Her father gave Erin a warning look that told her they were done talking for now. Anything else she wanted to ask—and there was a *lot* she wanted to ask Shelby Rae—would have to wait.

Shelby Rae had said she thought there was a woman involved. As far as Erin was concerned it pointed to one person more than any other—Bryn Owens.

IN WETUMPKA, I am my human's constant companion. Tammy Lynn and I go everywhere together, with the exception of some food establishments and the doctor's office. Two locations that could, indeed, benefit from the presence of felines. One sees these therapy dogs entering medical facilities, and no one bats an eye when they see them in the aisles of the grocery store. What, one wonders, is therapeutic about a bouncing, slobbering, untidy chunk of unbathed fur? I shudder at the thought. Felines are unquestionably far more calming influences.

I fear Erin may be rather less confident of my crime solving abilities than Tammy Lynn. The dreaded Jocko didn't help matters by snatching that bloody garment away from me and dropping it at her feet moments after I discovered it. She wants to find out who kidnapped her stepmother, and I confess I can't bear to see such a tantalizing mystery unsolved. I must convince her to let me stick closer to her so I can help her, but also keep her out of danger. It seems that no one but Erin and myself—and perhaps Noah—is interested in bringing the kidnappers to justice. While Erin slept this morning, I settled myself on a sunny table outside the gaudy master suite (think Versailles as reimagined by that Beiber fellow—I believe it's the only room Shelby Rae decorated herself) to listen to Bruce and his wife talking. She begged him once again not to call the police. I find that curious, considering the kidnappers could return at any time and strike again.

After my late morning nap and grooming duties, I do reconnaissance inside the house to see what I can find. The cadaverous housekeeper, who seems to set her own schedule, is in the kitchen, mopping. She's a tetchy sort, and complains frequently about her teeth not fitting correctly, leading me to wonder what she looks like without them. Grisly, I expect, because she's about ten feet tall, and has a face like a week-old kidney pie. But I leap from counter to counter so she doesn't accidentally swat me with her broom when I venture into the kitchen for a drink of water.

I take an equally indirect way out. Thank goodness Jocko is no longer my shadow, entrenched as he surely is on his mistress's bed. The housekeeper likes Jocko as little as she likes me. It puts me in a mind of the ancient proverb, "The enemy of my enemy is my friend." If only I could let her know my feelings about Jocko, she might be a little kinder to me.

Bruce is ensconced in his office doing paperwork, and doesn't even glance at me as I leap nimbly onto his desk. I pretend to ignore him as well. He looks completely knackered, but had managed a shower and shave so that he smells of gentleman's cologne and strong soap.

I spy what I'm looking for. The ransom note is half-tucked beneath a file, but I can see enough.

You're thinking that cats can't read human writing. While you would technically be correct, I don't need to be able to read it because I remember exactly what it said when Bruce read from it, right down to the mention of Shelby Rae being pretty.

It's the paper itself I'm interested in. I lie down with graceful care, *and for a moment I think he'll shoo me away. Instead, he picks up his cell phone and makes a call.*

The paper smells musty. It's not crisp and white, but faintly yellowed at the edges, and brittle. I've seen Tammy Lynn handle such paper. Letters from old files she's researching. Notes stuck in books. The writing on it isn't from a computer, either. The letters look to be typed on an old machine, not printed.

Are we looking for someone old? Who would have such a machine? I'm thinking of the typewriter off in a corner at the Wetumpka public library. Surely the New Belford library would have a typewriter. But I can't imagine someone being so foolish as to type a ransom note in a library, because libraries often have cameras. It could have been done anywhere—perhaps in someone's attic, on paper they found there. But I worry that Erin won't follow up on it. It's certain that Bruce won't.

Still, I think we can eliminate Bruce from the list of suspects. His only motive could be to terrorize or frighten Shelby Rae, and he seems to genuinely care for her. Humans are such strange, complicated creatures. I love them, but also pity them.

Seeing how miserable Bruce is makes me wonder how the victim herself is doing, and after a few more restful moments on the spacious desk, I stretch and make my way silently up the stairs.

JOCKO IS STRETCHED out on the master and mistress's bed, the lazy sod. As though he has done anything useful at all today. But Shelby Rae isn't with him. I wander by the en suite, but no one is inside. Hmmmm.

I hear a voice from an unusual place—Shelby Rae's enormous closet.

Before coming to New Belford, I'd only seen such a closet wonderland on television. Two separate aisles of dark polished shelves and drawers and racks of hanging clothes. Marble countertops with mannequin heads wearing hats of all sorts. Small, built-in cabinets hung with necklaces, and little drawers for earrings and rings and bracelets. Tammy Lynn would laugh at the extravagance. One would expect such a room—for a room it is—would be brilliantly organized, given that everything has its dedicated spaces. But, no. It looks like the Last Chance Sale at Victoria's Secret after a busload of tourists has swarmed through. Lingerie and skimpy clothing flopped onto the floor, dangling from hangers, and escaping from half-closed drawers. Even the countertops are littered with costume jewelry.

You can tell a lot about a person if you peek into their personal closet. But the mess was fortuitous because it let me get close to Shelby Rae, who stood at the room's single window wearing one of the simpler nightdresses in the room, without her noticing me.

Not only was she out of her bed, but she was talking on a small black flip phone of the type I'd seen older folks and the occasional teenager use. I believe it's called a burner phone.

I can only hear one side of the conversation:

"But I hurt all over."

"He's downstairs. He's doing absolutely *everything* for me."

Laughter.

"I better go. I'll call you."

More laughter.

I slip into one of the sweater cubbies before Shelby Rae turns around, and watch as she stands on tiptoe to put the phone on a high shelf. When it's hidden she starts out of the closet, but stops to look in the mirror and mess up her hair a bit more.

I wait a few moments to let her get settled in the bedroom before I leave the closet. When I finally emerge, I hear someone tap on the bedroom door and see Bruce peek in. He sees what I see—Shelby Rae reclining on her pillow, eyes closed.

One of us knows she isn't actually asleep.

· · ·

AFTER ERIN'S father took Shelby Rae upstairs to tend to her and put her to bed, Erin texted MacKenzie to see if she wanted to meet in town for lunch. The house suddenly seemed too small for the three of them. Of course, the idea that it was actually too small was absurd. But Shelby Rae and her father had been reunited in their own little world—a world from which Erin was excluded.

Exhausted, she showered and put on a pair of denim shorts and a sleeveless peasant blouse she'd bought at the international shop near campus. The blouse was embroidered with bright blue and yellow flowers twined with green stems, and she left the ends of the delicate red ribbon at the neck untied. The flowers cheered her up. It had been a strange, awkward time at the house, and while she was truly glad Shelby Rae was back safely, her return hadn't lightened Erin's mood. If anything, she felt more unsettled. It creeped her out that there really were people evil enough to kidnap her step-mother for money, and that the man she'd seen pick up the fifty thousand dollars was still out there. It wasn't that she was afraid. She was strong and watchful and could put up a much better fight than Shelby Rae had. But that person—or people, according to Shelby Rae—was not only in the New Belford area, but had been inside the house to leave the note.

Erin stroked Trouble, who had reclaimed his spot on her bed and was stretched out, eyes half-closed with contentment. "Keep watch," she said. "Don't let any crazy people in. Jocko's worthless as a guard dog." The cat lifted his head and squinched his cool green eyes at her. She had absolutely no doubt they understood each other.

THERE WERE ONLY a dozen restaurants in New Belford that

weren't fast food places, and Erin arrived at Gerald's on the Square at two minutes before noon. Gerald was long dead, and the owner of the revamped pub had kept the name, the worn handmade tables, and the mahogany bar, but had brought the menu into the 21st century. MacKenzie would be five to ten minutes late, as usual. Most people considered five or ten minutes late to be on time, but Erin had a dread of arriving somewhere even a minute late. It was something MacKenzie teased her about. Before Tionna's death, they would have met at Two Hearts Bakery for lunch. The bakery always had a fun herbal iced tea on the menu, and the chicken salad contained fresh French tarragon that Bryn grew in the little garden out back. The chicken salad came on homemade croissants and was served with fruit salad and two light-as-air pastel *macarons* for dessert.

Even if Bryn reopened Two Hearts, Erin knew she would hardly be welcome.

She ordered sweet iced tea for herself and lemonade for MacKenzie. How badly would she have preferred to order a cold beer, even if it was only lunchtime? At home, her father didn't mind if she had a beer or a glass of wine, as long as she wasn't driving. And there were plenty of bars around the UK campus that didn't look at IDs too closely.

At last MacKenzie arrived looking fresh and cool in a short, pink linen dress and open-toed, heeled booties that made her slender legs look even longer. Her brown hair was caught in two low pigtails. Erin greeted her with a hug, thinking that only MacKenzie could wear schoolgirl pigtails and look perfectly gorgeous. They sat back down and within ten minutes, Erin had caught her up to date with all of the recent drama.

"You mean your father's not calling the sheriff? Doesn't the

FBI have to investigate kidnappings?" MacKenzie swiped a carrot slice through the dish of hummus between them and took a bite.

"Keep your voice down, Mac. If they find out about it they *have* to investigate." Erin leaned forward. "Whoever did it is still out there, and they could do it again. That's why I told my dad we should tell Sheriff Bowen, but he won't listen to me. Shelby Rae is completely freaked out."

"Did they, you know, do anything sexual to her?"

Erin leaned back, surprised. She hadn't thought to ask, and Shelby Rae hadn't volunteered any details.

"Seriously, Erin. She should at least see a doctor, don't you think?"

"God, I don't want to go there." Erin sighed. "Dad is with her. She would tell him, right?" Her appetite, which had been voracious when they ordered, evaporated. She never could have predicted what having someone close to her being kidnapped would truly be like. If it had been her father who had been kidnapped, she would've called the sheriff, the FBI, and the local SWAT team, then grabbed the Mossberg to search every square inch of McClaren County. Somehow she hadn't felt so angry about Shelby Rae, and that bothered her. What if Shelby Rae had actually been raped or injured in some way that wasn't obvious? No wonder her father had wanted to get her back as soon as possible.

They ate in thoughtful silence for a while.

"Mac, I need to know who did this."

MacKenzie nodded. "Who else knows about it?"

Erin counted off on her fingers. "Me, my dad, and Shelby Rae, of course. Julie Berry. She showed up yesterday morning."

"Ugh."

"You know how she's never liked Shelby Rae." Erin put her

napkin by her plate. "But I can't imagine Julie being a *kidnapper*. Shelby Rae said there were two people, and one might have been a woman. Julie's bitchy but I can't see her being violent."

MacKenzie shook her head. "My mom told me it was harsh the way Mr. Berry left her for a waitress like that. Said she didn't leave her house for almost two months. When she came out again, she'd lost thirty pounds. I think we were only like five years old or something when it happened."

"So it's like the chicken and the egg thing. Was she crazy and kind of bitchy to start with, and that's why he left her? Or did his leaving her make her that way? She used to be so nice to me." Erin genuinely felt bad about thinking ill of Julie.

"Anybody else?"

Do I tell her about Noah? Erin was torn. It wasn't as if she seriously suspected him. She realized she hadn't texted him back about meeting for coffee. He probably thought she was blowing him off. The corners of her mouth dropped into a frown.

"Okay. Spill." MacKenzie crossed her arms, and gave Erin her most severe schoolteacher look. "Now."

"It's Noah Daly." Erin paused, watching the smile spread over MacKenzie's face. "What? Why are you looking at me like that?"

"You're blushing. You always blush when you like a guy."

"Come on. You don't know what you're talking about." Erin could feel the heat burning at her ears, and on her cheeks.

"He followed you around like a puppy dog on Sunday. I'd say the feeling is mutual."

"I was getting his mom some *glasses*, you idiot."

"Right."

"Then everyone got all excited about Bryn Owens being

parked out front, and Chief Deputy Wilkins running her off."
Erin remembered she hadn't told Mackenzie about seeing
Noah talking to Bryn. She was about to say something when
MacKenzie put up one hand.

"You haven't been on a date in six months, and *he* broke up
with his girlfriend right after Christmas. I know because she
does nails at the salon, and she's really cute and shy, but he
stopped going to her charismatic church with her, so they
broke up." She reached across the table and touched Erin's arm
with her cool fingertips. "I know it's complicated, because of
who his dad is. But he really *is* a good guy. Plus, your dad gave
him a job. Your dad's not dumb, right?"

"I'm not looking for some stupid summer romance," Erin
said. "I don't think I even want to stay here the rest of the
summer. After I find out who's messing with my family..." The
word "family" caught in her throat. When had she started
thinking about Shelby Rae as her family? "I'm going back to
Lexington. Get a part-time job and volunteer at the rescue
shelter there until school starts." She didn't add that she was
feeling awkward in her own house.

"When's the last time you actually had sex?" MacKenzie's
voice carried to the next table, where a homely man in his
fifties sat reading a book over lunch. He choked on his beer
and had a coughing fit.

Erin covered her eyes and bowed her head in an *I can't
believe this is happening* gesture. MacKenzie gave the man her
sunniest smile before turning back to Erin.

"No one says you have to fall in love with the guy. You
might as well have some fun. He's probably at least *clean*
anyway. It's not like he dates skanky girls."

"You are *unbelievable*, Mac." Still, a part of her wanted to
laugh. MacKenzie talked a good game, but she was very partic-

ular about whom she went out with. When her parents had let her start dating when she was fifteen, she had been the one to do everything first, and on her schedule. Her latest experiment was a Nashville DJ named Stryker whose parents had a country estate nearby that he visited with select friends. "He's kind of a snob," MacKenzie had told her. "I'm embarrassed for you to meet him. Maybe next time he comes up. *Maybe*."

"It's better than hanging around the house all the time with the wicked stepmother, right?" MacKenzie put a hand over her mouth. "Oops. Too soon?"

Erin waved it off. "No worries. I'm sure she'll be back to her bitchy self in no time." She woke her phone to check the time. "I guess Noah *did* ask me if I wanted to have coffee today."

"What did you tell him?"

"I haven't said anything, yet." Erin was defensive. "I couldn't make up my mind."

MacKenzie waited to answer until the server finished refilling her lemonade. "He lives with his parents, I think. You know his mom manages that huge gas and convenience store out near the interstate. I wonder if he'll move out now that creepy dad of his is out of jail. Noah really seems like too sweet a guy to have Jeb Daly for a father."

Erin is stunned. "What do you mean? Jeb Daly is out of jail? No one said anything. They're supposed to tell people. Victims' families."

"But it was Zach Wilkins who shot your mom."

"But it was *Jeb Daly's fault*. That's part of the reason he went to jail. Not just because of the robbery! When did he get out?"

"I thought you knew," MacKenzie said. "Now I feel like a moron. I think he got out last Friday."

"So he was out over the weekend, and Noah didn't bother to mention it to me?" That bothered her. A lot. He hadn't lied to her, but he hadn't told her the whole truth, either. For nearly seven years his father had been away, out of sight and (mostly) out of Erin's mind. She glanced around the pub. Jeb Daly himself could walk in any minute. The thought chilled her. Someday she would have to see him again. It had been one thing to think about going out with Noah, but knowing he slept in the same house as the criminal who was responsible for her mother's death? That was too much.

"I bet he didn't want to upset you. He couldn't exactly say, *By the way, my dad just got out of prison, and I know you hate him, but let's mess around anyway.* Don't be harsh, Erin."

"Why are you defending him?"

MacKenzie held up both hands. "Whoa. I care about *you.* See him, or don't see him. It doesn't matter to me. But it's been over seven years since your mom died. You've been doing great. Now you're freaked out all over again."

Erin whispered through a tight grimace. "Shelby Rae was *kidnapped.* On Sunday, I saw Noah talking to Bryn Owens where she was parked out front. What if he was helping her? What if it was Noah, his dad, *and* Bryn? Noah's job could've been to distract me. He could have easily slipped into the house and left the note." She slapped a hand on the scarred surface of the table, making the silverware rattle. "I feel like an idiot."

"Oh, come on. Noah?" MacKenzie's words were incredulous, but the look on her face was far less skeptical.

ERIN COULDN'T SHAKE her disappointment. Her car was parked in the post office's public lot, and as she walked there, she couldn't stop thinking back to sitting with Noah on the dock. She hadn't felt so comfortable with a guy in a long time, but now she knew it was possible she'd been completely wrong about him. What was the saying? *Like father like son.* In the far distance she could see the enormous American flag flying over her father's dealership. Noah was probably there, working. If she wanted to, she could just walk in and ask Earl, the service manager she'd known since she was eight years old, to have Noah come out and talk to her.

Did you and your dad kidnap Shelby Rae? Were you supposed to keep me out of the way? Is that why you hung out with me?

She tried to imagine his face when she confronted him. Surely he wouldn't have the nerve to lie to her face. But he probably had, already. They hadn't talked about his father, at all. Or her mother. Obviously those weren't safe subjects.

Still, she wasn't one hundred percent sure he'd done anything wrong. She prided herself on being able to spot the kind of guys who lied and cheated and to stay away from them. Despite his not mentioning his father being out of prison, nothing about Noah had raised any red flags. In fact, quite the opposite.

She was halfway up the steps to the post office parking lot when she saw Julie Berry's small gray Mercedes pulling out of the exit. Julie sat bolt upright, her slender fingers with their neatly trimmed, clear-coated nails wrapped securely around the wheel in the ten and two position. Erin tried to wave her down, but Julie, who was wearing a pair of once-fashionable, enormous Jackie O sunglasses, didn't notice her. How odd it was to Erin that Julie would drive a Mercedes instead of a car from her father's dealership, especially given that she had such a crush on her father. Did forty-five year-old women even get crushes?

Erin jogged a few steps, waving her arms, knowing she looked like a perfect idiot, but couldn't get Julie's attention. If there was one thing Julie was, it was a gossip. She loved being everyone's source for the latest. It had occurred to Erin that she just might know something relevant about Shelby Rae, or even Bryn Owens. Only the day before she'd been the first one to show up after Shelby Rae had disappeared. Could it really have been such a coincidence? She'd been defensive and a little strange. As much as Erin cared for her, and Erin really did care, she could believe that Julie actually had known already that Shelby Rae had been kidnapped.

When Erin got to her car, she pulled up Julie Berry's cell phone number and dialed. It rang five times and switched to voicemail. She left a message saying Shelby Rae had returned, but she needed to find out if Julie had noticed anything out of the ordinary at the party. "Anything at all," Erin said. "Maybe you heard someone talking about Shelby Rae or someone was looking for her, or acting strange?" She also apologized for not being able to give her more details about Shelby Rae's absence from the house. "I'll explain later when dad and I have a better idea of what's going on. Promise." It wasn't entirely the truth. Erin and her father already knew what had gone on, but not the when or why. But if she knew anything about Julie, it was that she couldn't resist you if you flattered her or offered good gossip.

ERIN TAPPED on her father and Shelby Rae's partially open bedroom door.

"Come in."

Trouble slipped inside the master bedroom just ahead of Erin and jumped up on the tall four-poster bed where Shelby

Rae was curled against a bank of pillows, reading a magazine. Trouble didn't notice that Jocko was buried in the comforter Shelby Rae had pushed to the end of the bed, and when the little dog's head popped up, Trouble went vertical at least six inches. When he came down, he stiffened his tail and stalked to a corner of the bed to settle as though it was what he meant to do all along.

Erin stifled a laugh. Jocko and Trouble were like an ill-suited comedy team.

Shelby Rae gave Trouble an irritated look, but she didn't shoo him off the bed. "When is that Tammy person coming back for the cat?"

"I'll take him out with me when I go. She'll be back in town next Monday, I think. She's going to email me if not. Are you feeling better? Is there something I can get you?"

"I'm going to get up in a few minutes. It's not like I'm one of those invalids. Lying around in bed is so boring, you know?"

Erin felt luxurious if she took a day to lie in bed and read books until the summer daylight faded. Her father encouraged her to relax while she was at home because he knew how hard she worked at school. This summer she'd only been hanging out with MacKenzie and volunteering a few afternoons at the animal rescue shelter up the road, and she felt a little guilty. She might as well have been tucked in the house reading. But then she would've been stuck with Shelby Rae, which was something neither of them wanted.

Shelby Rae slid her tanned legs off the bed, letting her satin nightgown drop to cover her thighs. Her hair was still a mess, but at some point she had at least gotten up to cut it so it was no longer so uneven. Sighing dramatically, she crossed her arms to pull the nightgown over her head and walked to her closet. Erin wasn't fazed by her habit of undressing in front of her.

She did it in front of the housekeeper as well. In some ways Erin admired her stepmother's lack of self-consciousness.

"We—I mean, I found your earring up on the path." Erin stood by the bed, stroking Trouble's soft fur.

"Which one?"

"The white enamel butterfly. I have it right here." She took the earring out of her pocket and looked at it. Its lower right wing still had dirt on it.

Shelby Rae came out in her bra and panties, taking a sundress off a wooden hanger. As she crossed the room silently on the rich blond carpet, Erin noticed that her upper chest was getting freckled with age and sun exposure. "Let me see." She plucked the earring from Erin's palm. "Huh. Wondered where that went. I lost both of them. But they're vintage, right? Cute. Too bad." She tossed the earring into the small trashcan next to Bruce's nightstand.

"So you weren't wearing them on Sunday?" Erin was confused.

Shelby Rae shook her head. "It was a barbecue." She rolled her eyes as if Erin should know better. Stepping into the sundress, she turned around and asked Erin to zip her up. When Erin finished, Shelby Rae headed for her vanity counter in the bathroom.

She brushed her hair and covered much of it with a scarf so only a fringe was visible. "I got an emergency appointment for my hair. I'm not going to let those assholes ruin my life *and* my hair. It was a weird and shitty thing for them to do."

"You're going out? Already? I don't know if that's a good idea, Shelby Rae. I still think you should go to the doctor."

"It's over. I want to move on."

"But you were kidnapped! How can you just pretend everything's normal?"

Shelby Rae met Erin's eyes in the mirror. "How am I supposed to act? You weren't the one it happened to."

Erin felt chagrined. "I'm sorry. I know you said you don't want to talk about it..."

"I still don't. I'm okay, all right?"

"What did the place they took you smell like? Did you hear any noises that might identify it? Maybe a train or traffic going by. Or did it smell like you were by the lake?"

"Look, it's over. I was scared to death, and at first I thought they were going to kill me. Why would I want to remember anything about it? They didn't treat me all that badly, except for when they threw me out of the van." She smoothed cover-up and foundation over the bruise on her face as she spoke. But Erin noticed that her hand shook a little bit.

"But if it was Bryn Owens, and some man, they're still out there. They could do it again. They could try to kidnap you again. Or Dad." Erin's voice trailed off. She didn't understand why her stepmother wasn't more of a basket case, why she was even considering leaving the house after what she'd been through. Was she just dumber than Erin had ever considered? *No. She's not dumb. She got my father to fall in love with her and marry her, even though they had nothing in common.*

Shelby Rae turned to Erin. "Or you, right? Your father told me you were always afraid of a boogey man coming to get you in the dark. He said you had night terrors until you were seven years old and used to camp out in front of their bedroom door in the middle of the night, and he would almost trip over you in the morning. They happened again after your mother died. Are you really worried about me, or are you just scared for your own sake?"

Erin took a step back. "What are you talking about? No!" She'd put the night terrors out of her head for so long. They'd come back for six months after her mother was killed, and her father had kept a blow-up mattress on her mother's side of the bed that she could collapse onto whenever she woke and was afraid to be alone.

"Don't be embarrassed, honey. We all get scared sometimes." The tone of her voice was gentle and reminded Erin of when they'd been close, before Shelby Rae and her father were married.

Now Erin felt like she was twelve years old again, and remembered the touch of her mother's hand on her hair in a way she hadn't in many years. The day her mother was killed, Julie Berry showed up at school in the middle of the day to take her to her house in town. Erin had known something was wrong, but Julie smiled unconvincingly and said she wanted to wait for her father to come and get her. She made her a grilled cheese sandwich with the crusts cut off, the way Erin's mother always did. But Julie had used Crisco instead of butter in the pan and the sandwich came out pale and limp, without the crisp swirls of darkened butter that were on the ones her mother made. She'd been too worried to eat more than a couple of bites.

For a long, long time, she'd felt like her world ended on that afternoon. A part of her would hold onto that feeling forever.

She didn't trust Shelby Rae with that part of her. Steeling herself, she returned Shelby Rae's gaze. The impulse to push Shelby Rae a little harder was one she couldn't ignore. She asked the question she'd been thinking about.

"Is there something you don't want anyone to find out about the kidnapping? Maybe someone in your family needed fifty thousand dollars, and you thought Dad would notice if you wrote them a check that big, so you faked it?"

Erin was so stunned by the slap that she hardly understood what Shelby Rae said next.

"Don't you *dare* talk about my family that way! You don't have the slightest idea what I've been through. Not that your father even cared that I was gone, either. Do you see him here in the room with me? I'm sure he's downstairs back to work. You've never liked my family because you don't think any of us are good enough for you. I'm sick of it, and I'm sick of you!"

Erin heard the last part clearly. Shelby Rae's cheeks, which had blazed with angry color, went pale as she realized what she'd done. But she didn't apologize.

"What's going on here? Erin? Shelby Rae?" Bruce Walsh stood in the middle of the bedroom, confusion etched on his face.

Unable to speak or continue looking at her father, Erin ran out of the room with Trouble on her heels. Jocko remained at the bathroom door, looking anxiously between Bruce and Shelby Rae.

Erin didn't want to try to explain what had just transpired to her father. She had a pretty good idea whose side he would be on anyway.

THERE WAS ALWAYS an air of a holiday about the dealership when Bruce Walsh wasn't in the office because it didn't happen very often. Noah had heard from techs who'd worked at other places that the owners didn't usually hang around much once the business took off. They came in just to show they were keeping an eye on things or to be there when a relative wanted a special deal on a vehicle. It helped that Bruce Walsh was a pretty nice guy. His people were happy to have him around, and when he was there they were conscientious about their jobs. But he'd been closeted in his office all Monday afternoon, and today he hadn't come in at all. People were starting to slack off a bit. Earl, the service manager, was in a sour mood, and Bruce Walsh was one of the few people who was good at joshing him out of it. Earl kept to himself, and no one knew where he lived or what kind of life he led when he wasn't behind the desk. But Bruce even occasionally got a half-smile out of him. Now Bruce was out, and only Noah knew why the light in the big, open office in the loft overlooking the show-room was really off.

Speaking of slacking off, he was irritated with himself for checking his phone every fifteen minutes to see if Erin had texted him back. Had he said something wrong? *She* was the one who had texted him before he'd been awake for ten minutes, right? Maybe he was being immodest, but usually when he asked a girl out, or they exchanged numbers, he got a lot of interest. Some of it was the wrong kind, of course. There had been that girl with the Shelby Mustang he'd met when he and Katelyn were fighting a lot the previous fall, who'd gotten his number then sent him a half dozen snaps of herself in her lacy neon-pink bra and panties. And one in which she had no bra on at all.

It had to be that photo that he forgot to delete—genuinely forgot, seriously—that Katelyn found. Katelyn had thrown the phone at him, calling him names he hadn't even known she knew.

The truth was that their relationship had been headed downhill for months. Katelyn's parents and the people at her Pentecostal church were pressuring him not so subtly about them getting married. While he was cool with their not having sex (Katelyn prized her virginity above all things, which was her privilege), the last straw came when her father took Noah aside after dinner at their house and asked when he and Katelyn were going to start talking to the pastor about premarital counseling.

Despite the row over the photo, they kept dating until right after Christmas. He sensed that Katelyn didn't want to give up, that she felt she could somehow convince him, or at least guilt him into being the guy she wanted him to be.

It wasn't that he didn't want to be married someday, but the idea of settling down at twenty-one with Katelyn, and having kids right away, before either of them knew for sure what they wanted to do with their lives, freaked him out. Katelyn came from a huge family and made no secret of wanting the same thing, and soon. That was fine for somebody else, but he wasn't sure he even wanted to have kids. The idea of being a father terrified him. His own father was a poor excuse for a human being, let alone a father.

Now his father was back, and he hadn't changed a bit.

TUESDAYS WERE SLOW, and Noah was packed up and headed for his car at five minutes after five. Still no answer from Erin. *Screw it.* She wasn't really interested. He guessed she'd really only texted him to let her know that Shelby Rae was home and all right.

A couple of the guys were going out for a beer, but he wasn't in the mood.

"Yeah, I saw you hitting on the boss's daughter, Daly," one of them said. "You headed out for dinner at the mansion?"

The other guy laughed.

"Piss off, Duke. Like she'd even look at your sorry ass." Noah kept his tone light, knowing that if he protested too much, it would just get worse. *Was I that obvious?*

Duke, who was in his early thirties and had already been divorced twice, made a scoffing sound and put on his solid black sunglasses against the late afternoon sun. "Too skinny for me. I like a woman of..." He made a squeezing gesture with his open hands. "You know. Substance."

The guy who with Duke laughed but then started rattling off names of women that Duke had spent time with who could definitely be described as skinny.

Seeing his chance to escape, Noah walked over to his bike to put on his motorcycle helmet. Nearly every other guy he knew who rode a bike rode bareheaded. He knew and half-agreed with the argument against helmets— that they wouldn't keep you from getting killed, but would protect you just enough so that you ended up brain-damaged. But it was hearing Katelyn's mother, a nurse, comment every time she saw a rider without a helmet ride by that always made him think twice. "There goes another organ donor," she'd say. "I guess we should all be grateful."

As Duke and the other guy got into Duke's tricked out vintage F-150, Noah cut a wide half-circle around them and pulled out onto Main Street. Maybe he should've gone with them. Tuesday night was one of the nights he used to ride out to Paul's Dine-Away by the lake, and pick up chicken dinners for himself and his mother because she was off work. But now his father was home and things were different. He didn't really want to go home, and there was no way he was going to buy his old man's dinner.

When he got to Ash Street, where he should've turned to get to his mother's house (he wasn't yet ready to think of it as his mother and father's house, and hoped he'd never have to again) he surprised himself by continuing on out of town toward the lake.

Yes, he was stupidly transparent. Long before he reached the Walsh property, he slowed down so that when he passed he could get a good look. There was Erin's Challenger, black and sleek in the circular driveway. The afternoon was clear, the light mellow, and the azalea bushes and blooming crape myrtle trees out front made the house look welcoming. Erin was home, but she wasn't outside. What if she had been? She'd have seen him, and that could have been embarrassing. She might think he was stalking her.

He wanted to kick himself. When had he turned into a middle school girl?

NOAH COUNTED two unfamiliar trucks in the driveway and another two cars in front of his house even before he was halfway up the block. None of his father's old friends had had the nerve to come by the house to visit while he was in prison. It wasn't like they were family friends, and Noah was glad. He knew a couple of them by reputation: Scott and Billy Attwell. They'd taken over their old man's body shop north of town, and now it was known for selling as much dope as paint jobs and fenders. His father had mentioned that they'd made the trip to visit him at the prison a couple of times.

"True friends," his father had said over the spaghetti and meatballs Annette made for dinner his first night home. He'd pointedly kept his gaze on his dinner as he spoke. "You really learn who your friends are in a situation like that." Noah had only visited at holidays for the first few years, when his mother insisted. Then he'd stopped going.

As he slowed to turn the bike into the driveway, a different truck, this one a spanking new black king cab, rumbled toward him. The low sun glinted off the windshield, and he recognized the driver's reflective aviator glasses and Cincinnati Bengals ball cap. The driver put his hand out the window in more of a stopping motion than a wave.

Noah stopped the bike and put his feet down to keep it standing. "Hey, Zach. How's the new ride?" Most of the rest of the town knew Zach as Chief Deputy Zach Wilkins, the officer who had accidentally shot and killed Rita Walsh. But he'd made a friend of Noah after Jeb Daly went to prison.

"It's not the boy's fault," Zach had told both the sheriff and Noah's mother. "He needs a guiding hand to keep him from his father's path." Noah's mother had been surprised but grateful. The shame alone of her husband's attempted robbery of the bank and his role in Rita Walsh's death had nearly overwhelmed her. While she knew Noah was a good kid, she'd thought it wouldn't hurt to have someone in the sheriff's office keeping an eye on him.

Zach had often shown up at Noah's soccer games and had helped him get a counseling job at an area summer camp. He'd taken him deer hunting several times, something Noah's father had never done. It had felt weird to Noah at first—doing things with a guy who wasn't his dad, even though he and his dad hardly did anything together—but Zach wasn't pushy, and now Noah missed the times they had hung out together. The other thing Zach did was to teach him about engines and working on cars. Zach wasn't a collector, but he liked to have a project. Noah's favorite that they worked on together had been a black 1982 Crossfire Trans-Am.

Noah was old enough to know now that there were men out there who preyed on vulnerable teenage boys, but he'd never gotten any weird or creepy vibes from Zach. He really just seemed to be a responsible, nice guy. Well, maybe *nice* wasn't the word. He was pretty macho, as Noah's mom would say. A man's man. Responsible, but not a sap.

"Looks like you've got a houseful. How's it going?" Zach raised his voice over the sounds of their rumbling engines.

Noah unsnapped and lifted his helmet off and shook off the sweat beading at his hairline. The guys inside the house were probably getting an eyeful, unless they were playing cards or video games already. "Hey, it's going okay. Busy at work and stuff."

"Welcome-home party?"

Noah glanced at the front of his house. There was a cooler he didn't recognize on the porch with a pair of torn up 12-pack boxes that had contained bottles of Pabst beside it. "Yeah, I was just coming home with dinner. Surprised the heck out of me."

Zach grinned, his straight white teeth gleaming beneath his dark mustache. There was something about Zach that reminded Noah of Burt Reynolds, an old movie star from the seventies that his mom was crazy about. She'd wondered aloud more than once why Zach wasn't married, he was that good-looking. There was never much gossip about him around town. Noah envied him, though, living alone the way he did on a nice spread south of town, with a big barn and plenty of land for hunting. It sounded good to him.

"You come on out to the house if you need to get away for a night or two. You can crash on the couch if you bring some of your mom's chocolate chip cookies."

It was a joke between them because Annette had often sent a Tupperware container of cookies with Noah when Zach picked him up, and Noah would eat most of them.

Noah thought briefly of asking Zach if he knew anything about Shelby Rae Walsh's kidnapping, but he remembered how

Erin had insisted that her father didn't want the police involved because of something the kidnappers had said. Besides, Shelby Rae was safe, right? But that whisper of a thought led him to Erin and the fact that she hadn't texted him back. He didn't want to be rude, but he wanted more than anything to be in his room, alone, even if the rest of the house was filled with strangers.

"Mom's chicken is getting cold. See ya, Zach."

Zach nodded and continued slowly past Noah on the street made narrower by the extra trucks and cars. Noah eased the bike down the grassy side of the driveway, weeds brushing at his boots. The grass badly needed cutting. He was sure he'd hear from his dad about it soon enough. The truth was that Noah would've cut it by now, but he didn't want to hang around the house long enough to do it with his father home.

He parked the bike in a smooth dirt patch under the side eave of the garage, and retrieved the chicken dinners from his saddlebags. The white pickup truck he brushed against on his way into the house had a confederate battle flag hung in the window. So his dad really was making new friends. He wondered if his mother had seen it. She'd be embarrassed and upset. Noah understood that some people considered the flag a piece of their heritage, but it didn't seem right to him that it should be constantly in the faces of people who felt deeply hurt by the symbolism. He headed to the kitchen door hoping he could slip in and avoid the party. But of course he'd been seen from the front windows.

"Come on in, son. Have a beer!" Jeb Daly called from the noisy living room. "Hey, I didn't even get to buy him his first drink," Noah heard him say. "Courtesy of the Feds, of course."

"Go on, just go in and say *hi*. If you don't, you'll hurt his feelings." Noah's mother was taking the chicken dinners from the boxes and arranging them on plates. "Honey, it was so thoughtful of you to get dinner for your father, too. I'll put it in the fridge for later. He had me get a mess of wings to heat up."

"Since when does he have feelings? Did I miss something?"

"Don't be silly. Take in that platter of chips and salsa with you while I finish the wings."

The living room was full of cigarette smoke and tough-looking men, local types who had never owned a jacket or tie. They were either overweight or chain-smoker thin, bearded, bald, or indifferently shaved. All wore cotton T-shirts and blue jeans in various states of repair. The television was on, and Scott and Billy Attwell were playing *Call of Duty* on Noah's old Xbox 360, with a third guy continually trying to give them advice. Scott and Billy were both buzzcut and wearing bright white T-shirts. Billy had a rebel battle flag tattooed on the outside of his upper arm, but the rumors were that the brothers were in deeper than just Southern pride. Four other men sat around the shaky folding table his mother called the *games table* playing poker with the same red, white, and blue chips he'd loved to stack and knock down as a kid. Besides the cigarette smoke—and not just cigarette smoke, but the grassy tang of pot as well—there was a kind of humming charge in the air, driven by the strung out bass of the Led Zeppelin CD on the old stereo. Despite the fact that it was supposed to be a party, its pleasantness felt forced. Tense. Noah wondered if prison felt this way.

He stood frozen in the doorway holding the chips and salsa, remembering the times when he was a little kid and his dad had let him open the pop tab of his beers and even take a sip. One night his mother had come home to find seven-year-old Noah getting sick in the bathroom because he'd sneaked a whole beer, and she had yelled at his dad in front of everyone, but it was Noah who later got the belt. There had been times, too, when the police would show up to break up a party that had gotten too rowdy, and he barricaded himself in his room until his mother made him open the door. Now that Noah was no longer afraid, he felt sorry for that little kid.

"Once we finish this hand we'll deal you in, boy."

"Nice to see he's not too old to help out his ma," one of the guys at the poker table said. "Always help your mom, and don't be an asshole to her because she had to squeeze you out of a space you can't even get your fist into." He was one of the older guys, older than Noah's father. The other players groaned at the image.

Noah forced himself to move forward and set the food on top of a stack of magazines on the cluttered coffee table. "Thanks. I've got stuff to do." Not wanting to piss off his father by disappearing too quickly, he wandered over to the television to watch the *Call of Duty* game, and exchanged nods with the Atwell brothers, who despite their lined smokers' skin and tats, looked to be only about thirty years old.

The guy who'd been giving the loud advice looked up at Noah from the couch. "So you're pals with Barney Fife, our friendly deputy?" He picked a flake of tobacco from his unfiltered Camel off his tongue, inspected it, and wiped it on his blue jeans. "That was his truck out there." It wasn't a question but a statement.

Noah was confused for a second, but finally remembered that Barney Fife was the name of an old television deputy. He shrugged. "He's okay."

"Shot that woman and locked up your old man. Seems like a strange kind of friend for you to have."

"I guess that's my business," Noah answered. His heart

beat harder after the words came out of his mouth, but he found he didn't care what this guy thought.

"Just sayin' is all." He appraised Noah with his dull blue eyes and turned back to the game. "What the hell did you do *that* for?" One of the onscreen figures had tried to jump off of a wall onto the other and gotten himself shot.

Grateful for the distraction, Noah glanced out the window. Anyone sitting in the living room facing the window would've had a clear view of the street out front. Probably more than a couple of the guys in the room had reason to want to avoid the cops. What about his father? Wasn't there some rule that he couldn't hang out with known felons? How like him to blow off the rules. And what about his asking Noah to say he was asleep on the couch Sunday night? It was like he was *trying* to get thrown back in prison.

"Mom told me to ask if you need anything else." He stopped at his father's chair. The hair on his father's crown grew in sparse, wide swirls, the scalp beneath it slightly pink and smooth like a child's. Did he know he was going bald? He wouldn't like it if he did.

"Tell her to bring some chicken wings on in if they're done."

"Hey, you work out at the dealership, right?" The full-bellied man who had complimented Noah on helping his mother put his hand up to indicate he was passing on getting more cards. "What kind of deal can you get me on a new truck? I got a trade-in."

After the guffaws of the other men at the table about the shape his old truck was in, Jeb answered before Noah could say a word.

"You've got it wrong, Carter. He works in the shop."

"You don't say."

A voice came from the other side of the room. It was the advice guy. "You remember that chick who worked the desk there a few years back? The one with the tits, and all that hair?"

"She was hot. Kind of stuck up, though." This from the guy at the table who looked something like Hulk Hogan and wore a shiny red bandana over his hair.

"Where the hell have you been?" Jeb asked. "She's the boss's wife, now." No one needed to add that it was he who was ultimately responsible for the death of Bruce Walsh's first wife. "Still looks damned good, too, right son? Did she ever put any moves on you?"

"Me?" Noah was genuinely surprised. "No way." Would they mention Erin, too? He didn't like the idea of these men talking about her. As far as Shelby Rae was concerned, he didn't really care what they said about her. She was a lot older and wore too much makeup. He supposed he should feel sorry for her because she'd been kidnapped, but he knew he only cared because Erin was upset about it.

"You got a girlfriend?" Bandana Man asked.

"Nope." Noah let it rest there, and no one pursued it. He waited while they finished their hand, then said he'd ask his mother about the wings. As he entered the kitchen, he heard, "Kid's wet behind the ears, Jeb. Hardly like he's your son at all. You sure he belongs to you?" Noah didn't hear his father's quiet response, but only the laughter erupting a few seconds later.

In the kitchen, his mother handed him a warmed up plate of the chicken he'd brought home.

"You go on and eat in your room if you want." She tucked a napkin beneath the edge of a biscuit for him. "That crew in there will eat us out of house and home before the night's over. There's plenty of beer, too."

"You want me to hide in my room? Like when I was little?"

She made a face. "Of course not. What do you mean?"

Noah dropped his voice to a whisper. "Dad can't afford for the police to show up. But if they do, maybe it's not such a bad thing."

"What's come over you? You can't talk about him like that when he's in the house. What if he hears you?"

"He's trying too hard with us. I don't trust him, and I don't trust those guys in there." Noah's voice was low and earnest. "What if they're planning something?"

She shook her head. "Don't say that. If you say things like that, you let them out there in the world and they might come true."

Noah wondered what sort of magic his mother believed in. Mostly he didn't want to see her hurt. But there was another dimension to it, too, wasn't there? Erin already saw his father as the man ultimately responsible for her mother's death. If he got involved in something else and got caught...He didn't want to think about it.

Why is what she thinks important to me? She was beautiful and smart and serious and had a strong sense of justice. That was the kind of woman he wanted to be with. Every other girl he'd dated before paled in comparison.

"Sure, Mom. You're right." He bent to kiss her on the cheek. "Grab me a Coke?"

She smiled. Why she seemed happy, he wasn't sure. But there was an edgy excitement to her happiness. He was sure she knew his father was up to something.

But when he started down the hallway to his bedroom she

stopped him, whispering. "He's got a lot of money on the table."

"Yeah. I saw. Did you give it to him?"

She shook her head. "I have no idea."

AFTER EATING his dinner while catching up on a Netflix series, Noah took a quick shower. As the evening went on, the voices from the living room got louder, and the smell of pot filled the hallways. He locked his bedroom door and tried to sleep. The wall opposite his bed vibrated with music, and even earplugs didn't keep out the background bass. He lay there, edgy and wakeful. Where had his father picked up so much cash, and what about the coincidence of Shelby Rae's name coming up? His father had seen her recently, even though he'd only been home for four days, and he and Shelby Rae were hardly on the same social circuit. How and when had that happened?

CHAPTER SIX

*I*t had been years since Erin had cried as hard as she cried that afternoon. Trouble cuddled close to her on the bed, his soft, purring body firmly against hers, acting as a kind of emotional shock absorber.

She missed her mother. She missed the short time she'd felt really close to her father. It had taken her mother's death for him to respond fully to her need for him, and her need for him had been great. But once he married Shelby Rae, he changed back to his old self. The Provider. The Guy Who Worked All the Time. Shelby Rae constantly complained about it, but Erin knew that's what he was really like. Over time, Shelby Rae's behavior revealed that she wasn't terribly interested in being a mother, so Erin didn't find it all that difficult to go away to college.

Why did it still hurt so much? Why did she even care what Shelby Rae said or thought? It was like the little kid in her had awakened and had found herself alone, and afraid. Who was she supposed to trust?

She slept for six dreamless hours, until the sun rested just above the treetops outside her window, and Trouble nudged her gently to remind her it was time for his dinner.

She walked through the strangely silent house. Curious, she opened the door into the garage and saw that both her father's and Shelby Rae's cars were gone. That struck her as odd, but she decided it was just as well. If either of them had been home, she would have gone out, maybe called MacKenzie. Wait. MacKenzie was with her boyfriend at the house he was renting, miles away. Or she might have called one of her other sort-of friends who were still living in town. The fact was that she felt oddly alone in her own home. In her own hometown. Was this what being an adult was like?

In the kitchen, she fed the drooling Jocko first. Her father or Shelby Rae had cooked up a big container of ground beef and rice and put it in the fridge. Taking out one of Jocko's special bowls, she put a cup of the food in it and heated it in the microwave. While he ate, his tags clinking against the porcelain, she spread the contents of a can of wet food for Trouble on a plate, then decided that some broiled trout was more his style. He tracked her, walking on the counter as she worked. Shelby Rae would have a hissy fit to see him up there, and Erin took a perverse pleasure in letting him walk wherever he wanted to.

Realizing she was also hungry, she grabbed some cocktail shrimp, tossed it with fresh spinach, veggies, and tiny tomatoes, and drizzled some bottled Caesar dressing over everything. Then she took an open bottle of Pinot grigio from the fridge and poured herself a glass. Not only was there no one to know, no one would even care. She settled down in front of the television with Jocko and Trouble on either side of her to watch *Pretty Little Liars*.

What she'd said to Shelby Rae about her faking the

kidnapping to get money for her relatives had been in the back of her mind, but she had surprised herself by confronting Shelby Rae. If it were true, it would explain a lot—Shelby Rae's not wanting the police involved, her not being afraid to go out —just her generally cagey attitude about the kidnapping. That Erin's father had possibly heard it (was he even still speaking to her?) was worrying. More worrying was how plausible it was.

Having a glass of wine and letting Trouble walk all over the counter made her feel a lot better. Rebellion for rebellion's sake wasn't in her nature, but at that moment it felt pretty good. Maybe she should go upstairs and accidentally give Jocko one of Shelby Rae's carefully shelved Manolos to chew on. Could cats be trained to pee on things? She looked at Trouble, who had been dignified even as he mangled small bites of shrimp and trout. Probably not this cat.

She texted MacKenzie to see what she was doing, and MacKenzie texted back that she should make the drive out because it was a good party, and there was plenty of room to stay the night. The message came with a half dozen wink emojis.

The last thing Erin wanted to do that night was hook up with some stranger, so she told her she'd come next time.

There was also a call she'd missed. Julie had called back while she was sleeping, but only left a very brief message asking Erin to call her right away. Erin tried, but got no answer.

Around ten, she heard Shelby Rae come in from the garage. She knew it was Shelby Rae because Jocko had jumped off the couch and run to greet her with his special bark: *I'm so glad you're back, I'm so glad you're back, I thought you were never coming back!* When Shelby Rae didn't come in to say hello, Erin felt relieved. They had nothing to say to each other. She was much more nervous about seeing her father, but when she went to bed an hour later, he still wasn't home.

Where was he, without Shelby Rae?

I'M A CHAMPION SLEEPER, *just like my feline forebears, but right now I'm restless. There's something unsettling in the air and though there's still an hour until dawn, I find myself prowling anxiously through the air-conditioned palace that is the Walsh estate. Finally I settle in the enormous, silent kitchen. I know of a mouse family that lives in the closet in the unused maid's quarters, but they're tiny and not much sport, so in the gray light I sit on the kitchen counter alternating my attention between a mouse searching the floor for crumbs and the quickening sky outside the window.*

If only Tammy would return. She's rather more experienced at sniffing out mysteries than young Erin, and I do enjoy working with her. I believe there's hope for Erin, but she sat like a lump on the sofa last evening when I was trying to get her to go up to Shelby Rae's room and investigate that phone. Not that I blame the girl. She's deuced unhappy, and that best friend of hers, MacKenzie, is a gallivanter. Perhaps Erin will let her guard down a bit and maybe trust Noah a little more. We shall see.

Erin's right, I believe, to show little faith in Shelby Rae. I wish I could have jumped into her car to see where she went yesterday. Her demeanor is noticeably untrustworthy. Although, I have seen traumatized kidnap victims before, and they can be unpredictable. Perhaps her performance on the phone was just that—a good performance.

Jocko is still asleep on his mistress's bed, so I'm alone as I ease through his dog door and onto the patio thirty minutes later. The birds are starting to awaken, and the feeders near the trees are busy with cardinals and red-winged blackbirds. My natural instincts are piqued, but I have no taste for bird games this morning.

Something is up that has nothing to do with the local wildlife.

The path leading to the docks is damp and cool on my paws. I love the soft feel against my sensitive pads. Contrary to popular belief, most cats don't mind a little dirt. It's easily whisked away with a concentrated bathing session.

Already the fish in the cove are surfacing to catch morning bugs on the water. Turtles line the submerged log beyond the first dock, waiting for the sun to rise and warm them. I wouldn't mind a spot of sunshine myself. A cold chill dances its fingers up and down my spine.

Beyond the turtles, there is no more movement near the water. No fish. No frogs. No singing birds. It's as though night is still abroad despite the lightening sky.

I continue toward the second dock, then pad past it. Hearing a movement in the woods above the path, I stop. Someone is coming. Twitching an ear in that direction, I pick up the sound of whistling. It's a mournful sound, not a happy one, and I don't recognize the song. I jump into the brush to watch.

Noah is alone. Instead of going up onto the dock, he sets his backpack on the ground and assembles his nifty telescopic fishing rod. He continues whistling as he ties a lure. Then he takes his boots and socks off, wiggling his toes like a happy child. There's no way for me to tell him I can sense that there are no fish around here now. Not a single one that he can catch and release, as is his usual practice in the morning. It's an odd morning habit for a young man to have, but some do look at fishing as a form of meditative relaxation. I only fish occasionally. A little dirt I don't mind, but I'm no fan of bodies of water.

While he stands, casting, waiting, I walk silently toward the water. There's a sense of disturbance in the air, and I have to know what it is.

With Noah still whistling quietly nearby, the first thing I see that's out of place is a bare foot in the mud. A human foot that's dark with mud and debris. It's a horrifying sight to see a single human foot out *here, and I find myself singularly relieved that there is a leg attached to it, and a body attached to that.*

I keep my nose close to the ground as I investigate. The body is a woman's. Her well-shaped, tan legs are bare, and from her knees upward she's half-submerged in the water, her eyes staring, open, and her arms spread as though she is crying out for an embrace. Tendrils of shortish blond hair swirl away from her head and float on the water's surface like the tentacles of a disorganized jellyfish. It takes me a moment, but I recognize her. A low, unconscious growl escapes my throat. This is no accidental drowning.

I wait, watching carefully for signs of life, but I know a dead body when I see one. Julie Berry is beyond help. Unafraid, I move toward her and rest my paw on her ankle. It's as cold as the disgusting mud in which I stand, colder, perhaps, than the summer-warmed lake. She's been dead for hours, at least.

Someone must be told. It's a known fact that whoever discovers a dead body is the first suspect, and the second is the person's spouse or significant other. I do know that Julie Berry's ex-husband doesn't live here, so it looks like Noah is about to have a big problem. But there's nothing for it. He must be the one to find her.

I jump onto the dock, startling him as he's about to cast.

"Hey, cat. You scared the hell out of me!" *He glances around, surely looking for Erin. When he doesn't see her, he looks disappointed.* "I've got nothing for you, dude. Just got started myself. I didn't even bring my creel with me this morning. Strictly a dry run."

I give him a throaty meow.

He shrugs. "I'm really sorry."

I meow again, and turn toward the body to direct his attention, but he goes back to casting. Humans can be so clueless. I repeat myself twice to no avail.

If cats could sigh, I would heave a large one.

As a last resort I jump down from the dock, and walk over to him, twining around his legs so that he almost loses his balance.

"Hey, what the heck, cat?"

What I do next is not very gentlemanly, I fear, but he clearly isn't getting the message. I bite him solidly on the big toe of his bare foot —not drawing blood, of course. I dash away and stand on the dock to meow at him repeatedly. He will listen to me!

This time he curses and drops the fishing pole to grab his toe. Erin, and certainly Tammy, would have laughed to see him jumping around as he was. But then they would not have been so obtuse.

Finally, scowling at me, he calms and says, "What is it?"

With considerable relief I turn and jump off the dock, within feet of the body, knowing that he will follow. When I land, I give another insistent meow! *just in case. But I needn't have.*

The sun breaks over the horizon, spreading Noah's shadow over me.

"Oh, shit."

Alarm and confusion flicker over his face. I feel sorry for him, and sorry that his life, and Erin's, are about to get very complicated. Finally coming to himself, he reaches for the phone in his back pocket. That's my cue to run to the house to alert Erin.

"YOU DIDN'T TOUCH ANYTHING, right? Like I told you on the phone?"

Chief Deputy Zach Wilkins, squatting in the mud near the body, looked up at Noah.

Noah already regretted calling Zach's cellphone before he called 911, but he'd been so freaked out he hadn't been thinking. Would it look bad to the rest of the cops? Surely Zach would put in a good word. "I waited right here. On the dock. I was just pacing, I guess. I've never seen a dead body before.

Not even at a funeral. You'd think I'd have seen one, right? Nobody I know has ever died. I don't even know the woman. I mean, I know who she is, but I never really talked to her except maybe on Sunday. Is that a problem? Do you think they—"

"Whoa, son. Take a breath." Zach came over to put a hand on Noah's shoulder. "You go sit on the bank, okay? Right over there." He pointed. "Call in to work and tell them you won't be there until later. I don't want you to get docked for not having cause."

"But what do I tell them?" *Hey, I found a body in the lake this morning. How weird is that? Be in later.* That didn't sound right. It sounded crazy.

"Tell them you're helping the police with a matter they're looking into, and that you'll be there as soon as you can. Mr. Walsh will know about it soon enough. Sheriff's giving him a call."

"If he doesn't know something's up already." Noah gestured toward the trees. From beyond them came the sound of approaching sirens. After he'd called Zach, he thought first of Erin. No one needed to start the day with a dead body practically in their back yard, and Julie Berry was a close friend of Erin's family. It seemed to him a horrible kind of coincidence that Erin's mother was killed, Shelby Rae was kidnapped, and now, Julie Berry was dead.

But it means I'll see her again. Sitting down on the bank, he had a brief fantasy of enfolding her in his arms, comforting her. *Stop it!* He told himself. Seriously, was that where he was going with this? That really did sound crazy.

Zach went back to the body, looking at it from different positions, but he didn't touch it. Noah had seen the woman's expressionless and strangely doll-like eyes. He remembered his mother's old baby dolls his grandmother kept in her attic. Their gazes seemed to see into some other world. Was Julie Berry looking at another world now? Was she looking down on them? He looked up at the sky as though he might see her soul there, hovering.

The sirens, close now, broke through his thoughts, reminding Noah he had to call Earl at the dealership. As he talked, he fumbled his words, and struggled to keep his voice under control. Earl asked if he'd been drinking, an unexpected note of humor in his voice. Everyone knew Noah was a straight guy, the one who was sober enough to drive the other guys home when their partying got out of hand.

"No. No. I had breakfast with my mom before work. No drinks."

"You're with the police? What's going on, kid?"

The sirens stopped, and Noah heard car doors slamming and voices shouting.

"I gotta go. See you later."

Jocko came running from the direction of the house, barking madly. Erin was right behind him looking about fifteen years old with her hair loose, and her face flushed with sleep.

When she got close, Noah stood, reaching out to stop her. "You don't want to go over there."

"What is it? What happened?" She tried to push past him, but he grabbed her arms.

A small crowd of uniforms appeared on the wooded rise above them and moved quickly along the path, their voices raised, radios crackling. Jocko ran in frantic circles, still barking.

"Tell me what's going on," Erin demanded. "Let go of me!"

"Promise you'll stay right here, okay? Just wait. I'll tell you everything." Reluctantly, Noah turned her loose and to his

surprise, she stayed where she was. Their attention turned to
the group spilling off the path: two EMTs, the sheriff, and
another deputy.

Erin called for Jocko, but he ignored her.

"Bruce! You folks stay right over there. Got it?" the sheriff
called. "This is a crime scene."

Only then did Noah notice Erin's father hurrying down the
path from the house, buttoning his sport shirt. Far behind
him, Shelby Rae, in a filmy robe, was also calling to Bruce,
telling him to *please wait, wait!*

Crime scene. Of course Noah knew they were standing at a
crime scene, but he hadn't been able to think of it that way
yet. This was where he came fishing. Where he and Erin
started to get to know one another. Now it was something else
entirely, invaded by the corpse of a woman they all knew.

Unlike Erin, Bruce Walsh didn't hesitate as he approached,
and Noah didn't try to stop him. He barely acknowledged
Noah's and Erin's presence. He'd finished buttoning his shirt
and was headed for Zach and the body in the water.

"What the hell's going on here? Who is it, Abel?"

Shelby Rae, breathing heavily, reached Erin and Noah.
Jocko, spotting her, came running and sat at her feet, vibrating.

Though Noah had to admit Shelby Rae had a certain sexual
appeal, he found himself unmoved by her dishabille. When she
adjusted a flopping strap beneath the edge of the nearly transparent robe, Noah looked away, before someone caught him
staring. It wasn't just her unconscious immodesty that drew his
attention. She had a bruise on her face she'd tried to cover
with makeup, and her hair was different. Blonder and shorter.

"Who is it? Is someone dead?" she asked. "Bruce, where are
you going?"

Ignoring the calls of both Shelby Rae and the sheriff,

Bruce didn't stop walking until he saw Julie Berry's bare legs, and the rest of her body. He froze as though he'd hit a wall.

"Dear God. It's Julie. That's Julie. What in the hell is she doing here?"

"Bruce, I need you to get on back." The sheriff waved him away.

"But it's *my* property, Abel. I should get a say."

"I'm sorry, Mr. Walsh. It doesn't work that way." This time it was Zach Wilkins telling him.

"I might have known you'd be here." Bruce's voice was filled with sudden venom. All the courteousness and forgiveness he'd shown Zach Wilkins since his wife's death disappeared.

Zach didn't respond but turned away to direct the EMTs where they should step to get close to the body.

"Noah Daly?" The sheriff stopped in front of Erin and Noah. He took a moment to greet Shelby Rae. "Ma'am. Hell of a morning."

"Sheriff." Shelby Rae gave him a wan smile.

"Yes, sir?" Noah felt a lot calmer now.

"Chief Deputy Wilkins says you found the body."

"I came fishing this morning. By myself. I didn't see her at first."

"What do you mean?"

Noah struggled to answer. He felt uncomfortable and conspicuous in his white work T-shirt. "I didn't see her until about five minutes after I got here." He hesitated.

"What?" This from Bruce. "What did you see?"

"Well, it was the cat, Sheriff. The black cat from the house."

"His name is Trouble." Erin pointed to the cat sitting

quietly a dozen feet away, seemingly staring out at the lake. "That's him."

The sheriff glanced that way but was uninterested. "And? Speak up, son."

"It was like he was trying to get my attention. To show me the body. I usually fish from the dock."

"But you didn't today?"

"No sir."

"So the cat took you to the body? That's what you're telling me?"

Erin spoke out. "He's a very smart cat, Sheriff. His owner says he's helpful with solving mysteries." She blushed slightly, and Noah wanted to defend her from the sheriff's skepticism.

The sheriff's eyes swept over the small group, and came back to Noah. Was it Noah's imagination, or was he looking at him accusingly? "You didn't see or hear anyone else?"

Noah shook his head. Who else might there have been? It hit him all of a sudden. The sheriff was thinking of his father, probably imagining that they had killed Julie Berry together.

Noah knew he hadn't done it. But there were no guarantees when it came to his father. His gut churned.

Finally, the sheriff turned around. "Bruce, you all go up to the house for the next little while."

Both Bruce and Erin started to protest, but the sheriff simply raised one hand. Behind Erin, Shelby Rae didn't make a sound. She was staring at the area where the body was. Noah considered it was a good thing that neither she nor Erin could see past Zach who stood over it.

"I'll see you up there," the sheriff said by way of dismissal. "Nobody go anywhere until after we talk again."

. . .

NOAH ENTERED the house right behind Trouble. He supposed the cat was some kind of hero having found the body, and Noah almost smiled to see how alert his ears and full black tail were, as though he were proud of himself. But smiling wouldn't be appropriate with Julie Berry so newly dead.

No one seemed to know what to do once they reached the kitchen.

Noah watched Shelby Rae sit down at the hand-hewn, antique table that once probably seated a family of ten. Like Erin, she looked younger this morning, but the difference with Shelby Rae was that he'd never seen her without makeup. He hadn't known her, until he started at the dealership, and he could see now why she was reputed to have won beauty contests when she was a teenager. Her eyes were large and vulnerable, and her mouth softer without her omnipresent bright lipstick. She was looking expectantly from Erin to her husband. At first she didn't seem to notice that Noah was there, and that was fine with him. He had just been...trespassing. Well, maybe not exactly trespassing. Erin's father had invited him to fish any time, but the last place he'd expected to be at seven-thirty in the morning was in the Walshes' kitchen.

The sun was higher, and Noah noticed how the crisp light showed the bank of windows along the back wall to be dirty at their corners and edges as though someone had only sprayed the center of the glass and wiped in careless circles. There were black hairs, presumably from the cat, on the counter closest to him. The light wasn't kind to Bruce Walsh's face, either. Unlike his wife and daughter, he looked older and very tired—definitely not the same outgoing guy he was at the dealership.

Erin paced, chewing at a thumbnail. He hadn't noticed her bitten nails before. That she was anxious in that way told him more about her than a hundred hours spent together could. She seemed to be ignoring him. Was she angry with him, or simply consumed with grief?

Shelby Rae finally broke the silence. "What in the world was Julie *doing* here? And what do they expect us to do? Spend all day waiting for Abel or one of his buddies to come question us? I don't think so."

"Shelby Rae, Julie is dead. She was one of our oldest friends." Bruce's voice was low and serious. "Of course there are going to be questions. We need to give them all the help we can. Somebody might have killed her.

"Don't patronize me," Shelby Rae said sharply. "I'm not an idiot. Just so they don't try to frame us or something because we were all here this morning." She looked directly at Noah. Her eyes were cold. "*We* were all home, anyway." Now her gaze moved to Erin. "Unless maybe you were on a sunrise fishing trip with your new friend here, Erin?"

She made the words *sunrise fishing trip* sound like a previously unknown sex act, and Noah opened his mouth to object. But Erin was on it, ready to defend herself.

"You heard me talk to Dad. You heard him tell me that something was going on outside before any of us went downstairs. Are you *deaf?*"

Shelby Rae shrugged. "I don't pay any attention to what you do anymore." She turned to Noah. "She's a big girl. She doesn't need my help like she used to." Her gauzy robe draped open as she leaned forward, exposing the rise of her full, satin-clad breasts.

Noah willed himself to look at her face. *Look at her face. Look at her face, not her chest.* How could he even be thinking about a woman's body? His boss's wife's body? He didn't even like her. Maybe he imagined it, but he could have sworn he saw the corners of Shelby Rae's lips twitch, as though she knew the brief internal skirmish he was having. *Caught you looking—can't help yourself, right? Poor guy.* But it was her reaction that instantly shut down his attention. She wasn't so special or attractive or sexy that he was inclined to play games with her, especially in front of Erin. In fact, he was now feeling a little grossed out by Shelby Rae's flirty act. That didn't mean that he thought she was involved in Julie Berry's death. He understood that she was the kind of person who was always acting, even when the situation didn't call for it.

"Well, Jocko and I are going back to bed. It's all so awful. Maybe she had a heart attack. It wasn't like she was young. She must've been almost sixty, right?"

"Forty-five." Bruce cleared his throat before continuing. "The same age Rita would have been."

Noah spoke up. "She *could* have been taking a walk and had a heart attack." He remembered the way her hair had floated around her head, as if trying to arrange itself. "Even if someone did kill her—and really, why would anyone?—they could've dumped her from a boat, right? It would have been easy." His father didn't have a boat, but a few of his buddies did. But what possible motive could his father have?

Bruce nodded. "That's possible."

"Did you see a lot of footprints?" Erin asked Noah.

"Some, but she was mostly in the water, so they could've washed away. Plus I didn't get a really good look until after Zach showed up."

"Oh, please." Shelby Rae sighed dramatically, which was, of course, the only way she knew how to sigh. "Come on, Jocko." She snapped her fingers and the dog sprang to attention from his bed underneath a built-in desk. "Let me know when all you Sherlocks have it figured out, and wake me up. But not before ten o'clock." She stopped to kiss Bruce on the cheek. "Join me?"

Bruce looked tired. "I'll wait for Abel. You get some rest."

"All right, darling. If he wants to talk to me, ask him if it can wait until this afternoon, please. I don't need this after what..." She stopped, glancing at Noah, who was sure she had no idea that he was aware she'd been kidnapped.

"I just don't need this," she finished, and went upstairs.

Noah watched after her. She'd been so callous. Could she just not hide her dislike for Julie Berry, or was she somehow involved?

CHAPTER SEVEN

"I know you'll be wanting to get on to work, so let's get these questions out of the way, son." Sheriff Bowen indicated the big striped sofa in front of the window to Noah, and sat himself down in a nearby leather chair.

The sunny library smelled pleasantly of coffee and books, putting Noah slightly off his guard. It was the kind of room he could spend hours in, reading or sketching or just daydreaming. But he was there to be questioned about finding Julie Berry's body, and he again felt conspicuous with his stained fingers and plain white T-shirt. Erin had said little to him, and she'd looked away when the sheriff told him to wait in the library for him.

"So your old man's back in town. How's he getting along?" The sheriff wasted no time. He took a sip of his coffee.

Noah bristled. No one could look at him without seeing his father. "How would I know?"

"He's living with you, isn't he? You and your mama? Zach tells me there was a crowd at your house last night. Probably your mama's friends welcoming him home."

Noah stayed silent.

The sheriff leaned forward, forcing Noah to look into his sharp brown eyes. "Zach tells me you're a good kid. I trust his opinion. Did you see your father leave the house last night, and was he there when you left this morning?"

Noah wanted to sigh with relief, but he stayed composed. At least he wouldn't have to lie. "Yeah, he was there last night. People stayed pretty late, but I went to bed." He wasn't going to volunteer the information that the living room had been filled with convicted felons and possible drug dealers. It seemed the sheriff already knew anyway. "I didn't see him this morning. My mom said he was crashed on the couch, but after breakfast I went out the back door. What does this have to do with the dead lady, anyway?"

The sheriff sat back in his chair. "Did you know Ms. Berry?"

Noah shook his head. "Not really. I saw her at the party on Sunday, but we didn't exactly chat."

As they talked, the sheriff occasionally scribbled in a small, leather-bound notebook. Noah was silent until the sheriff spoke to him again, one of the habits he learned from being his father's son. *Never answer a question a cop doesn't ask you.*

"She not friendly to you?"

Noah shrugged. "I don't know. We didn't really talk."

"What about Erin? You seemed very friendly with her on Sunday. She's a sweet girl."

"Sir, is this the part where the law tells me to stay away from her for my own good?"

The sheriff laughed out loud and slapped his thigh. "You obviously got your mama's brains, son. No, that's not really any of my business. That's between you and her and her daddy. But just between you and me, I gather Ms. Berry thought a lot of what goes on here was her business. She can't have been too happy if she figured out Jeb Daly's son was sweet on her little princess."

It was Noah's turn to laugh, and he tried not to let it sound forced. "I don't think she or Mr. Walsh have anything to worry about in that department. Erin and I are barely friends." From the way she was treating him, it felt like the truth.

"So what's this bullshit about the cat showing you where the body was?"

Noah was taken aback by the sudden turn. "It happened the way I told you. He got me to come up on the dock, and I looked down and there she was."

"Did you get down there to see if she needed help?"

"Should I have? I mean, her eyes were open and she wasn't moving at all. She looked pretty dead. Should I have?" *Does that make me look guilty, or like a bad person?* he wanted to ask.

The sheriff made a note.

"You come fishing out here often?"

Noah nodded. "Mostly *after* work."

"You ever see anyone else out here? Mr. Walsh, or maybe strangers?"

"That's why I like to come out here. There's never anyone around. And the fishing's pretty good."

"What time did you get here this morning?"

"I don't know. A little before seven. The cat showed up right after."

"And started right in to show you where she was?"

"Maybe. I don't remember."

"How did you get to the dock? Did you come down from the house?"

Noah wondered if the sheriff was trying to figure out if he'd been with Erin.

"My bike is parked up at the trail's head, in the field where everyone parked for the party. Didn't you see it when you got here?"

The sheriff shrugged. "I was a little busy coming in. Dead folks draw a crowd pretty fast." He paused a moment, as though thinking. "Your old man teach you to fish?"

"Probably the one useful thing he taught me besides how to use a credit card to open a locked door."

This time the sheriff gave a hint of a smile but didn't laugh. "He ever come out here with you?"

"He's only been out of prison a few days. He's been, you know, busy. And I didn't invite him, if that's what you're asking. We never talked about where I was fishing. If he knows anything, he got it from my mom."

"That's what I figured. If it was me, I'd be out there on the lake an hour after I got out. But people are different." He looked down at the notebook. "Guess that's all for right now. Might have some more questions later, but we've got your address." He asked for Noah's cell phone number and wrote it down as Noah told it to him.

When the sheriff stood, Noah stood also, unconsciously wiping his sweating palms on his thighs.

"So, you think it was an accident? Did she fall off the dock or have a heart attack or something?" Noah asked.

Shaking his head, the sheriff held up one large fist. "Nope. She's got a hole this big in her back. Shot at least once, maybe more."

"Really?" Noah was shocked. "I couldn't tell."

"No reason you would have if you didn't get close. There's not much blood visible with all the water. Exit wound is bigger than the entry." He put his hand on the library door's handle and looked closely at Noah. "You stay away from your old man.

SMALL TOWN TROUBLE

Get out of there if you can. He's bad news and he'll take you down with him, son."

Not knowing what to say, Noah quickly nodded and left the room. The sheriff followed him back to the kitchen. Erin stood when they entered but ignored Noah.

"Am I next, Sheriff?"

The sheriff asked for a refill on his coffee, and said he needed ten minutes to get a quick update from the deputies at the scene. Then he turned to Noah.

"You can go on to work, son. You're done here. We'll be in touch."

Noah said he'd be available for anything they needed. He almost mentioned wanting to help find who killed Julie Berry, but realized Erin and her father might not even have been told she was definitely murdered. Bruce Walsh told him not to worry about going into work, that he'd cover the day's wages.

"They'd just pester you all day, wanting to know what's going on. And it's a hell of a thing that happened this morning."

Surprised and grateful, Noah thanked him. Stopping in the kitchen doorway, he turned back to say goodbye to Erin, but she avoided his gaze, busying herself with the sheriff's coffee.

Why won't she look at me? What did I do?

He closed the door behind him without saying anything wondering if he would even see her again.

THE SHOCK of learning about Julie had pushed Erin's suspicions about Noah to the back of her mind, but as they'd walked back to the house, she remembered how he hadn't told her about his father being released from prison. And how she'd seen him with Bryn Owens. Now that Noah was gone, the pounding of her heart slowed, and she handed the sheriff his mug of coffee with a slight smile.

She didn't want to suspect Noah of anything. She didn't want to be angry with him. In fact, she felt like she'd give pretty much anything to be able to go after him, and ask him to tell her the truth.

"Bruce, Erin." Abel Bowen leaned against the big island, and set the mug down. "It's not good news. Looks like Julie Berry was shot, and I don't believe it was self-inflicted."

"Oh, God." Erin put a hand over her mouth, her thoughts about Noah evaporating. She sank into a chair. "Who would do that? Why here?"

Her father was silent but put a hand on her shoulder and squeezed.

"It's a shock, I know," Abel said. "Take a minute. I told the Daly boy about it."

Erin could hardly believe what she'd just heard. Julie. Murdered. People didn't just get murdered in New Belford. Her mother's death had been a horrible accident, and was hardly murder. Now Julie Berry had been shot, too. It was a strange and disturbing coincidence. Just then, Trouble glided into the kitchen and rubbed against her leg. After a moment, he jumped up onto the table. She didn't have the heart to send him back to the floor, and he lay down near her, purring.

"Julie didn't deserve this," her father said. "She always meant well." He swallowed hard and looked out the window.

"Listen, I'm going to head down to the dock. The boys have been texting me like mad. We'll talk some more when I get back. You up to it, Erin?" the sheriff asked.

Erin nodded. "I'll be okay."

"Good girl." Abel took another sip of his coffee and rested

the mug back on the counter before he went out the same door Noah had used just minutes before.

Erin didn't feel okay. Ideas swirled in her mind. Julie was a gossip, and she'd been desperate to stay close to Erin's father. Really, Erin had felt kind of embarrassed for her. But she didn't deserve to be murdered. Her mind went again to Noah. What if his father had killed Julie as some kind of sick revenge for being put in prison? Julie had been her mother's closest friend. He might be that insane.

"Pumpkin, are you really all right?" Her father's eyes were full of concern.

"It's just so unbelievable." Erin was overwhelmed with guilt. "She left me a message but I didn't get back to her. I tried to get her attention yesterday, but she didn't see me. What if I'd caught up with her? I was so distracted because of Shelby Rae coming back and...I'm sorry, Daddy. I know she was your friend, too."

"Honey, I wasn't as straight with Abel as I could've been."

"What do you mean?"

Her father stared down at the floor. It wasn't like him. He was always straightforward, even when it meant someone might get hurt. Now, he looked as guilty as she felt. *Don't tell me anything,* she wanted to say. *I don't want to know.*

"I was at Julie's late yesterday afternoon. She asked me to come by for a glass of wine. Said it had something to do with Shelby Rae being in danger. We'd just got Shelby Rae back, but she said it wasn't about the kidnapping. It was something she said I needed to know."

Erin waited for him to continue, still wishing she didn't have to hear what he was saying. *Please don't have killed Julie. Please don't tell me that.*

"I shouldn't have gone. It's just that Shelby Rae was acting so strangely after she got back. I was worried about her, especially since we didn't know anything about the people who took her. But there was something about Julie's call that made me think she had something to do with it. I don't know why—it was just a gut feeling."

"You saw her? Talked to her?"

Her father nodded. "Oh, yes. At her house. I got there and tried to be polite by taking a few sips of wine, but I just wanted her to get to the point."

Erin knew exactly what he meant. Julie always had an agenda she took a long time to get to.

"She lied about Shelby Rae being in danger just to get me there. Julie showed me photos, Erin. Photos of Shelby Rae with another man in her car."

"What?"

"The camera was far enough away that it was only clear it was a man. He was embracing her in one, but that's all I could tell."

There was a sound of movement from upstairs, and they were silent a few moments until it was clear Shelby Rae wasn't coming down.

Erin remembered Julie telling her she knew something about Shelby Rae. Erin hadn't taken her seriously.

"I didn't believe her. It didn't look like proof of anything to me, and I told her so. I was angry as hell. What did she expect? That I would leave Shelby Rae right then and there on the basis of a photo that was hardly even incriminating? It was ludicrous and I told her so."

What was in the photos didn't sound innocent to Erin. Maybe that was her dislike of Shelby Rae talking. Still, she didn't trust her.

"But why would someone kill her, Daddy? What was she doing when you left?"

"Before I left she threw the wine in her glass at me, and just missed. I'd never seen her like that." He looked hurt. Sad. "She said she knew who the man was, and that their relationship was monstrous. Disgusting. She kept calling Shelby Rae a white trash slut. It was like she'd lost her mind. I begged her to tell me what she knew, but she said I would have to wait because I treated her like a doormat. That I would find out for myself, soon."

"I don't understand why she'd do that to you. That sounds insane."

"I don't, either," her father said. "People have expectations of us sometimes that we don't even know about. But here's the thing." Now he looked into her eyes. "She called me, and someone might have seen me at the house. It won't look good. I'll have to admit she believed Shelby Rae was having an affair."

"And they'll think you didn't want her telling anyone about it."

"Yes. I went back later last night to talk to her again, and to get the photos, but the house was locked, and she was gone."

"Where were you in between?"

He shrugged. "Driving around. I couldn't face Shelby Rae. Or you. I was too upset. I grabbed something to eat and had a beer about halfway to Louisville. Then I turned around. I tried to call Shelby Rae, but I got a text from her that she was going out to see her mother, to tell her about what happened."

"Why are you telling me this? You shouldn't be telling me!" Now she was going to have to lie to the sheriff if he asked her

anything about her father. The thought of it made her sick to
her stomach.

"Because I love you, and I want you to know the truth. I
want you to know that if they say I had some kind of motive,
it's bullshit. I didn't kill her."

"There's no way I would think you killed *anyone*. Let alone
someone we cared about so much." She put a hand on her
father's arm. "*That's* ludicrous."

When her father's shoulders sagged a bit, she saw how
tense he'd been. He looked years older than he had at the
weekend party. Behind him, through the window, she saw Abel
Bowen ambling back to the house. She would do anything to
protect her father. Even kill someone if she absolutely had to.
But she hoped—oh, she so hoped—it wouldn't come to that.

Damn you, Shelby Rae. She settled her gaze on her father's
weary face, and put a hand over one of his. "It's going to be
okay, Daddy. No one will ever know you were there."

WHEN ABEL BOWEN RETURNED, he talked to Erin in the
kitchen while her father went upstairs to see how Shelby Rae was
doing. At first his questions were about what Erin knew about
Julie's life in general— who her closest friends were and whether
or not Erin knew of anyone who truly disliked her. Erin told him
she couldn't think of anyone. Julie was pretty popular at the
country club and did a lot of volunteer work in town, including
managing Rita's Friends, which focused on providing appropriate
work clothes and education for women transitioning back into
the workforce from situations of abuse, divorce, or years of child-
rearing. She said that sometimes Julie was a little abrasive, but
only because she liked to get things done. It was only a small lie.

"Did you see Julie yesterday?"

"No. Wait." Erin remembered trying to catch up with her after meeting with MacKenzie. "I tried to flag her down. She'd left a message on my phone to get in touch with her, and I wanted to talk to her about some other stuff."

Now Abel Bowen seemed interested. "Do you know what she wanted?"

Erin had to be careful. She'd asked Julie for information about the party, and whether she could remember anything out of the ordinary that could point to who might've kidnapped Shelby Rae. No one was supposed to know about the kidnapping. At this point it would only complicate things, when the two couldn't possibly be connected. It was time for a lie, and it felt shocking to tell it. "Sunday she said she was going through old photos and things and had some with my mother in them. She was really sweet like that." Erin felt emotion swell in her throat even with the lie about the photos. "She was really good to me."

Abel Bowen nodded sympathetically and gave her a moment to gather herself. Finally, he cleared his throat. "I know she worked on the charity with your father. How did they get along?"

"Oh they got along great!" *Do I sound too eager? Am I too loud?* "She came by the house yesterday morning for a meeting, but my dad wasn't feeling great because of the party."

"Does Shelby Rae work on the charity, too?"

Erin shrugged. "I guess. She helps with hosting fundraisers sometimes. But I wouldn't say she did a lot of regular work, like interviewing the women and stuff. Julie and my dad do most of that."

"They spend a lot of time together?"

Erin wasn't sure what he was getting at. "Who? Shelby Rae and Julie?"

"Your dad and Julie."

Now she understood. "Are you asking if Julie and my dad were having an affair?" She gave a scoffing laugh. "As if. They were friends, and that's all. Julie was my mom's best friend in the world." She didn't add that she'd noticed over the past couple years how flirtatious Julie tended to be around her father. Or that she'd seemed to be almost ready to move in the minute she learned Shelby Rae was gone.

The sheriff nodded. "You were home last evening, you said." He looked at his notes. "Was Shelby Rae home?"

"No. She was gone when I got home." She didn't volunteer that her father wasn't there, either, or that Shelby Rae got home first.

"How did Shelby Rae get along with Julie? Were they friends?"

Erin shrugged. "I wouldn't say they were friends." Was it possible Shelby Rae had killed Julie? Is that what he was implying? Julie might have even been blackmailing her. That would give her a motive way beyond the one her father might have had. She certainly got the impression that Abel Bowen thought it was a possibility. Did he know something, or was he just guessing?

ERIN KNEW she was taking a big chance by going by Julie's house so soon after the discovery of her body, but she headed there anyway with the key that Julie had insisted on giving her years ago. Parking the Challenger in the small municipal lot on the hill above Autumn Street, she double-checked her shorts pocket for the key and walked the half-block to where the stone wall along Julie's backyard met the road. It was a low wall, only about four feet high, yet it had seemed enormous to Erin when she was a little girl. She'd had to work to climb over it back then, but she was pleased to find she remembered exactly where the best toe-holds were. She was in the yard in seconds.

Julie's backyard was a gardener's paradise and was often a featured stop on the New Belford Garden Club's spring tour. The fuchsia blooms on the banks of azaleas were wan and edged with brown, but the dahlias and coneflowers and trellises of morning glories and giant pots of hibiscus and a dozen flowers Erin couldn't name showed their bright faces along the garden's winding paths. Best of all, for Erin, were the tall fans of exotic grasses and Japanese maples that screened her from the windows at the back of the house.

The house looked abandoned, and Erin was suddenly overwhelmed by its emptiness. She would never see Julie again. Never have tea with her again in the funny little room she called the solarium. It was the room in which Erin slept when she went to Julie's for overnights after her mother died, so that she would wake up bathed in morning sun, the smell of coffee and blueberry pancakes filling the house.

Julie had been her mother's closest friend, and now Julie was no more. The pain of Julie's death felt new, but also very old, like a reopened wound.

Knowing who killed Julie and why was important to her, but that wasn't why she was here, trying to figure out if there were already police in the house. Her father was very much alive, and he needed her help.

The key worked just as she'd known it would. Julie had wanted her to always have a place to come if she needed to get away from her own house and, Erin guessed, Shelby Rae.

Nothing looked out of place. From what she could tell, there'd been no fight, and there was no blood anywhere. She was grateful for that, because she knew she would've been violently ill if she'd found any. The only things she wanted to find were the photos Julie had shown her father so she could get them out of the house. There would be too many questions if the police found them.

Julie was tidy, but not obsessive. Yesterday's *Courier-Journal* lay re-folded on the coffee table, and in the kitchen, Erin stepped on a couple of flower stems on the floor near the sink. There were fresh bouquets of garden flowers in every room. Two wine glasses and an empty bottle of French merlot sat on the kitchen island.

"I was at Julie's early last evening. She asked me to come by for a glass of wine."

One of the glasses was nearly full. The other had only a dried spot of purple-red in its bottom. The full one must have been her father's. Or had Julie entertained someone else after her father left? Maybe she had drunk the rest of the bottle herself.

"Damn it." Erin looked around the kitchen. She didn't really want to be here, but she also didn't want anyone to know her father had been there.

The only thing to do was to wash both glasses. After putting on Julie's dishwashing gloves, she ran some hot water and soaped up the bottlebrush near the sink to clean them inside and out. When she was finished, she put them in the drying basket beside the sink. By the time she was ready to leave, they might be dry enough to put away. Then she rinsed out the wine bottle and put it in recycling, just the way Julie might have done it. The rug was a deep red oriental with an intricate pattern so there was no obvious spill where Julie had tossed wine at her father, so she left it alone.

Feeling a little ridiculous, she kept on the kitchen gloves as she went to search for the photos.

Her search was as methodical as she could make it. Julie wasn't all that complicated, and so her hiding places wouldn't be too difficult. Unless, of course, she was worried about someone else besides Erin's father finding them.

No, I'm not going to psyche myself out about this.

She started in the living room, at the enormous antique roll top desk that had belonged to Julie's husband. Her fingers were clumsy in the rubber gloves, but she riffled through the neatly organized papers and the desk's many drawers quickly. She even squatted down to look at the underside of the desk for signs of a hidden compartment. Nothing.

Nothing in the bookshelves or the highboy Julie used as a linen press for her many fancy tablecloths and napkins. Nothing among her several sets of china or neatly piled magazines on the coffee table. Every so often she would run to the front of the house to peer out the window for signs of the police. *Not yet.* One thing she did notice—Julie's car wasn't beneath the old-fashioned brick carport attached to the gracious house. She hadn't seen the car among all the police cars at the lake, either. It was good news, considering it might be a clue in Julie's death. But it did her no good at all when it came to the photos of Shelby Rae and the unidentified man.

Erin headed upstairs, daunted by the fact that the house contained four large bedrooms. It would be hard to escape unnoticed if the police showed up.

The photographs were important to Julie, Erin reasoned. So she probably kept them close.

In Julie's bedroom, Erin caught a glimpse of herself in an

elegant, full-length mirror. In her shorts and fitted blue T-shirt, long braid, and with her sunglasses on top of her head, she looked like her normal self—well, except for the rubber gloves. She found it hard to believe she was ransacking a dead woman's bedroom.

She looked swiftly through Julie's dresser drawers, trying not to mess things up too much. It couldn't look to the police like someone had been here, searching for something after the murder. Then she searched the tall jewelry dresser, marveling at Julie's collection of expensive jewelry. It made her understand how modest Julie really was. When she went out, she rarely wore more than a watch and earrings, and maybe a gold necklace. But the small drawers were filled with velvet boxes containing delicate diamond and sapphire and emerald bracelets and necklaces. There were tiny boxes with rounded edges that held diamond and gold earrings and several pairs of pearl earrings that glowed with exotic warmth. For a while she became lost in the jewelry, wondering why Julie never wore it. Though there weren't many events in New Belford where she might wear them without looking a little silly.

She jumped at the sound of a car door and ran to the window, feeling her heartbeat pounding in her throat. Not the police, but a pizza delivery car across the street. Her body flooded with relief.

Turning around, she surveyed the room. She hadn't searched the big closet yet, or the bed and bedside tables. Despairing of not only the very full closet, but also the other four bedrooms, she sighed. She was certain the photos must be in the house. Her father had seen them, and it seemed unlikely that Julie would've taken them anywhere with her.

Avoiding the closet for now, she went to the first bedside table and pawed through the debris that wasn't dissimilar to what was in her own—too many bookmarks, pencils, lip balm, lotion, eye drops, a small flashlight. Eyeglass cloths, Tums, a tin of mints. Julie's drawer also held a prescription bottle with a label that said *Lorazipam*. It was a drug that Shelby Rae also occasionally took "for her nerves." Though Erin couldn't imagine Julie joking about it as she washed it down with a glass of wine, as Shelby Rae did.

Before she went to the other side of the bed, Erin bent to look beneath the big four-poster. There was no awkward dust ruffle, and she could see across the rug beneath straight to the other side. When she was little, her parents had had a similarly high antique bed—Shelby Rae had insisted on an entirely new bed when she married Erin's father—and Erin had loved to lie on her back underneath it looking up at the slats and slipping her small fingers between the rough-cut, slightly uneven slats and the box springs. She had imagined hiding treasure there, or even a knife or other weapon, just in case. No one would ever guess it was there.

Now she stretched out, the worn, hand-loomed rug soft against the back of her legs, and scooted beneath the bed. For a second she had that momentary thrill of fear that the bed might fall on her, but took a deep breath and focused on looking for something hidden in the slats.

It was a big bed, and she wished she had the flashlight she'd seen in the bedside table drawer. Taking off the rubber gloves, she ran her fingers along the wooden slats, wary of splinters. She'd been at it for two or three minutes and was beginning to feel stupid when her searching fingers hit the corner of something that bent as she touched it. An envelope.

Yes!

Erin didn't have any time to celebrate and only confirmed that the envelope held photographs of Shelby Rae in her SUV with a man Erin didn't recognize. She stuffed the envelope into her slim leather crossbody purse, and glanced around the room to make sure nothing was out of place. Satisfied, she ran down the stairs to put the gloves back in the kitchen. Could they get fingerprints off of rubber? She wasn't sure. But the thought of stealing the gloves and having to dispose of them made her feel like a true criminal, and she wasn't really a criminal, was she? She hesitated, uncertain, and was about to put them in the cabinet beneath the sink when someone banged on the front door. It was not a polite banging, either.

She hurriedly wiped the two wineglasses dry, set them on the counter, and ditched the gloves.

The voice from outside was muffled, but she heard it clearly enough.

"Police. Open up the door, Miss Walsh. We know you're inside."

THE CHIEF DEPUTY loomed over Erin, who sat in a wing chair by the fireplace in Julie's living room. As New Belford had grown, the sheriff's department had gotten bigger, and only a very few of its members were known to her. This woman wore a name tag that read PIERCE in big block letters, and her thin, sun-worn face and pale eyes gave her a rugged look that belied the graceful hang of her brown and black uniform. She looked like a fashion model, thirty years on. A second, male deputy, was stationed at the front door.

"The lady next door said you arrived here about twenty minutes ago. How did you get in?"

"I have a key. Julie gave it to me years ago."

"What have you been doing since you arrived?"

As soon as Erin had heard the voice at the door, her mind

had begun working. She was nervous but she knew she had to make her lie convincing.

"I guess I was afraid Julie's relatives would take the things she had that were my mom's. There's a painting my mom did in college, and some clothes Julie was keeping for me. She'd told me she'd found some photographs, too, that I should have."

Deputy Pierce looked around the room. "Where is everything?" Her voice was skeptical. She seemed the kind of person who expected everyone to lie to her.

Erin wrapped her arms around herself. "I got here and I guess I was too sad to really look for anything. I did check her bedroom and all the bookshelves for the photos, but I couldn't find them. It's like they've disappeared."

"Really? You didn't find any photographs at all?"

"Just her family albums. She said there were some from high school she forgot she had. She and my mom were both cheerleaders at New Belford High School before it closed down and got consolidated."

The deputy didn't seem impressed. "Did you tell anyone you were coming here? Mrs. Berry's body was found near your house yet didn't you think the house might be off-limits during the investigation? Her family might consider this trespassing. I know I do."

It sounded entirely possible to Erin. Julie's only family was an older brother and sister-in-law, and their adult children weren't very pleasant. They never came to visit Julie, and she never visited them.

"I guess I didn't think about that." The emotion clouding Erin's voice was genuine. Julie was dead. There would be a funeral, and Erin would never see her again. "I panicked. I wasn't thinking about them. Only about my mother. And Julie." She stared at the floor.

"May I see the key you used to enter the house?"

Erin dug the key out of her front pocket, relieved she hadn't put it in her bag.

"Wait here." The deputy walked to the back door, opened it, and inserted the key in the lock. As she turned the key, the deadbolt slid out. When she turned the key again, the deadbolt disappeared, and she shut the door firmly to relock it.

Guess I won't be going out that way. What will the sheriff say? She thought of Abel Bowen and how nice he'd been to her. He'd probably be both suspicious and pissed off to hear she'd been at Julie's house.

To Erin's surprise, the deputy handed her back the key. Erin noticed the perfect buff manicure on the woman's long fingers. The nails weren't long, but were beautifully shaped.

"Hey, Pierce." They couldn't see him, but Erin assumed it was the deputy guarding the front door.

"Yeah?"

"Need to talk with you a minute."

Pierce nodded to the unseen deputy. "Right there." She looked at Erin. "Sorry. I need you to stay here for a moment. I'll be right back. Please don't touch anything else."

"Sure."

When Pierce was gone, Erin's hands went to her bag as though to reassure herself that the photos were still inside, though she wouldn't dare look. Her being in Julie's house was suspicious enough. She'd left the lake house while Sheriff Bowen was talking to her father. What would he say when he learned she'd gone to Julie's? She hoped he'd be glad, and hadn't decided to tell his friend the truth under questioning. The worst that could happen right now was that she might be taken to the police station. At least her father would understand, but Shelby Rae would be ape-shit.

Except she wouldn't be here at all if Shelby Rae hadn't been sneaking around. And maybe, just maybe, Julie wouldn't be dead. Although she didn't know for sure that the two things were connected, the coincidence seemed way beyond happenstance.

Finally, Deputy Pierce returned. She didn't look very happy, but her voice was oddly smoother. Kinder.

"You can go, Miss Walsh. We're requesting that you don't take anything from the house at this time. We need to do a thorough investigation in order to determine if a crime was committed here, or if there's evidence pertaining to Mrs. Berry's death."

"All right."

"Did you bring anything with you into the house? Bags or boxes to take things with you?" This was said with a slight tilt of her head, that made Erin think of the deputy as a model, asking a friend if she'd brought her makeup with her to a shoot.

Erin gave her a slight smile. "No. Nothing." She stood, self-consciously tugging at the edges of her shorts. What made the woman so friendly all of a sudden? She started to the back door.

"You'll need to go out the front door. Please don't return without checking with us first. Sheriff Bowen says you can contact him directly."

Ah, so that explained what was up. Abel Bowen had vouched for her. But it could also mean he would ask her himself what she was doing there. "Thanks. I won't." Erin was almost to the front door when the deputy spoke again.

"We'll be in touch, Miss Walsh. I'm certain we'll need to

get your fingerprints to eliminate any confusion. We'll contact you."

When she was out of the house, Erin tried not to break into a run. Only then did she realize how terrifying the whole incident had been. She felt like her chest would burst. The thought of going right home made her feel even worse. She needed to tell her father that she had the photographs, but she needed to be alone for a little while, away from the police.

As GRATEFUL AS Noah was to Bruce Walsh for giving him the paid day off, there was no way he was going back home. His father was probably just getting up, perhaps having a beer and frozen waffles or Pop Tarts for breakfast. As a kid Noah had frequently asked his mother why he was only allowed to have oatmeal, generic Cheerios, or shredded wheat for breakfast, while his father ate cookies and doughnuts and soda.

"Because I said so. Because I want you to have teeth when you're old." She might have added, *because I don't want you to end up like your father*.

His father would only grin at him and wink. But he never so much as gave one doughnut to Noah when his mother was out of sight, even when Noah begged. His father was irresponsible, but not exactly playful or generous.

Normally if he had a day off, Noah would go fishing. He tried to imagine ever returning to the Walshes' place to fish. The image of Julie Berry's body would be forever linked to the swampy weeds and bracken near the lake's edge. How could he be anywhere near there without thinking of her lying in the shallow water, her blank eyes staring at the sky?

The weather was good and he took his motorcycle out on the county highways he knew well, avoiding the rough and gravel roads that were better handled in a car. There was very little traffic, and he finally relaxed. Maybe *relaxed* wasn't the word. The problem was that it was full on summer, and as the sun got higher in the sky, it burned down on him even though it wasn't yet noon. The helmet felt glued to his head, but at least it wasn't evening, so the bugs weren't a plague.

After a couple of hours, he was tired and ready to come back to town. A part of him wanted to go to work to get his mind off Julie Berry's stiff body, and Erin's cold-shouldering. Work saved him from getting too far into his own head.

He rode by the police station, but he didn't see Zach Wilkins' truck. Maybe he was still out at the Walsh estate. How long did it take to process a crime scene like that?

Zach could give him information about Julie Berry. It bugged him that her death had happened right on top of both his father getting out of prison and Shelby Rae's kidnapping. He wouldn't ask him for specifics.

Why do I care? Erin's the one who really wants to know this stuff. It's none of my business. I'm just a grease monkey with a parolee for an old man.

He slowed the motorcycle to a couple miles an hour below the speed limit as he entered town. He was about to turn left at the old furniture store that had been turned into medical offices when he saw Erin's Challenger parked in front of The Village Bean. As he circled the block to get a better shot at a parking place, he tried to imagine what he would say to her when he got inside. Would she be alone, or perhaps with MacKenzie? How was she feeling after what happened that morning to her friend, so close to her own house? Parking the bike, he told himself he would never know what she was doing there if he didn't go in and ask.

· · ·

ERIN WASN'T at a table near a window, so he figured she didn't
see him come in. That was good. He was afraid she might run
away to avoid him.

He deliberately didn't look for her when he entered, and
went straight to the counter to order a sweet tea. He pondered
buying a couple of the giant, chocolate chunk brownies to
share with her. But he didn't know her all that well. She could
be allergic. Or hate chocolate. Or she might think it was
creepy as hell that he'd offer her a giant brownie just a few
hours after she'd seen somebody she loved dead on her own
property.

Turning away from the counter, he scanned the room. Erin
sat beneath a vintage poster with a French clown superim-
posed over a cityscape of Paris. She had a piece of quiche on a
plate in front of her and was poking at it with her fork without
much enthusiasm. She looked tired, but was still beautiful.
Today her strawberry blonde hair was twisted into a thick
braid that lay over one shoulder. What a shitty time she'd had
lately. She'd never come right out and said she disliked Shelby
Rae, but it wasn't hard to guess. For a fleeting moment he
wondered if Erin had done something, hired someone to make
Shelby Rae disappear. She probably had enough money, but
not all rich fathers were generous. Erin was obviously irritated
with Shelby Rae on Sunday, but to kidnap her then bring her
back and drop her beside the road? The idea sounded stupid,
even to him.

A woman brushed past him and he quickly apologized.
How long had he been staring at Erin? Then, as though finally
sensing him watching her, Erin looked up. He held his hand up
in a wave that felt pretty lame. Why did he always feel clumsy,
like his limbs were about as useful as giant sausages when he
was around her?

She didn't smile, but she didn't look away quickly, either.

Putting the most positive spin on the situation he could, he walked over to her table. Small talk with women wasn't his greatest strength. His father talked to his mother like she was a moron. Or he screamed at her—particularly when he was drinking.

"How's the quiche?"

Erin glanced down at her plate and put her fork down. "I don't know why I ordered it. I'm not really hungry."

"Can I sit down?"

Erin shrugged. "I guess."

Noah pulled out the chair across from her and sat. She moved her knife an inch farther from the plate, slid her coffee cup an inch or so his way, marking her territory, putting up an invisible wall between them. It was clear she thought there needed to be some distance between them, and he suspected she didn't realize she was doing it.

"Are you angry with me about something?" Confrontation was something he hated, but he couldn't stop himself. The idea of there being a big disagreement or issue between them felt wrong, and he wanted to fix it.

"Do you think this is really the best time to talk about it?" She watched him evenly. Her eyes were tinged with red, and she looked like she hadn't slept much recently. "Somebody died. Maybe you didn't know her, but I did. You're not actually involved, right?"

Noah shook his head. "You know I'm not involved. I was in the wrong place at the wrong time, and that cat made sure I saw her. I didn't do anything to anybody." He slid back the chair, feeling defensive. "I was just wondering if you were all right. That's the only reason I came over here."

"Really? The only reason?"

"Yeah, I guess so." He hated the animosity between them. Why wouldn't she just say what was going on? She couldn't possibly blame him for Julie Berry being dead. It made him sick to think that she might.

Erin picked up her paper cup of coffee and looked past him as she sipped. They were frozen in their unhappiness. Finally, she spoke.

"Why didn't you tell me the other day your father was out of prison?"

Noah stared at her. It hadn't occurred to him to tell anyone about his father getting out. While his being in prison, obliquely responsible for Rita Walsh's death, had become a dominating fact of his life, he tried to forget it as often as he could. It was tough because everything in his life seemed to happen because of it, or in spite of it. There was no space in his world for any other possibilities. He'd imagined he knew the way it affected Erin and her father, but what did he really know? If *he* couldn't bear the fact of his being out of prison, what must it be like for Erin? His father was his father, the jerk who went to prison, leaving him and his mother to fend for themselves. To Erin, his father was the murderer of her mother.

"Wow. I feel like an asshole. Of course I should've told you." He wanted to explain, but knew it would just sound like an excuse. "I don't know what to say."

"I just want to know why you hid it. Was it because you knew I'd be upset, and you wanted to hang out with me? Because that would be creepy. Or did it not matter to you at all?"

"Erin." He scooted his chair closer to the table. "Why would *you* think I'd do something like that on purpose?" He glanced around them. No one was close enough to hear what they were saying. "I asked my mom to come to your party so we could both get away from him. You think I wanted people to know and talk about it? It's bad enough everyone sees me and thinks of him."

Erin didn't speak, and at least wasn't interrupting, which was good.

"Everyone expects me to screw up or steal something. Or they expect me to be perfect so they can be extra sure I'm not like him. I know that's not an excuse. I didn't mean to upset you. I swear. I wasn't even thinking about him when I started talking to you, except to think it was cool that you were talking to me at all. You've got every right to tell me to get lost."

The tension in her face relaxed the slightest bit. "What about Bryn Owens? What were you doing with her, out in front of our house?"

"Bryn? I don't know. I saw her and said hello. It was kind of weird that she was there, but nobody told me she was stalking you all."

"Really? Weren't you friends with them or something?"

Noah felt a flare of warmth around his face. "Not exactly. They went to my mom's church. I haven't gone since I was a kid." He wasn't sure how much Erin believed him. But it was the truth, really. He hadn't actually been friends with them, and those few minutes with Tionna behind the bakery—well, that hadn't been friendship. More like momentary lust. Tionna's revenge on Bryn for their fight. Noah wondered if Tionna had ever told Bryn. Maybe they'd laughed about it later. But no, he was sure Bryn would have made it a point to give him hell if she knew.

They sat in silence. Noah sipped his tea. Erin stared out the window, thinking.

Finally, Noah put his hands on the table and leaned forward. "I'm not my dad, Erin. You know that, don't you?"

She nodded, slowly. "Yeah, I know." Then, "What about your dad? Do you think he had something against Julie? Or Shelby Rae?"

These were thoughts that Noah had had himself.

"He's an asshole, but I don't think he's stupid enough to kidnap anybody." He didn't mention how flush with cash his father was. There was something going on there, but he didn't think it had anything to do with the kidnapping. It would be too bizarre. "Or murder someone." He really hoped he was right about that.

"What if he wants to get back at my dad?"

"Doesn't it make more sense that he'd want to get back at Zach? I mean, *he's* the one who killed your mother."

Erin's eyes clouded.

Did I really say that? "Hey, I'm sorry. That was stupid."

"It's okay. I didn't mean to imply your dad was a murderer. That was wrong of me."

"I know he's not a good guy. I hate that he got your mother killed." Impulsively he put a hand over one of Erin's. She didn't take it away. "I'm really, really sorry it happened. There's hardly a day that I don't think about that. Especially when I see you, Erin. And I want to see you more. I know that probably makes me sound crazy. But it's true."

"DON'T RUSH ME, Bruce. Julie isn't going to get any deader."

I watch from behind an enormous potted ficus tree as Shelby Rae comes down the stairs, followed by an exhausted-looking Bruce. Jocko precedes them both, his tongue hanging out like the foolish creature that he is. It's my hope that he doesn't spy me out in his canine eagerness.

"That was beneath you, Shelby Rae. I know you never liked her but she only ever wanted to help. Especially Erin. You were there. You know what it was like for her."

When Shelby Rae reaches the bottom of the stairs she deftly swings around on a narrow high heel, surprising us all.

"No. Julie Berry wanted to be helpful to *you*, and you know it. I'm glad she's dead because now I won't have to worry about her trying to take you away from me. She's wanted you from day one after Rita died, and I bet even before that. You think I didn't know how she talked about me? Like I was white trash. She had the nerve to wear black to our wedding. Did she think I wouldn't notice?"

Poor Bruce. I wouldn't want to be in his uncomfortable position for the world.

Drat! The intrepid Jocko is trotting my way. Now that his mistress is back in residence, he thinks he's the four-legged king of the house. Too bad for him he's only a jester. When he sticks his nose into my hiding place, I give him a swat, and he backs away. He's lucky I didn't use my claws this time. He doesn't yelp, but walks sullenly back to Shelby Rae. I do believe I almost have the blighter in hand.

"It takes two people to have a relationship," *Bruce says.* "I've never been interested in Julie that way. We've been over this a hundred times. Why are you acting so jealous now? She's dead, for god's sake."

I follow them into the kitchen and settle to watch out a window. Listening to them is more interesting than stalking mice. With Shelby Rae there is always drama.

"Why did you go to see her yesterday?" *Shelby Rae's voice is strangely low.*

"What are you talking about?"

"Yesterday afternoon you were at her house. I saw your truck. You weren't being very sneaky if you were trying to hide it." *Shelby Rae steps close to him, as though she were about to kiss him. But her tone is accusing.*

Bruce doesn't back down. "Why do you think I went by there? You seem to think you know."

"I *don't* know, but I can guess. She was telling you some bullshit lie about me, wasn't she? I told you she hated me."

"How do you know that's what we talked about?" *He doesn't seem surprised, which puzzles me. How does Shelby Rae know, indeed, unless she spoke to Julie Berry first? Or Julie Berry had threatened her? The plot thickens, and the game is, as they say, afoot.*

"She told you I was having an affair, didn't she? God, she was such a snobby bitch. Believing whatever suited her. And *that* ugliness suited her to a 'T'."

"If you know so much, then you also need to know I didn't believe her. You're my wife, and there's never been a day when I wasn't glad you agreed to marry me. It doesn't matter what she said. I won't even ask you if it's true."

At first Shelby Rae is indignant and tosses her hair like an angry filly in the paddock. "Oh, sure. You say that—"

Bruce, in the manner of a rough hero in a steamy novel, suddenly wraps his arms around her and pulls her to him. I'm inclined to avert my eyes, but both Jocko and I are strangely riveted on the scene. Shelby Rae doesn't resist, but pushes herself against him, caressing the back of his head as they kiss. One of Bruce's hands slides down her silky pink dress and shapes it around her generous bum. Now I do look away, embarrassed for them both. Jocko gives a little whimper and walks glumly to settle in a tight curl on his bed in the kitchen.

One must excuse humans their mating indignities. I turn my head decisively back to the window. During the next ten minutes, the sounds Shelby Rae is making seem to indicate that she is having a rather pleasant time. Alas, Jocko. I feel for the poor sod. Humans really should be more considerate of their creatures.

When they finally gather themselves, Shelby Rae is back to her giggling, coquettish self. She takes a languorous stretch, almost worthy of a feline, and sighs. "I wish you'd done that a week ago. I've missed you so much. I was afraid you didn't want me anymore." She pouts. *This actress should be made a dame of the commonwealth just like Judi Dench.*

"Baby, I get so wrapped up in work. I promise to do better."

"I'm going to hold you to it. We should maybe—I don't know—take a little trip together. Vegas? We had so much fun last time."

"Anywhere you want to go. And it was my pleasure." *Bruce Walsh raises his bushy eyebrows and gives his wife a look that embarrasses me all over again. Though they're the ones who should be embarrassed.* " We're going to be late meeting Abel, so we better leave."

Shelby Rae touches him on the shoulder. "Do you think it will take very long?"

Bruce kisses her tenderly on the cheek. "Not long."

"I won't mention I saw your truck at Julie's house. There's no need to complicate things. I'm sure they'll find the poor woman was the target of some stranger who came through town. The world just isn't safe these days, is it?"

Poor woman! Whom does she think she's fooling?

"I love you, sugarcakes." *Bruce takes her in his arms once again for a lingering kiss.*

Oh, bollocks! Am I going to be forced to stare out the window again? Fortunately, this time things don't go any further, and they leave the house for the police station. How I would like to be a fly on the wall during that meeting.

There's something wrong in the Walsh home. One or both of them is hiding something. Bruce is being secretive about his meeting with

Julie Berry, and I know he told Erin that he not only went by there in the afternoon but later, as well. He didn't share the second visit with Shelby Rae. Why not?

How did Shelby Rae know what Julie Berry was up to? I wonder if she was being blackmailed.

Even more interesting, they're both lying to the sheriff. There's a lot going on here that adds up to something dangerous. I'm convinced that Bryn Owens has nothing to do with this. The mystery lies closer to home.

CHAPTER EIGHT

*N*ow that he and Erin were at least somewhat back on track, Noah felt like a weight had been lifted from his shoulders. There *was* a track, he was convinced. She thought his plan to ask Zach Wilkins some questions about Julie Berry was a good one. After their talk at The Village Bean, they parted ways until he would pick her up later that evening to go out to Zach's place. He couldn't wait to see her again.

At home, he showered quickly and dressed, choosing a funky black and white fitted western shirt he'd picked up on his last trip to Louisville and black jeans. It wasn't that he thought they were on a date, but he suddenly wanted to impress her. To be his best self. The guys at the dealership would give him six kinds of hell if they saw him.

Screw them.

"Well, don't you look dressed to kill, son?"

When Noah had gotten home the house had been empty. Now his father stood in the kitchen doorway, a six pack dangling from his hand. He twisted off a beer and held it out to Noah.

"No thanks. Gotta go." Noah gave him a conciliatory smile and started past him.

"Hey, wait a minute. You got a date or something? Your mom said you dumped that little Christian girl last winter. Must be the boss's daughter then. She's a tasty little thing. I like that you're thinking big. Imagine me father-in-law to the Walsh girl. Ha!"

Noah didn't like the idea of his father even thinking about Erin. He clenched his fists, then relaxed them. He couldn't let his father see he was getting to him.

"Why don't you have her out here to dinner some night? Your mama's such a fine cook, and I bet she'd be pleased to see you with a girl like that. She always did want better for you. Though nobody could do better than your mama. She was a peach when she was a girl. Not that you'd know it now. She's let herself go a bit."

Again Noah bit back his anger and breathed deeply. He wanted to punch his father until he understood that every bit of pain his mother had felt, every wrinkle on her face was due to *him*, Jeb Daly, a man who had married an unspoiled teenager then turned into a real criminal, a man who eventually quit legitimate work to let his wife support him.

"Yeah. I'll ask mom. Thanks. I'll see you later, Dad."

Noah finally got past him and opened the kitchen door to go to his bike.

"Not tomorrow, though. I'm getting out of this place for a couple days. I need a break from the four walls. Feeling caged, you know?" He grinned at his own joke.

"Are you allowed to leave town? You got permission to go somewhere?" Noah wasn't sure about all the specifics of his father's parole, but he didn't think it included being allowed to hang out somewhere out of town with his dope-growing friends.

"Aren't you nice to worry about your old man?" He shook his head. "Everything's under control. Nothing to worry about at all. I don't check in until Friday afternoon." He put the six-pack down on the counter. "Hey, wait." Reaching into his front pocket, he pulled out a thick fold of bills. Peeling off a hundred, he held it out to Noah. "You take that girl out somewhere nice. On me."

"That's okay, Dad. I've got money." Where had that money come from?

"Oh, come on. I had luck playing cards the other night. I'm sure it was because your mama kissed them for me."

Noah's stomach turned. The thought of his mother charmed again by his father made him sick. But he took the bill his father held out. The last thing he needed was for his father to have reason to be pissed off at him. No way he was going to spend it, though. It might be counterfeit or contaminated with drugs. Who the hell knew with his old man.

"Thanks, Dad. Have a good trip."

THE SUN HUNG low in the sky behind Noah as he turned the bike down Erin's driveway. The garage door was open, and the bays were empty. Only Erin's Challenger sat in the driveway. He was somewhat relieved not to see Shelby Rae or Bruce Walsh again. It felt like a hundred years since he'd found Julie Berry's body, but it had only been early that same morning. There was no longer any sign of the police or crime scene techs. Was there still crime scene tape down near the dock where he'd found her? She'd looked so alone. Her body was surely at the morgue by now, but he could only picture her lying in the muddy water.

Seconds after he shut down and got off the bike, Erin emerged from the garage, Jocko darting out in front of her to bark madly at him.

Noah took off his helmet and squatted to pet the excited Jack Russell. "Hey, buddy. What's up?" A moment later, Trouble padded over the mulch to sit a few feet away. He looked anywhere except at Noah, and languidly switched his tail back and forth.

"That cat sure likes to play hard to get," he said to Erin.

"Oh, he's jealous of Jocko. You'd think he owned this house, and that Jocko wasn't here first." Erin rolled her eyes. "He's a sweetie, but kind of silly."

Noah noticed she'd also changed her clothes since he saw her a few hours earlier. Her light blue sleeveless romper showed off her long, lightly freckled legs, and though it was buttoned all the way to the base of her throat, it gave her a sexy lean look. He liked how her hair sat in natural waves about her shoulders.

"You look great," he said. Erin blushed. "You probably want to grab a jacket or something. And some shoes. You don't want to be on the bike in sandals. Sorry."

Erin bent to pick up Trouble, and he put his paws on her shoulders, looking around with interest. "Do you mind if we take my car and bring Jocko and Trouble with us? They've been alone so much, and Dad and Shelby Rae haven't been home all afternoon. I don't know where they are. These guys get lonesome. And maybe Trouble will help us out. I told you Tammy Lynn said he was good at mysteries, didn't I?"

"You want to take them out to Zach's?"

"It's not like he lives in town, right? We can take my car."

She tilted her head and said with a smile, "You can drive if you want."

THE DRIVE FELT TOO short to Noah. He could've driven the Challenger for hours. Both the cat and dog were standing on Erin's lap with their faces out the open passenger window. Erin thought it was so cute she couldn't stop taking pictures of them, and Noah couldn't disagree.

"I've never seen a cat like Trouble," he told her. "It's almost like he's part human. Like he understands what we talk about. It's kind of weird."

"Damn it. I forgot to bring the photos I found at Julie's house." Erin sighed. "I wanted to show them to you. Julie told my dad she saw Shelby Rae with a guy in her SUV. That she was having an affair, and that she thought it was—what was the word?" She thought a minute. "Yeah, *abominable*. Like the guy was a monster or something."

"Julie's house?" Noah was confused.

She told him about being caught by the deputy in Julie's house earlier that day, looking for the photos her father had told her about. He was surprised she didn't tell him earlier at The Village Bean. Shelby Rae might have been having an affair? If there was a stranger involved it put a new spin on her kidnapping, and Noah said so.

"I know, right?" Erin stroked Trouble's back. "Maybe that's too much information to share with Zach. I mean, we don't know if it's true, and it would really embarrass my dad, you know?"

Noah thought about the things he knew about his own father. Embarrassment wasn't the issue, but he felt similarly reticent because he was sad for his mom. "I hear you. It's interesting though." He didn't say anything about the way some people at work talked about Shelby Rae. It was only gossip. "So, check. No mention of Julie's gossip about Shelby Rae."

When they turned on to the private gravel road leading to Zach's place, Jocko barked, shivering with excitement.

"What's that about?" Erin laughed. "What a goof. He loves to go places. I think he's been lonesome."

Noah liked the ramshackleness of Zach's two-story farmhouse. There had been nights when he slept on Zach's couch, comforted by the settling creaks of the house, as well as the scuffling of mice. A sturdy, if uneven, porch wrapped around the front and one side of the house. On the other side was a set of painted stairs leading to the second floor. Zach called it a mother-in-law's apartment, and Noah knew it was empty. He secretly hoped Zach would let him rent it one day so he could move out of his mother's house.

As Noah parked and turned off the Challenger, Trouble sniffed the air and jumped out the passenger window. Before Erin could stop him, Jocko scrambled up onto the window, scratching the door's leather with his back nails. Then he was out, chasing after Trouble, who beat him to the porch and was sitting in front of the door as though waiting to be let inside.

NOAH HAD an urge to grab hold of Erin's hand as they walked to the door. *This isn't a date, this isn't a date* he told himself. *Her friend just died. It's not the time.* The urge was strong and difficult to resist, but resist it he did, and settled for resting his fingertips gently on her back as they walked up the porch stairs, as though to steady her. She didn't startle or jerk away, as he feared she might. Would he ever stop being so nervous around her?

Zach opened the door. Noah always felt glad to see him because he was a real friend. It didn't matter that his dad despised the fact that they were friends—especially now that Noah was twenty-one. Zach was still in his uniform, though his collar was unbuttoned and his face was peppered with dark, end-of-the day whiskers. He was taller than Noah, about six two, and although he was bulky with muscles, his face was long and thin, and he had deep brown eyes, rimmed with lashes Noah's mother said she envied. If there was anything off about his face at all it was his pointed, narrow nose that was a shade too small. But it had been broken once, which at least had made him look impressively tough to the younger Noah.

"Come on in, but leave the animals outside. I'm allergic to cats, and I've got the General shut in his crate, but he'll smell the terrier and piss all over the place later."

Erin nodded and scrambled to grab Trouble as he tried to slink past Zach's legs. "Come on, Jocko. Let's go. Come on!"

Jocko looked back at her and was eventually convinced.

"They can hang out on the porch. I doubt it will be full dark before you leave, so nothing should get them."

"The General's a boxer mutt," Noah said by way of explanation. "He's a great dog. But he would probably try to chase Trouble off."

"That's a fact." Zach led them inside after Erin set Trouble on the porch swing.

Noah and Erin settled on the couch, and Zach brought them glasses of lemonade. He opened a beer for himself and poured it into a glass.

"So, what's up?"

Noah shifted. "There are actually two things we'd like to ask you about. I know you probably can't tell us a lot about Julie Berry. Not sure if you even know anything yet."

"Well, now that it's a murder investigation, there's not much I *can* share. We're looking for her Mercedes and doing a lot of interviews with folks to figure out who saw her last. You already know she was shot." He gave Erin an apologetic look. "What's the other thing?"

Beside Noah, Erin straightened up. Noah waited for her to speak.

"This is really confidential. My dad and Shelby Rae didn't want to tell Sheriff Bowen. Shelby Rae says she's afraid to."

Zach raised an eyebrow. "And?"

She told him how Shelby Rae was nowhere to be found after the fireworks and there were signs of a struggle in one of the cabanas. Then how her father found the note, and she found Shelby Rae's bloody white cover up on the path to the field.

"Wait. Shelby Rae was at the lake this morning. So she was kidnapped, and came back okay?" He looked confused, but also, Noah thought, shaken.

"My dad paid the fifty thousand dollars right away. She was back Tuesday morning."

"He *paid?* Jesus. Why didn't you people call us? It's a miracle she wasn't killed anyway. Or your father wasn't hurt. Talk about idiotic."

Noah bristled. "They were doing the best they could. The police don't always get people back. Shelby Rae got released, didn't she?"

"Yeah," Zach said. "She got released. *This time.* Now whoever it was knows your old man's a soft touch. She could be taken again. Or you could, Erin." He looked at her, but it was a look without compassion. Noah had rarely seen Zach so irritated.

Erin stood up and walked to the window. Jocko had leapt onto the porch swing and barked when he saw her.

Zach sighed. "All right. Water under the bridge. What did Shelby Rae say about whoever took her? Was it one person? Two? Where did they take her?"

"She's not sure about where." Erin turned from the window. "She says she thinks it was a man and a woman—something about the way the woman wasn't quite as strong and her hands were smaller. But they didn't talk or give her anything to eat. Just water. After my dad paid the ransom they dumped her out on our road, blindfolded. They made the bindings on her hands loose enough that she could get out of them when they were gone."

"Does she still have them? We can maybe trace them. What about DNA? Did she scratch them or something? I'd like to talk to her." Zach was earnest. "People shouldn't get away with shit like this. Unbelievable. Maybe it was someone with a beef against your father. Everybody likes Shelby Rae. I can't imagine anyone wanting to hurt her."

Noah didn't look at Erin. He knew she wouldn't agree, and he wasn't sure he agreed himself.

"What about Bryn Owens?" Erin asked. "She was there at the party, right? Well, not at the party, but she was waiting out front in her car."

"You think Bryn Owens would do something like this? Really?" Zach was skeptical. "I guess it's possible. I did have to run her off, and your father said he's been getting unpleasant notes from her because of Tionna and the lawsuit. But it's hard to believe she'd resort to kidnapping. According to her, she wasn't even after money in the lawsuit. She believes the dealership shouldn't have let Tionna drive that car away. That it was gross negligence."

Noah interrupted. At least he was familiar with these details. "Earl said she refused to wait. The negligence was on her part. I know it sounds harsh, but there's no reason Earl would lie about it."

"I think it's important that she was at the house," Erin said. "She had to be trying to see who was there and when everyone would be gone."

"I ran her off," Zach said. "She didn't hang around."

"Maybe she came back." Erin was adamant.

"I followed her all the way to the bakery and watched her go inside. Before she went upstairs, she flipped me off and shouted she'd report me for harassment. It wouldn't have gone anywhere of course, but it was unpleasant enough. I left on patrol, but I drove by her place a couple of times. Her car was still there when it got dark."

Erin sat down again. "Someone could've picked her up."

"Possible, but unlikely." Zach took a long drink of his beer. "I can look into it more. But I'd really need to talk to Shelby Rae first. She's the one with details."

"You can't. Let me try to talk to her again to see if she'll change her mind. She doesn't act much like it, but she has to be worried that they'll come after her again. I doubt she's all that worried about them taking me." Erin gave a wry laugh that made Noah feel bad for her. It sucked that she had a stepmother she didn't get along with. What if his own mother did get divorced and remarried? It's possible she could get together with someone even worse than his father. He thought back to the way she'd looked up at Bruce Walsh. Had she really been flirting with him? The thought made him uncomfortable. *No way*. She couldn't think about his boss that way. But if *he* thought he could possibly have a relationship with Erin, wasn't it only fair that his mother should be able to pursue someone like Bruce Walsh? Not *actually* Bruce Walsh of course. No. Erin's voice startled him out of his wayward thoughts.

"Um, where's your bathroom?" she asked Zach, sounding a little embarrassed.

"Past the kitchen. First door on your right."

THE FLOOR of Zach's old farmhouse creaked as Erin went to the back of the house in search of the bathroom. Things had gotten too intense talking about Shelby Rae. Shelby Rae's insistence that none of them should talk to the police was maddening, and Erin felt like she couldn't rest until she knew what had really happened. And somehow she was certain it had to be connected to Julie's death. Even though she had no proof, she felt like Shelby Rae was lying about something.

One never knew what to expect of guest bathrooms, especially those in houses belonging to bachelors, and Erin was pleasantly surprised that this one wasn't too bad. It could almost be called retro. The vanity and walls were all of the same rough knotty pine, and the decoration was mostly framed certificates and photos of Zach with various dignitaries. There was even one that showed he'd been made an honorary Kentucky Colonel the year before. Her father kept *his* certificate in his office at work, saying it was good for business.

As she was washing her hands she read the large, gold and black lettered certificate on the wall beside her. LOUISVILLE WESTERN HIGH SCHOOL. It was dated fifteen years earlier. She hadn't known he was from Louisville. Who else did she know from Louisville in New Belford? A few kids from her high school who had transferred. And, of course, Shelby Rae, who had been—as she told everyone who asked about her life

—homecoming queen, a sometime model, and a pageant winner. But Erin had no idea which high school she'd gone to, so she made a mental note to ask.

That would be a fun conversation, given the way they were getting along these days.

When she was done in the bathroom, she took a wrong turn and ended up in a hallway with several dim rooms along it. At first she thought to hurry back and find the living room, but she was too curious about Zach not to look. He was, after all, the man who'd killed her mother.

The first room she came to was a cluttered bedroom with a low platform bed piled with messy sheets and a quilt. A trail of men's clothes littered the floor—socks and underwear and T-shirts, sweat clothes. Though a second deputy's uniform hung in a clear dry-cleaning bag on the door like a rebuke to the mess around it. Erin wrinkled her nose. It smelled like sweat and despair.

What a funny thing to think. Like something from a novel. But still, that's what it smelled like. Sadness.

She knew she should hurry back to the living room, but she quickly peeked into the next room, where the light from the hall shone eerily on the stuffed creatures on the wall: a duck and an antelope, and the head of a buck with an eight-point rack. As someone who couldn't wait to be a veterinarian, the sight of those dead animals broke her heart. She understood hunting for food, but Zach had probably not eaten the antelope, and obviously hadn't eaten the duck. She whispered an apology to the remains of the animals, glad that her father wasn't a fan of hunting trophies. On either side of the windows sat two large gun safes. Besides the safes and trophies was a reloading rig where Zach obviously filled his own shells for hunting. MacKenzie's father had a similar one, and he'd shown

MacKenzie and Erin how to load 12-gauge shells. Erin had thought it pretty fun because then they got to go out and shoot clay pigeons.

One long wall was lined with hooks hung with hunting and fishing clothes: waders and coveralls and camo jackets and pants, mostly green and tan. But there was plenty of gray, white, and black, too, for winter hunting. She noticed a single, dark hoodie, but couldn't tell if it was blue or black, like the one the man who had picked up the ransom had been wearing.

Then she heard a low, threatening growl from deep inside the room, and she jumped back into the hallway.

"What are you doing?"

Erin gave a nervous laugh. Zach stood at the end of the hall, silhouetted in the light. Noah came up behind him.

"You okay, Erin?"

"Just a little embarrassed." She smiled awkwardly at Zach. "Took a wrong turn."

"You're lucky the General's in his crate. He's not fond of strangers." Zach reached past her and firmly closed the door.

"He wouldn't hurt Erin," Noah said good-naturedly. "The General's a good guy."

Zach gave a kind of a grunt and followed Erin and Noah back into the living room. Erin's pulse was pounding. Lots of men had dark hoodies. If she suspected every guy with a dark hoodie of being the kidnapper, she'd probably have to suspect half the guys she'd known in high school, including Noah.

Once they were seated again, she tried to catch Noah's attention to let him know she wanted to leave. There were more questions she wanted to ask, but she was spooked. Zach didn't seem as nice as he had. Of course nobody liked strangers snooping around their stuff. Maybe she wasn't being fair.

"How are things at the house?"

For a moment Erin thought Zach was talking to her, but Noah answered.

"You know. Weird. As usual." He cast a shy look at Erin and shrugged.

"You tell me if Jeb gives you a hard time. Have you thought about moving out? He's got a number of job possibilities, I'm told. Your mom and he should be able to manage without you."

Erin wondered what sort of jobs an ex-convict like Jeb Daly could have waiting for him, but she didn't want to ask. Beside her, Noah seemed uncomfortable. She already knew he didn't like to talk about his father, so she interrupted.

"Not to change the subject or anything, but do you know Shelby Rae's uncle? His name is Travis, and he was acting kind of strange at the party. Super touchy with Shelby Rae. But I guess he always is." Erin found it hard to keep the distaste from her voice. "When I was younger, he always talked to me like I was a little girl even though I was like fifteen. He creeps me out. And I know Shelby Rae gives money to her family."

"What are you saying? Did he assault you?" Zach leaned forward.

"No, no. Nothing like that. I just wondered if he maybe wanted more than she was able to sneak to him and her family. Maybe he knew fifty thousand dollars was what my father kept on hand in his safe. It would explain why Shelby Rae was let go unharmed, right?"

"Yeah, Travis isn't major league. Did a little time for forgery, but not much. He's a gambler, and spends a lot of time on the riverboats. It's possible he could owe folks some money."

They were all quiet a moment.

Erin finally spoke. "I don't know why Shelby Rae's got so

much family around New Belford. It's not like she grew up here, right? She's from Louisville." Before anyone could answer, there was a crash above their heads.

"What was that?" Noah looked up at the ceiling.

Zach's face clouded as he also looked up. His hands clenched his knees, and then he stood. "I'll be right back."

Before he left the room, he retrieved a handgun from a drawer in a table beside the door. He held it so the muzzle was pointed down as he turned back to them. "Wait here."

With the door open, Jocko began to bark.

JOCKO'S EXCITEMENT grabbed my attention as soon as we arrived. He's no rocket scientist, but he definitely exhibits plenty of signs that our visit to Chief Deputy Zach Wilkins' bucolic farmhouse was one of import to his minuscule brain. It was almost as if he expected a warm welcome. When the lord and master opened his front door, I was a bit stunned that he didn't at least let Jocko in. Back at the morning's murder scene, Chief Deputy Wilkins was pleasant to Jocko, but extremely dismissive of me, so his barring me from the house was hardly surprising. But once Erin set Jocko on the porch swing, he settled down to sleep in a most feline way and didn't move even when I set the thing swaying. What a useless skive that fellow is.

I watch through the window. Erin does not seem happy to be here, though she was happy enough on the trip over. At least she and Noah are spending time together. I was worried they'd had a row earlier in the day. Young love is often fragile. Still, I have no doubt she and Noah are just right for each other.

With Jocko sleeping, I find myself painfully bored. Hot as well. I investigate the half-full bowl of water near the front door but discover it's stale with canine drool, and there are no ponds or leaking hoses in sight. Returning to the porch swing, I give myself a vigorous bath so the swing will shimmy, just to annoy Jocko, but nothing wakes the foolish beast.

Not in the least weary, I give up and decide to explore the area. The surrounding land, with its dull pastures and sagging, gray outbuildings, looks dry, as though the life has been sucked out of it. There's no springy, well-watered lawn, as at the Walsh estate. We're only a mile or two away from Erin's home as the crow flies, but it's an entirely different countryside. A pair of dusty horses stare over the fence. One rolls in the grass, giving itself a writhing scratch worthy of a Labrador Retriever.

The scent of mice and voles is everywhere, and most of the trail scents lead into cracks around the old house's foundations. For a bit of fun, I stalk a chipmunk that quails inside a fallen planter, but that doesn't last long. It's dreadfully hot, and the rattling window air conditioners tell me it's much more pleasant inside the house. Truly, there seems to be nothing interesting here.

When I return to the porch, Jocko is gone. Inside? That would be a smack on the snout for me! I pad around and find him on the outside staircase. He spots me and gives a small jump, a sign he's glad to see me. Then he dashes up the stairs to the landing outside the door and gives an encouraging yip. Humoring the daft git, I climb the stairs. He seems to want me to see something there. Now I'm interested.

There's room on the outer ledge of the window right beside the door of the upstairs apartment for me to secure my footing. And just enough room in the window opening for me to slip my body through it. I land deftly on the floor. Jocko can't follow but keeps his yapper shut.

Given the dog's excitement, I expected some horror on the other side of that window. Secluded rooms are often full of mystery, and this apartment is musty and appears little used.

Inside, blinds cover the door, as well as the window I've entered, but the rest of the second floor windows—the ones that can't be easily viewed from outside—are uncovered, so that the room is filled with a murky light.

I nearly jump out of my pants when I realize there are numerous people silhouetted in the room—people who have no heads! I give them a warning hiss, but they don't move. With a shudder, I realize the figures are not human at all, but mannequins. Each mannequin is female-shaped with a generous bosom and rounded hips—nothing like those skeletons one sees in fashionable stores. Two of the mannequins wear glittering evening gowns, and a third wears a tiny skirt and matching fitted sweater with some kind of logo on it.

While I am a cat of the world who believes everyone should be allowed to express themselves in any clothing they desire, I find these fabulous ensembles uncharacteristic choices for the whiskered and gruff Chief Deputy Wilkins, and about six or seven sizes too small. Instead I envision him in generous tweeds and sensible low heels such as her majesty wears when visiting Balmoral Castle.

The light is fading fast, so I take in the rest of the room quickly. There's little furniture except for a few tables, a shabby bean bag chair of uncertain vintage, and some rusting folding chairs that would be at home in any church basement. Wait! I hurry over to a table in a corner where an old typewriter sits in a field of dust. I'm put in mind of the typed ransom note. I try to pull the ribbon free, but it gets tangled. I'll have to take some other clue to Erin. Because clues are exactly what I'm looking at. Zach Wilkins is surely involved in Shelby Rae's kidnapping.

The clothing on the mannequins is curious, but equally curious are the photos pegged to enormous cork boards on the opposite wall. Hundreds, perhaps even a thousand photos of one person—first of her as a smiling, round-faced middle-schooler holding some kind of certificate, of her blowing out birthday candles, or finishing a foot race, or posed with a bat or soccer balls. Her scowling in Halloween skeleton makeup, taller now. On a school bus, waving from the window or

mugging for the camera beside a friend whose face has been oh so care-
fully excised from the photograph. Then the pageant photos—in dresses
and swimsuits, her hair elaborately coiffed, her body tanned, her
makeup perfect. She's young and lovely and would be perfect if not for
a certain glint of shrewdness in her eyes that's visible even in the dark-
ening room. It's a look with which I'm only too familiar.

In the later photos—behind a desk, in newspaper wedding photos,
in a sports car, sipping a glass of wine—she's much more recognizable
as the woman I know. But even in these newer pictures, the faces of any
other people have been carefully cut away. And in the wedding photos,
the excising is particularly savage and pronounced as though the person
doing the cutting was angry or in a hurry.

There's something very odd and spooky about this deputy having
all these photos and clothes. But the strangest thing is an elaborate tiara,
its faux gems and cheap metal yellowed with age, resting in a Lucite
display box in a place of honor on an otherwise empty table.

How can I alert Erin? It's clear that Chief Deputy Zach Wilkins
is obsessed with Shelby Rae and may be a danger to Erin and her
family. At this very minute she's sitting in the man's living room, no
doubt giving him details and information that might make it easier to
cause all the Walshes harm.

If Jocko and I go downstairs and start causing a ruckus, there's no
guarantee they won't just secure me in the car with the windows
cracked until they're finished. I wish they would cut their visit short.
Chances are they're giving the deputy far more information than he is
giving them. It's obviously in his best interest not to tell them a thing.

There's no sign that anyone has been imprisoned in this apartment,
in fact no sign that anyone spends much time up here except for a few
candy bar wrappers in a rubbish basket and a used coffee mug at one
edge of a table. The best thing for me to do is to get one of these old
photographs to Erin and hope she understands where it came from. I'll

have to steal it and hide it near Erin's car so I can get it home without the deputy seeing me.

I choose a photograph of the girl in a pageant gown looking like a dog's dinner. In fact it's the selfsame gown that one of the mannequin wears. Taking the end of the pushpin in my mouth, I tug, careful not to swallow the thing, and let it drop to the tabletop. But the deuced photo floats down through the crack between the table and the wall, and in my haste to retrieve it, I whip around only to knock the coffee mug to the floor. The crash resounds on the bare wood.

They will surely have heard that downstairs, so my time for planning is over.

Careful to avoid the shattered crockery, I find the photograph. It takes me several good bites to secure the thing in my teeth as the photographic paper is thick. Finally, with the taste of old paper on my tongue, I scamper to the window and ease my way out. The paper bends a bit, but it can't be helped. As I leap down the stairs two at a time past Jocko, he begins to bark. Below, heavy footsteps rush across the porch. Worse luck, a motion light mounted on the eave just above the apartment door floods the side yard with light.

"Cat! Get down here!" *The irate deputy starts up the stairs, aiming a gun at me. Jocko growls and nips at his ankles.*

If I didn't have a photograph impaled on my fangs, I would laugh as only cats know how. Midway down the stairway, I leap off its side to the ground. It's a good distance, but I'm a champion jumper even with my mouth full. The deputy won't catch me.

"Wait. Don't shoot the cat!" *Erin's terrified voice follows me into the warm night.* "Leave him alone!"

Bless the child. Thank goodness she came out in time.

I disappear into the darkness, confident that Erin will understand I'm smart enough to find my way back to her house on my own.

. . .

"You almost shot my cat!" Erin was furious. "How dare you." *Just like you shot my mother, you creep,* she wanted to add.

Zach Wilkins stood over her, equally angry. "Your damned cat shouldn't have been messing around in my place. He's lucky he's not dead."

Erin was glad Noah put a hand on her shoulder to hold her back because she was *thisclose* to shoving the deputy.

"How could the cat have even gotten in upstairs?" Noah kept his voice even, his hand on her shoulder. "I mean, he's a cat. What could he do? But we've got to find him. He doesn't even belong to Erin."

Erin *was* worried. She felt foolish about bringing Trouble to Zach's with her. While she was confident that he was more help than mischief-maker, he hadn't been allowed into Zach's house and had probably been irritated at having to stay on the porch with Jocko. Maybe he could find his way home. Trouble really was a smart cat. But what had he been doing upstairs?

"Window's open to keep it from getting musty up there." Zach now sounded defensive rather than angry.

Erin picked up Jocko. He was growling low in his throat, and Erin was sure it was because of Zach and the gun. She stroked him gently behind one ear. *I don't like him either, boy.*

"Let's go after him. You've got more flashlights in the gun room, right, Zach?" Noah started toward the front door.

"Sure."

Jocko followed behind Erin and Noah as they searched. Zach walked ahead of them all, leading them toward the garage and the nearby shed containing his tractor and deck mower. The grass and dirt in the path of the flashlights showed gray in the light.

Erin called for Trouble again and again, and was only answered with the hooting of an owl.

When Zach threw open the doors to the shed, something scrabbled quickly into a corner. Erin gasped and lunged to grab Jocko to keep him from running in after it.

"Raccoon," Zach said dismissively. A blur of gray fur disappeared through a hole in the wall. There was nothing else alive inside the shed that was larger than a mouse.

The garage was a newer metal building with a glaring lamp over the door, and its interior was hung with overhead fluorescents. A smattering of last fall's leaves, and gravel from the driveway, covered the floor. But the only occupant of the big garage was a classic 1972 Camaro with its hood missing and its engine partially disassembled.

"You've done a lot of work." Noah ran a hand approvingly along the Camaro's body.

"As much as I can. Anytime you want to come out, you're welcome. But I guess that would be what they call a *busman's holiday*, yeah?"

Noah looked down at Erin and she saw the pride in his eyes. "Zach got me started working on cars. You should've seen the '82 Trans-Am we fixed up and sold. It was badass. Zach split the money with me."

Erin nodded, but she really didn't want to chitchat about old cars. What she wanted was to find Trouble. She looked back at the darkness beyond the door. Because of the light around them, the barn was a barely visible rectangle in the distance.

"What about the barn? He could be hiding there."

Zach led them out of the garage and slid the enormous door closed. "It's possible, but I want to wait until daylight.

The barn's got a serious rat problem. I've got traps set everywhere, and I don't want you two getting hurt."

Seeing the concern on Erin's face, he put a hand up. "No
worries about your cat. Cats are smarter than that. But most of
the lights in there are burned out. If he's in the barn he's probably already holed up for the night."

ERIN DROVE home with Noah in the passenger seat, Jocko on
his lap. The car felt emptier without Trouble.

"He might even be home when we get there. Maybe he's
running through these very fields." She gestured to the darkness outside the window, trying to sound more positive than
she felt. In her mind she couldn't stop thinking about the
phone call she would have to make to Tammy Lynn if they
didn't find Trouble. She wished she hadn't taken him to Zach's
in the first place.

"What do you think he was doing up in that apartment?"
Noah asked. "I wonder if he really did go in through the
window like Zach said he did. Wasn't it weird how he and
Jocko both ran to sit on the porch as soon as we got there?"

"I don't know what that was about. Except Jocko likes
everybody. Shelby Rae says he'd move in with anyone who
would have him. Except he seemed to change his mind about
Zach." When Noah didn't answer, she realized she'd probably
insulted Zach, and Noah obviously cared about him a lot. Was
it going to be a problem? Zach had been nice to answer their
questions, even if he wasn't terribly helpful.

A few moments later, she turned the Challenger into the
driveway and parked. The garage doors were all closed, which
usually meant both her father and Shelby Rae were home.

"I'd ask you in, but it's been kind of a long day. Who knows if Shelby Rae is even speaking to me tonight, and if she is she'll probably be rude to you, too." It wasn't that she didn't want to spend time with him. She was tired and concerned that she'd crossed a line, but she was also anxious to see if Trouble had made it back yet.

"That's okay. Hey, do you think you'd come to my house for dinner tomorrow night if I asked you?" Noah sounded nervous. "My dad is gone for a couple nights, and my mom's a great cook. I know she'd really like to see you again. You were so nice to her at the party, with the glasses and everything."

Erin thought of the silent dinner she would probably have with her father and Shelby Rae. Even a firing squad sounded better.

When they both began to talk at the same time, Erin laughed and said, "You first."

"If you want to do it some other time, that would be good, too."

"No! Tomorrow night would be great. Honestly." She wanted to thank him about a hundred times but put a lid on her enthusiasm. She didn't want to sound like a dork. "You really think Trouble will show up?"

"Yep. Any cat that can escape Zach and his revolver is no dummy. I bet he didn't even use up any of his nine lives." He smiled and opened the car door. Jocko jumped out and ran for the doggy door at the back of the house. In the mellow glow from the dome light, the dimple in Noah's chin was more pronounced than ever and his eyes were a deeper brown. "Great. I'll text you my address. See you tomorrow. 6:30." Then he was quickly out the door.

Erin got out of her side of the car. Should she wait in the driveway to see him off or go inside to look for Trouble? Her decision was made for her when Noah secured his helmet and cranked the bike. Then he waved goodbye and disappeared down the driveway. She felt a small stab of sadness. Was she just upset about Trouble, or was she a little disappointed that neither one of them had attempted to kiss the other goodnight?

Once inside the house, Erin went to her room and searched upstairs for any sign of Trouble, but there was none. Downstairs, after looking in all the unoccupied rooms, she quietly entered the family room where her father and Shelby Rae were watching a *Real Housewives* on television. Or rather her father was snoring lightly in his favorite recliner, and Shelby Rae was reading something on her phone. Shelby Rae glanced up.

"I wish you'd let me know you took Jocko out with you. Text me or your Dad. I thought he ran off. The only sign of anything was that motorcycle in the driveway." Now Jocko was settled on the couch, his head lolling against Shelby Rae's leg. Shelby Rae wore silk lounging pajamas, and her newly-cut hair was pushed behind her ears. Her face was scrubbed of makeup and glowed with expensive moisturizer. Bare-faced, Shelby Rae was truly pretty. Erin never understood why she rarely came downstairs without layers of makeup on.

"Sorry," Erin whispered. "Jocko really wanted to come, and I didn't know you'd be home before I was. Hey, have you seen Tammy's cat?"

"Ugh, no. When is she coming back, anyway?" She darkened her phone and picked up the television remote to turn off the battling housewives.

Erin's father startled awake. "Guess that means it's time for bed." He gave Erin a pleasant smile as he stood, his eyes wide and strangely cheerful the way some people's are when they wake to find other people watching them. "Have fun tonight?"

When Erin nodded, he said, "Good. Good. This is one day I'm glad has come to an end."

He kissed Erin on the cheek, and she felt the roughness of his late-day beard. "Night, Dad. Love you."

"Don't stay up too late, Shelby Rae. Come up soon."

"I'll be up in fifteen, honey."

Sometimes Erin thought Shelby Rae exaggerated her affection for her father just because she was around. Or maybe she'd just become too suspicious of her stepmother recently. Nothing had come of the row about the tattoo. Erin wondered if Shelby Rae was saving it up for some other attack. She followed Shelby Rae into the kitchen.

Shelby Rae loaded a few remaining things into the dishwasher while Erin rifled in the fridge for a snack. Strangely enough, she was less regular about meals at home than she was at school.

"You're dressed up. You have a date with that Daly boy?" There was no sign of teasing or rancor in her voice. Only curiosity.

"Not really a date. We went out to see Chief Deputy Wilkins. I wanted to know if he could tell us anything about Julie. He and Noah are friends. But you probably already know that." Erin didn't look at Shelby Rae, but waited.

"Good Lord, why would I know that? I don't care to know anything about the social life of a Zach Wilkins *or* a car mechanic. I'm surprised you would bother with a boy like him. Especially with how he was involved in your mother's case. Does your father know? He asked about the motorcycle in the driveway. He knows it was the Daly boy's."

Erin laid out the goat cheese, some grapes, and her favorite nut crackers on a plate. She wasn't going to let Shelby Rae's snobbery get to her. She shrugged. "We're just hanging out. No big deal."

"It's not a big deal that Noah Daly found Julie's body? Seems pretty coincidental to me. He could be a suspect."

"Oh, my gosh," Erin said. "Speaking of coincidence...the weirdest thing."

Shelby Rae plucked a small cluster of grapes from the colander and popped a grape in her mouth. Erin had a sudden memory of giggling with her over a plate of chicken salad and strawberries at a tearoom in Louisville after they'd gone shopping for school clothes. She must have been thirteen or fourteen. It seemed like a lifetime ago.

"What?"

Erin put down her plate. "Zach Wilkins has a Kentucky Colonel certificate and his high school diploma hanging in his bathroom. He's from Louisville, too. Did you know him when you lived there?"

The question took Shelby Rae by surprise, and Erin watched her eyes change as she considered her answer. Finally, she gave a smile that was more of a grimace.

"I *did* know him in high school, but we weren't friends or anything. He was kind of a loser. Not somebody I ever would hang around with. You know, he wasn't on the football team or anything like that. He skipped school a lot to go hunting. None of *my* friends did. We weren't hillbilly like that."

"You never told me why you moved to New Belford. It seems weird that you would choose to come live here."

Shelby Rae made a scoffing noise. "Yes, I did tell you. My aunt had cancer and I came down here to help my uncle take care of her. I was the only one who would do it. My Uncle Travis can be a waste of space sometimes, but my aunt was good people. I know *you* don't like Uncle Travis. At least you don't like me helping him out. Or my mother. Some people just have bad luck with money. Not something *you* ever have to worry about."

Erin didn't rise to the bait.

"Did you meet Chief Deputy Wilkins again after you moved here?"

"Sure. I mean, he was a cop, right? I saw them all at the dealership from time to time. Is there something wrong with that? It's not like I could escape seeing him after Jeb Daly robbed the bank. *Everybody* knew him. It's my opinion he should have left town after everything was straightened out and Jeb Daly went to jail. It was strange the way people just went on with their lives—your father giving Jeb Daly's son a job, and being pretty nice to Zach. Well, mostly nice." She paused a moment and looked at Erin shrewdly. "Did Zach say something to you? Is that what this is all about?"

"About what?"

"Did he say anything rude about me, about high school or anything? Or about me marrying your dad?"

Erin shook her head. "No, he didn't say anything about you at all," she lied. Zach had talked about Shelby Rae needing to be interviewed. Erin had just been curious about their having grown up in the same town, a big town at that. But now she really was interested. Zach now knew about the kidnapping, and he was going to investigate Bryn Owens some more for them. They had told him not to mention the kidnapping to anyone else, hadn't they? *Damn.* She couldn't remember.

Something about Zach Wilkins bugged her, and she felt like it was more than the fact that he almost shot a fleeing Trouble.

After Erin reassured Shelby Rae again that, no, Zach had

said nothing unpleasant about her, Shelby Rae wandered toward the stairs.

"Turn the lights out, will you?" she asked. "Good night."

It was the most pleasant her stepmother had been to her in a week.

ERIN HUNG out in the kitchen a while, watching Netflix on her iPad, hoping Trouble might come through the pet door. Weary after half an hour, she loaded her dishes into the dishwasher and started it. She thought about Julie, and how very quiet her house must be now that she was dead and the police were gone. Because they'd once been so close, she felt badly about how irritating she'd found Julie lately. But the photographs she'd had of Shelby Rae with the man in her car bothered Erin. Now they sat in a shoebox in her closet, perhaps some kind of evidence linked to Julie's death.

Was it possible Shelby Rae was involved? She didn't want to believe it, if only for her father's sake. It wasn't like Shelby Rae couldn't just divorce him if she didn't love him anymore. He would surely give her all the money she needed, after begging her to stay. It was almost painful to Erin to know how much her father loved Shelby Rae.

She should've told him right away that she'd retrieved the photographs, so he didn't worry, but it was too late now. Even Shelby Rae was probably asleep. She also needed to know if he'd told the police he'd gone to Julie's house.

By the time she reached her bedroom, Erin was so tired she barely had the energy to swish the toothbrush over her teeth. She went to her closet and took off the romper, stuffed it into her hamper, and threw on a long T-shirt to sleep in.

The next day would be a long one, searching for Trouble,

volunteering at the shelter, and having dinner at Noah's house. *Oh no, what should I even wear? Should I take dessert?* Her mind was suddenly filled with more questions, more worry.

But the questions and worry evaporated when she discovered Trouble lying on her bed, busily washing one of his long legs. His soft black fur was dotted with burrs and bits of dirt, making him look untidier than she'd ever seen him. Lying on the bed close beside him was a creased and tattered photograph. Erin picked it up and held it near her bedside lamp. The paper was pocked with tiny punctures, like from an animal's teeth, around the edges. It was a photograph of a teenage girl in a pageant gown hung with a sash that read *Miss Jeffersonville*. The girl's smile was radiant, and she held a bouquet of yellow roses in one arm. Her opposite hand was raised to steady the tiara not quite centered on her head.

Erin had seen a similar, more formal photograph in an album Shelby Rae had shown her years earlier. But this photo was a snapshot, taken just below the stage, from the audience. Erin was sure Trouble had brought it from Zach Wilkins' place.

She touched Trouble lightly on the head, not wanting to interrupt his grooming. "Trouble, you're brilliant."

CHAPTER NINE

"*N*oah, if you don't calm down, you're going to drive us both crazy before lunchtime, and breakfast isn't even over." His mother laughed as she set a stack of pancakes in front of him.

He'd gotten up an hour earlier than usual before work to dust and vacuum the living room and dining room and clean the guest bathroom. It wasn't that he didn't think his mother kept a clean house. In fact he'd had cleaning chores himself since he was a kid. It was just that he wanted all signs of his father out—the ashtrays, the smudge rings on the tables from where his father's friends had left beer, the dirty fingerprints on the bathroom light switch. (Okay, maybe those were actually his.) If only his father would stay away, now that he was gone. It was almost like he was off in prison again. Almost.

Where *was* his father? His mother said one of the Atwell brothers had picked him up in his truck. "I hear things about them. What they do out at their place. I don't think your father should hang out with them, but he doesn't listen to me," she'd said.

No. He wouldn't think about his father right now.

"You've got stuff for tuna casserole, right? I'll stop at the store and get bread. Asparagus, too. What if she doesn't like asparagus?" Asparagus was Noah's favorite vegetable, and he thought everyone should like it. He liked Erin and he liked asparagus. It wasn't possible that she didn't like it, too.

"Why would you want tuna noodle?" his mother asked. "That's not very fancy. I could pick up steaks or something. We're not *poor*, honey."

Noah found it hard to explain. He wanted to be honest about the kind of people he and his mother were. They didn't try to be people they weren't. Even though he planned to eventually go to college to study architecture, he didn't ever want to be the kind of person who was ashamed of where he'd come from. He'd long ago stopped thinking of his father when he counted his family, even if there were people in town who didn't want to let him forget. In fact, he saw himself leaving New Belford behind one day. He wondered how Erin would feel about that.

"You make the best tuna casserole on the planet, Mom. Who wouldn't be impressed by that?"

She laughed again and gave him a little push on the shoulder. "Go on, you!"

When he arrived at work and was putting his lunch in his locker, his phone buzzed.

Erin: Trouble came back last night with a picture. I think it came from Zach's! Shelby Rae as a teenager. Isn't that freaky????

Noah: Maybe he got it in your house?

Erin: It's kind of torn up with lots of teeth marks. Ripped too. He was covered in dirt and stuff. I bet that's why he ran away. So I could see the picture.

Noah wasn't quite sure what to answer. He was skeptical that Zach would have a photo of Shelby Rae. Why would he even have anything to do with Shelby Rae? Shelby Rae was pretty, sure. Men flocked around her and talked about her. But Zach had never been like that. He hardly even dated, and had never had a woman living with him that Noah could remember. Maybe Erin was grasping at straws, trying to find anything and anyone connected to the kidnapping or Julie Berry's murder. He really couldn't blame her. But Zach?

Noah: Bring it with you later and the others. I want to see them.
Erin: What if Zach is the one who kidnapped Shelby Rae? Do you think he's dangerous? Wow I can't believe I said that. You know, --my mom.

Now Noah really didn't know how to answer.

Noah: Is Trouble okay? Not hurt?
Erin: Sleeping like a champ. I'm volunteering at the shelter this afternoon. Have to talk to my dad at work later. Maybe see you there? Or I'll just see you tonight. I feel like we're getting close to something. Bye!

I feel like we're getting close to something. Noah read the line again. He hoped her idea of getting close to something wasn't just making assumptions about Zach. Even if Zach had an old photo of Shelby Rae upstairs, would it mean anything? Noah didn't want to think so. He trusted Zach.

The morning rushed by. Everyone in the service department was so busy that they hardly had time for breaks or even talking. A lot of people had their cars in the shop getting ready to take vacations tagged onto the upcoming Fourth of July holiday. Every year the Rotary Club sponsored a picnic and fireworks display at the county fairgrounds. Last year he'd gone with Katelyn and her family, and it had been a disaster because one of his friends who'd just turned twenty-one surprised him by bringing a beer over to where they sat eating. Katelyn's family didn't believe in drinking alcohol and didn't approve of anyone who did. Plus, he half-suspected his so-called friend had done it on purpose to insult Katelyn's family. Noah believed in the concept of live-and-let live. Embarrassed, when the guy walked away, Noah had poured the beer in the grass and dropped the can in the trash.

Katelyn had given him hell later.

Now, ten minutes before lunch, his phone buzzed again with a text message, and——hoping it was Erin again——he snuck it out of his coveralls pocket. Noah didn't recognize the number, but the message got his attention.

> Son need a favor. A buddy in a delivery van is going to be pulling up behind your bike in about 15 minutes. He's got a package I need you to bring me right after work. Won't take you long. Directions coming.

Noah texted back right away that he didn't have time. He didn't mention that neither did he want to have anything to do with his father or strangers with packages that almost certainly contained enough drugs to get him sent to prison for a long,

long time. But the only answer he got was a few lines with directions leading to someplace about fifteen miles out of town.

He sent an answer. No I'm not coming.

No response. Of course there wouldn't be. His father's silence indicated that he expected no backtalk.

What can he do to me? Though he knew he could handle any kind of crap he got from his dad for disobeying, he also knew his father was just as likely to take out his anger on his mother.

It was his father's dumb luck that it was one of Noah's days to take the early lunch shift. As soon as the clock hit noon he grabbed his lunch and backpack and went outside to his bike before anyone could ask him where he was going. Sure enough there was a yellow and white delivery van stopped behind it, a man with neat brown hair and sunglasses behind the wheel. He also wore an official-looking white shirt with yellow pockets. When Noah approached the van, the driver put down the window.

"You Noah Daly?"

"Yes."

The driver shoved a large brown padded envelope at him. "No need to sign."

Noah hesitated and the driver pushed it another inch toward him. "Why can't you just deliver it to my old man?" But Noah took the package anyway.

The driver turned away and put the van in gear. "Don't ask me questions. Do I look like goddamn *Wikipedia?*" He drove slowly until he reached the dealership's exit, then turned onto the road leading out of town and quickly picked up speed.

His hand shaking slightly, Noah stowed the envelope in his backpack and took the backpack inside to his locker.

Right after lunch, the afternoon went from bad to weird.

Earl paged him to come to the service desk. That was rarely a good thing. He didn't like surprises at work. As soon as he got to the door he saw this was one of those not-good times.

"This nice young lady says she'd like you to service her Escape, Noah. Told her you'd be happy to."

Katelyn stood in front of the service desk, her bright pink purse swinging from one hand. She looked different, more relaxed than when he'd seen her last. Her sunglasses were atop her head, holding back her deep auburn hair, and she was wearing dressy shorts and a sleeveless white blouse unbuttoned generously from the top.

"Noah!" she shrieked. "Am I *ever* glad to see you."

An uncharacteristic hint of a smile played at Earl's mouth as he turned back to the computer screen.

"Katelyn. Hey." He froze as she threw her arms around him. She smelled of hairspray and lemon and something sweet, like a little girl. "You got a new car?"

"I got a job of my own. Phone sales and marketing for a data company. It's super fun, and I got my own apartment, too. Well, with two other girls, anyway. It's really great living away from home."

"That's great. Sure, I can service your car. No problem. It's good to see you." It *was* good to see her, but he still felt awkward. Katelyn had an oddly manic look in her eyes. He wondered if she wasn't giddy with the freedom of being out from under her parents' thumb. She'd been so adamant about doing everything they said, living her life exactly as they planned it. But she did look even prettier now, nervy and vibrant.

"Maybe we could get something to eat later. It's my day

off." Katelyn looked up at him, her blue eyes wide and appealing. "I've missed you."

Behind her, the door from the back hallway opened and Erin, looking weary and sad, came in. She looked from him to Katelyn and back to him again. Katelyn's body language was obvious, and Noah reddened slightly.

"Um, sorry. I've got plans," he said. "I need to get to work."

Katelyn hadn't yet noticed Erin. "My cell number's the same. My parents stopped paying for my phone, but the phone company let me keep my number when I got my own account. Call me, okay?"

Something in Erin's face changed and became determined instead of sad.

"Hey, Noah," she said brightly.

Katelyn turned around.

Erin nodded to Katelyn and gave her a quick smile. Katelyn's own smile faded a bit. Without saying anything to Katelyn, Erin stood on tiptoe beside Noah and gave him a quick kiss on the cheek. "See you later!" Then she continued out the door to the parking lot, leaving both Noah and Katelyn staring after her.

NOAH HEADED out of work the minute he could and, wearing the backpack with its mysterious contents, got on his bike. Inwardly he was still smiling about Erin and the kiss she'd given him. Talk about a surprise. Katelyn had definitely gotten the message. And he was pretty sure he'd gotten a message, too. A message that definitely distracted him from his errand.

If things went well, he would make it back to the house in time to grab a quick shower and change before Erin arrived.

The place where his father wanted him to bring the package was an old concert grounds called Honeysuckle Jamboree that had been popular with groups of hippies in the seventies, but was now mostly overgrown and padlocked. It was rumored that various cult-like groups rented it out from time to time, and there were tales of weirdness and devil worship, but Noah suspected the stories were probably bullshit. He'd give anything not to know his father was hanging out there. Surely it was filled with plenty of types he was disallowed from being around. That was his father all over. Oblivious. He hoped he could just drop the package off and go, and that his father wouldn't make him come inside. He silently prayed that he didn't get pulled over, and that the cops weren't watching the place. If the package contained drugs, he would be screwed. But he couldn't take the chance that his father would punish his mother if he didn't deliver.

The temperature hung in the low eighties, the best he could ask for in late June. He almost felt guilty to be enjoying the ride and the beautiful weather. He couldn't wait to bring Erin out on the bike. When all this stuff was over, he imagined them maybe riding down to Kentucky Lake for the weekend, or to horse park near Lexington. Later, he could ride over to see her at U.K. What if he could get in there himself? It was a dream that had begun to feel more possible.

He reached the sagging, open farm gates of the jamboree within the half hour. A woman and two men, all in black leathers, sat around a bright white folding table just inside. Noah idled his bike without entering and texted his father that he'd arrived. The road leading into the jamboree had once been paved but was now broken up and mostly uneven gravel, hell for motorcycles. But one of the men, a bearded guy in a leather vest without a shirt beneath it, got up and waved him in, smiling. Noah thought about refusing, but decided it wasn't a good idea.

"How can we help you?" the woman asked after Noah parked and walked over to the table. Though she was wearing leathers, her lips were bright pink and her chin-length hair was blonde with pink stripes in it. Her face was round, and her bosom pressed upwards out of her bright pink shirt. Except for the leathers, she looked like a kindergarten teacher. "Do you have a ticket?"

Noah didn't see event signs or any suggestion that there was any kind of festival going on. The men watched him silently.

"You know, I'm just dropping something off for my dad. Jeb? Daly?"

His father's name didn't seem to ring any bells. At that moment Noah's phone vibrated. His father was asking him to ride down and meet him. Noah said as much to the people at the table, and one of them nodded and stepped away to talk on a radio. Within two minutes, Noah was on his bike making his careful way down the hill.

The jamboree had definitely seen better days. He rolled past a weedy parking area that was populated with several dozen pickup trucks and vans. Quite a lot of the vehicles were new and shone in the summer sunlight, but the rest were dusty and covered with decals and Confederate battle flags and skulls. He wasn't stupid. He was getting a bad feeling about the festival, or whatever it was.

As he turned on a wide curve, he heard distant metal music. The festival area spread out below him contained dozens of more trucks and at least a hundred motorcycles. A crowd of people was gathered in front a huge stage where the band was playing, and music echoed through the bowl-like

hollow. An enormous banner with the words UNITY
BROTHERS printed on it fluttered above the stage. At one end
of the banner was a white fist outlined in black, and at the
other a swastika.

Oh, shit.

Of course he'd heard rumors about white supremacists, but
he'd imagined that they were all from somewhere else. In fact,
many of the license plates he'd passed were from out of state.
This wasn't the Kentucky he knew, and it made him sick. Then
he saw his father being driven toward him in a golf cart by a
homely young blonde with a badly receding chin. She looked at
Noah shyly, but he found it impossible to smile back at her. He
raised one hand in a half-wave.

"You made it, son! Come on down and have a beer with the
old man." His father patted the girl on the knee and swung out
of the golf cart. The girl pulled forward and circled to go back
down the hill. A sign reading STAFF hung from the back of
the cart.

Noah parked the bike. "What the hell is this place? What
are you doing here?" he asked quietly, jaw clenching.

His father put an arm around him and squeezed, hard, a
broad, fake smile on his face. "You and me got a lot of catching
up to do!" Pulling Noah closer, he said, "Got the package? It
took you long enough. People are waiting, and they aren't
patient."

Noah shrugged off his father's arm and started taking off
the backpack.

"Not here, you moron." His father jerked a thumb at a
copse with an unlit fire pit. Logs and long, forked sticks had
been arranged around it. Were they setting up for s'mores later
in the evening? Noah wanted to laugh, imagining skinheads

like the Attwell brothers roasting marshmallows, but he kept his mouth shut.

In the copse, he squatted with his open bag in front of him, digging out the package. Before he handed it to his father, he carefully peeled off the delivery label—which he was certain was as fake as the delivery guy had been—and stuffed it in his pocket. "Why'd you get me involved in this? I'm not going to jail because of you and your asshole friends. You know probably half the guys here are Feds, don't you?" He shoved the package at his father.

His father was on him like a striking snake, grabbing Noah by the collar of his T-shirt. But Noah was unbalanced and fell backwards, his father landing on top of him. "You don't sass me like that, son. Ever. You live in my house and eat my food and sleep in the bed I got you when you were too little to wipe your own backside. You do what I say, hear me?"

His face was so close Noah could smell the cigarettes and beer and lunchmeat on his breath and was sickened. He could also feel the hard pressure of the gun in his father's waistband. There was a greater cruelty in his father's eyes than he'd ever seen before. Jeb Daly was desperate, and Noah knew it.

Noah maneuvered his father off with a move he'd learned in high school wrestling, and now he was looking down into his father's startled face. "Don't *ever* grab me like that again. You're the one who doesn't belong in our house, and I'll leave only if I think Mom is safe around you. And that time hasn't come yet. I don't know if it ever will. Leave me alone, and leave her alone, or I'll kill you." He was breathing hard, expecting his father to resist. But now he saw a brief flash of fear before it was quickly replaced with mocking bravado.

"Well, looks like the little boy's balls dropped after all. Get off me, faggot."

Noah got up quickly and grabbed his backpack. Slinging it over one shoulder, he didn't look back at his father but strode out of the copse.

"I know where you live, you little prick!" his father called after him. Then he began to laugh, and the sound of that laughter followed him, haunted him, even after he started his motorcycle.

The people at the gate were busy with a line of incoming cars and paid no attention to Noah leaving. But Noah had plenty of time to check out the cars and, in one truck, he saw a man he recognized—Earl, from the service desk. He didn't think about it until much later, but was fairly certain that Earl *wasn't* there to buy drugs.

Noah's mother, Annette, as she'd asked Erin to call her, handed Erin a glass of lemonade. "I think there's only one kind of lemonade, and that's fresh-squeezed. You know when you go to a fair or festival, and you see those vendors saying their lemonade is fresh?" Erin nodded. "Well, they put almost half a cup of sugar in the water and just a tiny bit of lemon. Which you wouldn't think because sugar isn't that cheap and lemons aren't that expensive when they're in season. You can hardly drink it, it's so sweet."

Erin took a drink from the glass she'd been handed, praying the lemonade wouldn't make her tongue curl. To her relief, it wasn't too tart at all, but simply tangy with a hint of sweetness. "It's delicious. Thank you."

Annette sat on the other cushioned porch chair. The chairs' paisley green cushions looked stiff and new against the well-used, gray chair frames, but Annette herself was relaxed. Erin was grateful because she was nervous. It felt good to stay away from home for a while. In her shift at the shelter, she'd cleaned half the cat kennels, wearing a special vest in which snuggled a tiny, orphaned kitten that needed constant body warmth. Then she'd walked a couple of the dogs and took a greyhound out for a run. Shelby Rae was in the bedroom with the door closed when she stopped home to shower and change and feed Trouble, but she didn't bother to talk to her. Things had ended okay with her the night before, and there was no need to push it.

Where was Noah?

Annette looked at her watch as though she'd just read Erin's mind.

"Noah said he'd be home right after work. Said he had a stop to make at the store, but it shouldn't be taking this long. I'm sorry. You seem to be stuck with me." Annette smiled.

Erin worried that she was making Annette uncomfortable. The two things they had in common were Noah, and the crime that had gotten her mother killed. Neither seemed perfect subjects for conversation.

"Noah said you're manager at your store, now? How long have you worked there?" Erin occasionally stopped at the big store to get gas on her way out of town, but she'd never run into Annette because she always paid outside.

"It took quite a while. Seven years. I like the regular hours and the benefits. So many different people—we've got our regulars, but since they put in the lot and pumps for the semis we see people from all over. You'd be surprised how many women drive trucks or work in pairs with their husbands." Annette paused. "You know, before that I worked at the salon here in town."

"Really? I didn't know that." Erin was surprised.

"I did nails and maintained stock and kept the books." She

lowered her voice a bit. "Shelby Rae always used to come in back then. *Very* particular about her hair and nails. I did her nails, but she probably doesn't remember. I gather she goes out of town for her hair now, and to that new spa up the road to get her nails done."

Erin suspected that Shelby Rae remembered exactly who Annette was but only pretended not to. She didn't remember them speaking at the party. "I don't have any idea where Shelby Rae goes. Probably somewhere they charge her a lot of money so she feels special."

Annette laughed with some relief. "She's insecure, I think, living in that big house. Married to your dad. I remember she talked about feeling nervous in town, living alone."

"Why was that?"

"It was probably because she was used to having people around. After her aunt died, she could've gone back to Louisville, but she decided to stay, and just moved out of her uncle's house."

Erin grimaced. "Uncle Travis. He gives me the creeps."

"Unfortunately, sometimes we can't pick our family."

Erin thought of Noah and his father. But Annette had chosen to marry Jeb Daly.

"Did Shelby Rae date anybody around here back then? I never heard about anyone, and it would be weird I guess to ask her now. It's not really my business." Julie Berry had been certain Shelby Rae was having an affair, and sometimes old boyfriends could be new lovers.

Annette furrowed her brow. She looked like Noah when she was thinking hard. "You'd imagine a pretty girl like Shelby Rae would cut a swath through the town, but she really was kind of quiet that way. Very self-possessed and proud. There was a teller at the bank, I think, and a teacher at the high school. Then there was one guy she talked about but it seemed to be more a—what do they call it now? Friends with benefits kind of thing. One of those *it's complicated* relationships like you used to see on Facebook. You don't really see that anymore. Facebook isn't as fun as it used to be."

Erin struggled with the notion of Shelby Rae as self-possessed and proud. She'd spent so long thinking of Shelby Rae as a little trashy that she sometimes forgot she had been so kind and very *normal* after her mother died. She'd even been admiring of Shelby Rae's skill with make-up and girly things. Her mother had been pretty and tailored and had worn very little makeup. So different. "Do you remember if she ever talked about my dad? I mean, after my mom died, of course."

Annette looked abashed. "Oh, of course after. She wasn't like *that* at all."

Erin twisted the cocktail napkin Annette had given her with her lemonade. "I guess I was so young, I didn't really know what to think."

"You were just a little thing. I felt so bad for you. So responsible."

This was a discussion Erin dreaded. She wasn't there to make anyone uncomfortable, so she turned the subject back to Shelby Rae. "The guy that was complicated about with Shelby Rae. Did their relationship go on any longer? I mean, like after she started dating my dad?"

"I'm sorry, I don't remember the details very well. I *do* remember being surprised when I heard the guy she was dating told her he just wanted her to be happy, and that she deserved to have everything she wanted." Annette frowned. "She wasn't very nice about it, I'm afraid. At least that's what I heard. I really shouldn't repeat salon gossip. It was so long ago."

Worried that she'd embarrassed Annette, Erin started to

reassure her, but they heard the rumble of Noah's motorcycle coming down the street. Annette looked relieved. But Erin's thoughts about Shelby Rae were confused. Had she been reading her wrong all along? And who was the guy who was so chill about Shelby Rae pursuing her father?

NOAH GREETED THEM, saying a surprisingly shy *hello* to Erin and kissing his mother on the cheek. He carefully removed a slender bouquet of purple irises from his backpack, and handed it, with a bag of asparagus, to his mother. "Oh, damn. I forgot the bread. I'm an idiot." He shook his head.

"Don't be silly." Annette opened the storm door and took the asparagus and flowers inside. "I'll make some biscuits. Won't take fifteen minutes."

"I hope you don't think biscuits with tuna noodle is too weird," Noah said. He looked tired to Erin, the corners of his mouth tight with stress.

She smiled. "I love biscuits *and* tuna noodle. My mom used to make tuna noodle all the time, but Shelby Rae's a hopeless cook, and my dad could never *quite* get my mother's recipe right. I've made it, though. Even though Shelby Rae says it's white trash food." Realizing what she just said, she colored and was glad Annette had gone inside. "Seriously, *I* love it. If that makes me white trash to Shelby Rae, whatever." But Noah seemed more distracted than bothered.

"Give me ten minutes, will you? I just need to get cleaned up real quick."

Erin thought he looked fine in his white T-shirt and jeans, but she didn't say anything.

"Will you keep my mom company in the kitchen?"

She followed him inside. The air was fragrant with the

casserole in the oven. Annette already had the ingredients for the biscuits in a bowl and was mixing them together.

"I'm just doing drop biscuits. Why don't you grease that sheet for me, and take the casserole out and set it right on top of the stove?" Erin did everything Annette asked her to do. It was comforting to be around calm and efficient Annette. There was no obvious sign that Jeb Daly was living in the house at all.

ERIN WASN'T sure if dinner was particularly delicious, or she was simply happy to be there with Noah. He seemed anxious that she should like the asparagus and was delighted that she ate the undressed, steamed stalks with her fingers. Asparagus wasn't her favorite vegetable, but she ate everything on her plate, including two biscuits dripping with butter.

After Noah cleared the table, Annette cut two large slices of peach pie that she'd gotten at a local Amish stand, and put them on the table. "Why don't you two take your pie out to the porch, and I'll clean up in here. There's a radio drama on the public station on in a few minutes I want to listen to."

Noah laughed. "Mom, I told you I can get that on a podcast for you any time so you don't have to listen when it's on."

"Just go outside, Noah. I swear, sometimes you can't take a hint." She smiled, and Erin blushed and picked up the plates.

On the porch, they sat side-by-side on the glider in the faded sunlight. Children rode bikes up and down the street, shouting to one another. When she and MacKenzie were kids, MacKenzie had also lived in a neighborhood, and Erin loved to visit her there. Erin's family's house by the lake was isolated and she'd often felt lonesome.

"I don't know if I can eat all this," Erin said. "I haven't had biscuits in forever and couldn't stop eating them."

"No worries. I'll help you out." When he grinned, his eyes smiled too, and Erin was doubly glad she'd come to the house. It was really the first time they'd been alone and relaxed since they'd sat on the dock together. She hadn't thought about Shelby Rae or her father or Julie once since they'd sat down at the table.

"So, that was Katelyn today?" she asked, playfully. "I remember her from school, but we didn't hang out with the same people."

"Yeah. Wanted me to service her car. Sorry about that." Noah shook his head. "I had no idea. I haven't seen her in months."

"Why should you be sorry? Oh, here." Erin switched plates with him, making sure he got the bigger piece of pie. The biscuits had been delicious and filling. "She didn't look very glad to see me."

Now Noah laughed. "*I* was very glad to see you. What was that about, anyway?" He looked straight at her, his eyes questioning. "Did you mean it, or were you just messing with her?"

"Mean what?" she asked, playing dumb.

Noah put their plates on the low table in front of him. "This." He kissed her gently, and Erin felt as though her heart would burst.

ERIN WAS dreamy about Noah and their kiss all the way home. She couldn't remember the last time she'd felt so happy. But the spell was broken when she opened the door from the garage and her father came hurrying in from the kitchen. He was still dressed in the sport coat he'd worn to work.

"Oh, it's you." His mouth wore a disappointed frown.

"Gosh, thanks, Dad," Erin teased. Then she realized he was genuinely distressed. "What's wrong?" She followed him into the kitchen. An open bottle of scotch sat on the island, an empty glass beside it. Touching the bottle lightly she said, "Is this dinner? Where's Shelby Rae? Her car's gone."

"Damn straight her car's gone. She texted me about an hour ago saying she decided she was driving up to the hotel at French Lick for a couple days to recover from the kidnapping. I don't know what's happening, here. Maybe Julie was right. Maybe she *is* having an affair. I should go after her." He put a hand in one pocket and took out his car keys.

"Oh, no you don't," Erin told him. "You've been drinking. You don't need to be out on the road. Shelby Rae's a big girl."

"I've had two fingers of scotch, and I'm hardly drunk. I'm worried about my wife!" He spoke so sharply that Erin took a step back. Jocko came to sit on the floor in front of him and looked up, obviously concerned. Trouble stood at his post near one of the back windows, watching them all.

"Did you ask her about it, Dad?" She'd shown him the photos she'd retrieved from Julie's when she'd gone to the dealership before heading to the shelter. They hadn't been able to come to any more conclusions or identify the man in the photos. But she didn't tell him about the photo that Trouble had come home with. She still wasn't sure what it meant.

He shook his head. "No. I didn't ask her about it. Things haven't been right this week. I should've told Abel Bowen the minute I saw that note. I can't believe I didn't, and then when she came back I was just so damn grateful that I wanted to forget all about it. She could be suffering from post-traumatic stress. She's been acting so strangely."

"Maybe you can drive up to French Lick to be with her tomorrow. Or I can drive you up there tonight."

"Hell, who knows if she's even there?" He seemed to blink out of his funk for a moment and stared at her. "Where've you been? You look nice."

Erin shrugged, not wanting to make a big deal about having dinner at Noah's house. "Just out for dinner."

"Who with? MacKenzie?"

It was unlike her father to sound so suspicious. She wondered if it was the scotch. She didn't recall him drinking as much as he'd been the past few days. "Don't worry about me. I'm fine. It's no big deal."

"First Shelby Rae, now you."

Erin got a glass and filled it with water from the fountain in the refrigerator door.

"Were you with Noah Daly?"

"Does it matter?" she asked, trying to sound nonchalant.

Her father poured another finger of scotch in his glass, but he didn't pick it up to drink it. Yet. "Abel told me that piece of crap father of his is out of prison. I don't want that man around you."

"He wasn't even at the house. He's out of town or something, and Annette made us dinner. That's all." Did he think she was stupid enough to *want* to see Jeb Daly? "Listen, why don't you go lie down for a while? You can go after Shelby Rae in the morning. You know how she is. She could be back before lunchtime with a whole other plan."

"I just wish she'd answer the damn phone."

They were quiet a minute. Finally, Erin went to stand near him. "Dad, this isn't right. There's something going on with Shelby Rae. Maybe it was the kidnapping, but I don't understand why she would leave you alone like this."

Her father looked exhausted. "Maybe I left *her* alone too many times. Your mother and I worked together all the time for so long, until she wanted to be home when you got off the school bus. She understood how much work it is having a business. But Shelby Rae's young and wants to be out having fun. I'm not saying that's what she's up to now, but she might be punishing me."

"That's ridiculous. It would be so childish, and you don't deserve it."

"I don't know about that," he said. "There's no fool like an old fool."

TROUBLE AND JOCKO followed Erin upstairs, but once they reached the door of her father and Shelby Rae's bedroom, Trouble darted inside.

"Trouble! Come on." She wanted to close her bedroom door and preferred to have Trouble inside. After he'd run away from Zach's place, she was wary about him going out through the pet door. Jocko followed her into her father and Shelby Rae's bedroom where she turned on the lights. Trouble wasn't in sight.

"Let's go, Trouble. I'm tired." She heard a noise in Shelby Rae's dressing room. Shelby Rae would have a fit if she found black cat hair all over her clothes. Very little of her clothing was black. She was much more partial to red and bright whites and light colored leggings and brightly patterned shirts. "Like a party, all by her own self," MacKenzie often joked.

Erin entered the closet and turned on the lights. The noise was coming from an upper shelf. She looked up and saw Trouble's dark head and one of his paws working together to move something along the shelf.

"What in the world are you doing?"

Trouble gave her a chiding *meow*, as if to say, "I'm doing something important, and could use your help, missy!"

Before she could chase him off the shelf, he gave a forceful swipe of his paw, and the thing he was pushing tumbled to the floor, bouncing off her foot. Erin blurted out a curse word her father would not be glad to hear her use, and bent to rub her stung toes. Trouble jumped from the shelf to the marble-topped counter running down the center of the dressing room and stood watching Erin.

"That wasn't nice, cat." She grabbed the thing Trouble had knocked from the shelf. It was a silver phone, the old-fashioned flip kind often sold as a cheap burner phone. Erin had never seen Shelby Rae use it before. She didn't open it but quickly stuck it in her pocket lest her father see it. Picking up Trouble, she held him against her shoulder and scratched him behind the ear. "You clever, clever cat."

Trouble began to purr.

She waited until she was in her bedroom with the door closed to turn on the phone. It blinked to life. There were no sent or received text messages, but the list of calls was long. Calls that went only to and from a single number. Erin didn't recognize the area code, but that made no difference anyway since it was a burner phone, and because people could move to another state and still keep their old numbers. A stream of ideas flowed through her mind. She could try to convince the police to trace the number. But which police? Sheriff Bowen or Zach? No, she couldn't ask Zach. If the photo of the young Shelby Rae had come from his house, as she suspected, he couldn't be trusted with it. Sheriff Bowen would have to be told the whole kidnapping story. No way they could get into that without it becoming a problem. Her father was adamant, as was Shelby Rae. Erin couldn't bear to hand the phone over to her father if Shelby Rae was using the phone to call her lover. How much else should he have to bear? What about confronting Shelby Rae? Now, *that* was a possibility. Except it would have to wait. She couldn't exactly text her stepmother and say, "The cat and I were snooping in your dressing room and we found a secret phone. Why do you have it, and whom have you been calling, please?"

Knowing it was her only choice, before she could change her mind she hit *redial* and listened as the phone on the other end rang. She bit her lip. What would she say if someone answered?

Finally, the call was picked up in the middle of the fourth ring. But no one said a word, and there were no sounds in the background. She plunged ahead. "Hello?"

Silence.

Whoever was on the other end hung up, and a chill ran down Erin's spine.

ERIN PULLED the duvet up over her shoulder to try to stop whatever was patting her rhythmically. It stopped for a moment but then continued on her head: *patpat, patpat, patpat.* "Quit!" She waved a sleepy hand in the air near her head and came in contact with a wall of soft fur. "What are you doing, cat?" she said into the pillow.

Opening her eyes a crack, she saw that it wasn't quite light outside yet. And what was that sound? Over on her desk, her phone was vibrating. *What now--and so freaking early?*

Trouble gave her a final pair of *patpats* on her head, then jumped over her to sit right in front of her face, staring at her with serious green eyes.

"Why don't *you* just answer the phone?" Erin sighed and
rolled out of bed, shivering in the air conditioning. "All right.
All right."

The phone read "6:05," and it wasn't the phone ringing, but
a text notification. From Shelby Rae.

> Don't tell your dad but I'm in trouble and need your help!!
> I'm at the fishing cabin and have made a terrible mistake
> but I can't come home and let him see me. Please please
> bring Jocko. I have to stay away for a while and I want
> him with me. Sorry to be weird. Will explain!

Erin had to read the message several times to get it
through to her foggy brain. What kind of stupid game was
Shelby Rae playing? Telling her father she was going to
French Lick, but then going to the fishing cabin. What kind
of trouble could she be in that she would ask *her* help?
Shelby Rae never asked her for any kind of help, unless it
was to watch Jocko when she wasn't going to be home. And
Shelby Rae didn't want her own husband to know what was
going on. As much as Erin wanted to protect her father,
hiding this would be an outright betrayal of him. Vulnerable
as he'd been lately, he was still an adult, and he needed to
deal with his wife—a wife who was obviously in way over her
head with *something*. They had to find out what that something was.

Erin threw a robe on and, animals in tow, rushed to her
father's bedroom to knock on the door. "Dad?"

The bed was empty. He'd probably fallen asleep on the
couch again, just as he had the night Shelby Rae was
kidnapped. She prayed he hadn't drunk himself to sleep. The
alcohol was beginning to seriously worry her.

He wasn't anywhere downstairs. She went to the kitchen, where the overhead lights were still on.

"Hey, Dad? Where are you?"

Jocko ran to the kitchen door and pushed through the pet door. Trouble stayed close to Erin. There was no sign of her father. The whiskey bottle was gone, and so was the glass. On the island where they'd been was a note clipped onto the wire message holder they sometimes used.

Slept a couple of hours. Driving up to French Lick to see if Shelby Rae's okay. Will call you later. Love, Dad

It was less than two hours from the house to French Lick. She wished she knew what time he'd left. If this was how complicated and awful marriage could be, she knew she never wanted any part of it. Whoever she eventually married would have to be completely honest with her. Always. Could Noah always be honest with her? She wasn't sure.

What she needed to do right then was get dressed, feed the animals, and get out to the other side of the lake and her grandfather's old fishing cabin to talk to Shelby Rae. She could call her father on the way and get him to turn around, if he hadn't reached the hotel already.

NOAH GOT out of the shower, still thinking about his time with Erin. He felt a rush of happiness when he pictured her face, so soft and beautiful in the summer evening light. After they kissed, she'd rested her head on his shoulder like it was the most natural thing in the world, and they'd sat like that for several minutes, rocking on the glider until his mother came out bearing cups of decaf coffee. Erin had quickly lifted her head, but Noah took her hand, not at all embarrassed. His mother didn't comment, but just asked if they wanted more pie. Erin stayed another half hour and he had kissed her again, out by her car.

"Breakfast in five." His mother gave two brief raps on the bathroom door. "Good morning."

"Hey. Out in a minute." When he was dried off, Noah went to his room and put on his jeans and T-shirt. The morning was cool and pleasant, but he hadn't gotten up early enough to go fishing. If he was honest with himself, he knew that the last time he'd gone, he'd mostly just wanted to be close to Erin. But look what that had gotten him. He'd discovered Julie Berry's body, and the police had told him they'd probably want to talk to him again. Was it because he'd been the one to find the body, or because of who his father was? He suspected it was a mix of both.

Thanks again, Dad.

His father would be home that afternoon, and as brave as Noah had been the day before, he was still a bit afraid of him. Jeb Daly was known to be a sneaky, clever man. And even though Noah knew he could take care of himself, he also knew he would die before he let something happen to his mother.

Boots on, he reached for his phone. There was a message notification, but he didn't remember hearing the phone buzz. Maybe he'd been asleep, or in the shower? He smiled to see Erin's number, but his smile faded as he listened.

She said she was headed out to her grandfather's fishing cabin, where Shelby Rae was hiding. She'd called her father and he was also coming to the cabin, but she wanted to let Noah know. Then she gave a nervous laugh. "Does that sound silly? Maybe that sounds silly. Anyway, I don't really know what's going on, but if I end up staying up there with Shelby Rae, I didn't want you to think I, you know, disappeared. It's off of Walsh Fork Road—clever, huh? There's an old sign at the beginning of the driveway, well it's kind of a crappy, rocky road rather than a driveway. Right after the big curve, you'll see a sign with a turtle wearing a sailor hat. I can't believe nobody's stolen it. Okay. I just wanted you to know. I had a great time last night. Bye."

It was a strange message, but the most significant thing about it was that she sounded nervous. He looked at the time. She'd left it nearly an hour earlier.

"FIND ANOTHER BODY, did you? Or you just going to work part-time, now that you're dating the boss's daughter?" Earl sounded disapproving.

"I'll be in later this morning. Promise." Then Noah told a lie. "Funny you should say that. It's actually something I'm doing for Mr. Walsh, right? I'm sure he'll tell you about it later."

"Mr. Walsh going to come in and do the oil changes while you're gone?"

Noah laughed. "Come on. You haven't had me doing oil changes in three months. You've got Andrew on them."

Earl gave a little grunt. "Just be here by eleven. We got a full afternoon."

Noah hung up wondering what he would find at the cabin. Erin said Shelby Rae was *hiding*. What did that even mean? From whom was she hiding?

It took him twenty minutes to get to Walsh Fork Road, but the area was familiar because he spent so much time riding the backroads on his bike. Somehow he'd never connected Walsh Fork Road and the old turtle sign with Bruce Walsh and his family, but it made sense. On a wall of Bruce Walsh's office there were photos of Erin's grandfather as a teenager, dressed in his sailor's uniform on the deck of a WWII destroyer.

The cabin was at the end of the gravel road, only about fifty feet from the lake. Its porch had been jacked up and the roof looked new, but its worn gray logs and narrow porch marked it as having been built many, many decades ago. Beyond the building and its moss and dirt yard, mist floated inches above the water's surface. A mated pair of mallards just offshore quacked softly, uninterested in Noah's arrival. The only anomaly was a small satellite dish pointed at the sky in the clearing behind the cabin.

Erin's Challenger was parked right beside the cabin on one half of a tidy rectangle of fresh gravel.

Noah parked his bike and ran to the car. Not only was it unlocked, but Jocko and the black cat, Trouble, popped up from the backseat. Jocko barked frantically at him and backed up into a corner of the seat. Trouble came forward and jumped neatly to the ground and licked a paw. Then he looked up at Noah, waiting.

"Guys, where's Erin? I can't believe she left you out here with the car closed up." It made him worry. The air was mild, and the car was in the shade, but in no time it could've become an oven. No way would Erin have left the animals that way. Also, Erin's keys sat in the console.

He turned around and called, "Erin! Where are you?"

Jocko finally scrambled from the car and ran to the porch to scratch at the front door. But before he could get a real scratch in, the door drifted open at his touch. He dropped his small forelegs to the ground and ran inside. Trouble and Noah followed.

The inside of the cabin was dim with pale morning light, but it was bright enough that Noah could see that some sort of altercation had taken place. Three wooden chairs, as well as a table, had been overturned. Broken glass lay scattered over the floor so that Noah had to call Jocko back before he cut himself. The coffee table between the couch and the giant television had a half-filled wine glass on it, along with a plate of stale-looking cheese slices. But the wine bottle lay near the television, its blood-red contents soaked into the tawny Berber rug. Still, there was no sign of Erin.

He went into the tiny bedroom. There was definitely evidence of a woman, probably Shelby Rae, having been here. A filmy satin robe lay half off the bed, and a messy pile of lingerie sat atop the dresser beneath the window. There was even one of those silly, lace-trimmed sleeping masks on the bedside table.

A sound behind him made Noah jump. He turned around to see Trouble pawing around inside an open bag resting on a chair. The colorful bag looked familiar, and Noah walked over to examine it. He picked up Trouble and set him on the bed. Trouble jumped off immediately as though the bed were on fire and stood resolutely on the floor. "Suit yourself," Noah said. He bent to examine the bag. Where had he seen it? He put his hand inside and grasped a rubber-banded stack of bills. Then another and another. It was the bag the man on the four-wheeler had carried away from the barn. No doubt there was fifty thousand dollars in the bag if the criminals hadn't yet removed some of the money.

There was something else in the bag—a half-dozen photos. In five of them, Shelby Rae sat in the driver's seat of her car with a man wearing a ball cap beside her. But in one, the man was embracing her. The cap he was wearing was a Bengal's ball cap, and Noah was certain the man was Zach Wilkins. These had to be the photos Erin had described to him on the way to

Zach's house, but she hadn't said anything about the hat. Had she brought these to the cabin to show Shelby Rae?

Erin's message said she was on her way to the cabin because Shelby Rae texted that she needed her, but had the fight in living room been between Erin and her stepmother? It seemed too bizarre. Erin's was the only car parked outside. Where was Shelby Rae? How was Zach involved?

Noah tried Erin's phone, but it went straight to voicemail, which meant it was probably off. He ran outside again, shouting for Erin, but got no answer. The only place he could think to look for the two women was at Zach's place. A sick feeling bloomed in his gut when he thought about taking Erin. What if he'd put her in danger?

When he hurried to his bike and got on, Jocko and Trouble ran after him. "No, guys. Not gonna work."

Trouble leapt onto the motorcycle and looked forward, ready to ride.

"Fine. Get in the car. Erin wouldn't want me to leave you guys here, anyway." Picking up Trouble, he carried him to Erin's car and opened the door. He deposited the cat in the front seat and tried to get Jocko into the back. But Jocko immediately clambered up front, so he could ride shotgun with Trouble.

ERIN STRUGGLED TO SIT UP. Her knees and arm were bruised and the side of her face hurt badly where Zach had punched her. She tried to move her wrists, but the zip ties he'd put on her were tight. Her feet were bound, too. There was no getting away, or even out of the main room of Zach's upstairs apartment when she could hardly move. Shelby Rae was only five feet away from her, similarly bound. Surprisingly he hadn't gagged either of them. That told Erin he was confident no one would come looking for them. He'd gotten away with so much, she suspected, that he didn't think he'd be caught. Or, perhaps, he was going to kill them.

One wall of the room was filled with hundreds of photographs. Erin had good eyesight, and could see that they all appeared to be new and old images of Shelby Rae. There was a blank space on one board that she suspected had held the photo Trouble had brought to her. *Trouble, please be okay. And Jocko. What did Zach do to you?* She twisted around to get a better look at the three mannequins in the room. Mannequins wearing pageant gowns and a cheerleading uniform. Surely they had once belonged to Shelby Rae. It was like the whole room was some kind of shrine to Shelby Rae.

Shelby Rae herself was sobbing, her makeup streaked below her eyes. "I didn't think he'd bring you here. I told him to leave you alone. Why couldn't you stay out of this?"

"What's he going to do to us?" Erin's jaw stung when she talked.

"I told him it had to stop. All of it. He killed that nosy Julie because she threatened to tell Bruce we were having an affair. *I* didn't hate her. I knew she didn't have a chance with Bruce no matter what lies she told him. There was no way she could get me to leave him. Oh, why did you come here?"

Erin twisted her hands, trying to figure out how to get out of the ties. She remembered watching a video that demonstrated how to do it, but she couldn't recall what the details were. She looked around the room for some edge she could saw the things off with, and noticed an old typewriter on a table in the corner. It wouldn't help them, but it explained where the ransom note had been typed. "I didn't exactly get here on my own. How long have you been here? Did you text me to meet you out at the fishing cabin, or did he just use your phone?"

Shelby Rae shook her head. "He's got my phone. I don't know why he's gone so crazy. He's never been like this before."

It was hard for Erin to keep the disgust out of her voice. "How long have you been sleeping with him? Since before you married Dad?"

The sobs began anew. A thin stream of mucous ran onto Shelby Rae's upper lip. "You don't understand. We were never lovers. *Never.* We dated a little in high school, but then he went in the Army. He showed up in New Belford after he got out of the police academy. I hadn't even kept in touch with him. He was always so sweet to me, but he never tried to date me or anything like that. We were just friends, I swear. But after I married your father we agreed that we probably shouldn't really talk to each other any more. And we didn't, really. Not until a couple months ago." Her voice trailed off.

Erin didn't know whether to believe her or not. She didn't trust Shelby Rae any more than she had before just because they were both being held captive.

There had to be a way out. If only she could get over to the open window beside the door to see if anyone was outside. She'd heard Zach's truck start up again after he dumped her in the apartment and told her to *shut the hell up*. She suspected he'd left, but she couldn't be sure.

"Okay. So Zach was kind of your friend, then he wasn't, and then he was. What happened? What changed?"

"I don't think I want to tell you." Shelby Rae sounded like a chastised little girl.

"He's got about a thousand pictures of you! And those pageant dresses, tell me they're not yours?" Erin jerked her head at the mannequins, which looked tatty and old in the sunlight. The dresses were grubby as though they'd been handled frequently, and it filled her with disgust. "There is something very wrong with him, Shelby Rae. He's psycho. He *murdered* Julie."

"I know! I know! But I didn't know he was going to do that. It was all supposed to end when I came home. I was only out at the cabin. Nothing else was supposed to happen. It wasn't like either one of us even wanted the money. I only wanted your father to..." She stalled again, and Erin wished badly she could shake her to keep her talking. Maybe that only worked in movies.

A horrible thought began to grow in Erin's mind. The money. The kidnapping. "You weren't really kidnapped, were you? It was Zach who came to get the money, wasn't it?"

Shelby Rae moaned.

"What did you do? Tell me!"

"You don't understand! Ever since the lawsuit started, your father hasn't been a real husband. He was so caught up in it. It was like he couldn't get enough of being at work, and of talking to the lawyers. It was like some kind of stupid war campaign. He was never home. He never wanted to take me anywhere or do anything because he said he was too distracted. What was I supposed to do? The stupid lawsuit wasn't the end of the world, but I couldn't make him see that. I couldn't make him see *me*."

"Tell me you didn't do what I think you did. Oh, my God, you're an adult! You're not a fifteen-year-old whose boyfriend is hanging out with his buds too much and wants payback. What is *wrong* with you? Daddy and I were afraid you were going to be killed!" Erin thought Shelby Rae would've been cried out by now, but her eyes filled again, and she began making a high keening sound.

"Please! Stop it. Stop it, now, Shelby Rae."

Shelby Rae eventually stopped crying and did her best to wipe her face on the shoulder of her peach-colored shirt. It was hot without air conditioning in the apartment, and her shirt already had patches of perspiration.

"I thought if Bruce saw he might lose me, he would get it. It wasn't like I gave him any reason to leave me. Ever! I was gone two nights, and he didn't even stay at home the whole afternoon after I got back. What does that tell you?"

"It tells me he was glad you were safe, and you may not know it but he left because Julie was trying to cause trouble for you and him. And don't tell me how broken up you were about the whole thing because you went to the stupid hairdresser after you woke up. I don't get you at all. Didn't it ever occur to you that Zach was way more of a stalker than a friend?"

Shelby Rae looked away. "What if he kills us? He's lost his mind."

Erin caught the change of subject, but, really, what other subject was there? If Zach killed them none of the other questions would matter a bit. He was some kind of obsessed psychopath. She hadn't paid enough attention when she and Noah had been there the night before. They'd done a great job of revealing information to a man who knew what was going on before they even got there. Is that why he'd turned on Shelby Rae? Maybe he thought she and Noah were getting too close, and that Shelby Rae was weak. The hoodie she'd seen hadn't seemed significant to her because she hadn't wanted to believe it was significant. So much simpler that way.

"Did you give him a hard time about killing Julie?"

"Of course I did. I didn't even want to see him again. But when I told him I was going up to French Lick to get away, he talked me into meeting him at the cabin so we could figure out what to say if the police somehow arrested *him* for it. That's where he told me he was framing Bruce for it, like I would think it was a good idea." Shelby Rae spoke angrily. "He broke every agreement we had. Fifty thousand dollars. It was all his, but he didn't even care about it. He wasn't supposed to do anything to you *or* your father."

"Shhh." Erin turned her face to the open window and whispered. "Listen." She could hear a car rumbling slowly over the gravel. It didn't sound like a truck. It sounded like her Challenger. Noah had been to the cabin and figured out where she was.

I CONFESS *I'm a bit wobbly getting out of Erin's car. Noah is a fine driver, but his urgency led him to drive like a maniac over the rough backroads between the cabin and here. Jocko is similarly unsettled. As soon as his feet hit the ground, he stumbled toward the brightest patch of grass he could find for a nibble to settle his stomach.*

Noah is remarkably sure-footed, despite his panic. On the way here, I believe he reached Erin's father on the phone and directed him to meet us. Even though I'm certain I can handle the situation, it will be good for Noah to have some support. Erin is surely here, and that deputy, Zach, is no doubt hiding nearby. The big, black truck belonging to him is nowhere to be seen, but I'm no gormless fool. Best to flush out the cad and deal with him immediately, lest he ambush the lot of us. But before I can lead Noah on a search of the farmhouse, Jocko begins to growl low in his throat.

"What is it?" *Noah crouches beside the dog, whose ears are alert and whose hackles are raised. He stares at the distant dilapidated barn. I give him a warning meow, but he doesn't even turn around. Stupid git. He and Noah will not be deterred, but start jogging toward the* barn. *Resolving that it's as good a place to start as any, I run ahead of them through the sparse grass.*

I don't enter through the main door with Noah and Jocko but slip in through a hole in the wall. The interior is dim and battered by years of hard farm use. Above is a series of lofts, some intact, others broken and sagging with age, and I leap from pillar to post until I reach one. But it's not hay I'm in search of.

Below, Jocko is busy sniffing the ground. Noah has found some-thing near the big doors—rounded shapes beneath giant black tarpau-lins. He pulls the tarpaulins back, revealing two vehicles: Shelby Rae's SUV and a small Mercedes I recognize as being Julie Berry's from when she visited Erin's house on Monday. Now my suspicions about the deputy are confirmed. He's involved in both Shelby Rae's earlier kidnapping and Julie Berry's murder. I'm relieved to see Noah is getting a leg up on things. He'll make a top-notch detective yet. I wonder if he's figured out that Shelby Rae is probably here as well. Her car may be hidden, but is she a captive, or is she an accomplice?

Leaving Noah to his investigation, I hurry to finish my explo-ration of the barn. It's large, and there are many places to hide—and hide captives. There's plenty of debris: plastic buckets, rusting tools, burlap, mouse-eaten bags, and more than one pile of metal pipes. I make my way down to the stalls and discover nothing except ancient hay, and a great, rotting rat in a trap with a blanket of fat, buzzing bottleflies hovering over it. The smell is beyond horrific, and I hurry away.

As I cross the barn, a slight vibration of the air teases my whiskers and I sense real danger nearby. Noah is leaning inside Shelby Rae's SUV, with Jocko at his feet. It will be one of the regrets of this life that neither my cry nor Jocko's alarmed barking alerts Noah in time.

Chief Deputy Wilkins slams the SUV's door against Noah's legs, causing him to shout out in pain. Stunned, Noah tries to right himself, but the man throws the door open again and hits poor Noah with a shovel on the back of the head. Noah slumps to the ground. As the brutal deputy pulls back the shovel like a cricket player readying himself for a second slog, Jocko flings himself at the man's ankles and sinks his tiny fangs in. At the same time, I launch myself at the deputy's back, my claws sinking into the skin beneath his T-shirt. He stumbles, screaming bloody murder, and I nimbly jump off, abandoning him to the tender mercies of the snarling Jocko. I reckon the tosser will be distracted enough to leave Noah alone for a while as he recovers himself. That is, if he can get away from the dog.

My mission now is to secure Erin's safety and stop Chief Deputy Wilkins.

The only sign of life in the ground floor of the deputy's house is the irate barking of what sounds like a very large canine that's running from room to room. It's only because I have superior hearing that I'm able to hear Erin's hoarse cries from the first floor above the din.

I zip up the outside stairs to discover that the window through which I entered the other evening is still open. I ease my way through the opening and Bob's your uncle, I'm inside.

"Trouble!"

Erin is on the floor, her feet and hands bound, leaning against a wall. Her face and neck glow with perspiration in the overly warm room, and there's an alarming purple bruise on the side of her face. But she's smiling, obviously chuffed to see me, and I leap gently onto her lap to touch my nose to her neck to comfort her. Surely the rotten deputy has done this to her. We shall have our revenge.

"I don't know why you're so happy." *The other human in the room is Shelby Rae, and she looks like a stretch of bad road. Her clothing is grubby and damp, her makeup melted.* "What good is a stupid cat going to do us?"

If I were a less dignified chap I would do something rude to indicate what a stupid cow I think she is, but that might embarrass Erin.

"I told you I heard my car. It's Noah. I'm sure it's Noah.

He found Trouble and Jocko at the cabin." *Erin addresses me.* "Is he out there? Can you get Noah to come up here?"

"You're crazy." *Shelby Rae sounds disgusted. Perhaps I can find a way to make sure Erin is rescued and she is not. Horrible woman.*

I can't produce Noah, and his survival depends on the passing seconds. The best I can do is find something to help release Erin from her bonds. I quickly examine the things around her wrist. As they're not metal, perhaps they can be cut.

"See? He's just messing around." *Shelby Rae scoffs like an old fishwife.* "Probably looking for food."

Doing my best to ignore the woman, I jump up and pad around the tables to look for scissors, a knife, anything sharp. I discover a cup full of pens and shiny objects.

"Is there a craft knife or something in there? I should've thought of it before." *Is Erin addressing me? No.* "Come on, Shelby Rae. What *is* there? We've got to get out of here before Zach comes back."

"I guess he does cut stuff up."

"Like the faces out of photographs? That's not creepy or anything." *Erin sounds angry.*

I knock the cup over and its contents spills onto the floor. In the midst is a shiny metal craft knife with a lid over the blade of the sort I've seen used for crafts at the Wetumpka Library. Voilà! Carefully, I pick it up in my mouth and, to cries of delight from Erin, carry it to her, setting it behind her back, within reach of her fingers.

"Erin, don't. You'll cut yourself!"

Erin ignores her stepmother.

"Trouble, you're brilliant." *With intense concentration, Erin feels along the knife's handle and carefully eases off the lid. Both Shelby Rae and I watch her, concerned, as she saws at the zip tie at her wrist. I have faith but Shelby Rae tells her again and again to be careful as though she thinks it's helpful.*

When I see Erin wince, I know she's cut herself, but she gives no other sign. Shelby Rae doesn't notice. Time passes slowly though it's only been a minute or two. We need to get to the barn and get the police, the real police, here quickly.

Erin gasps and brings the hand holding the knife in front of her. When she brings the other around, Shelby Rae sees that it's bloody and gives a little shriek.

"I'll live." Erin cuts the ropes from around her ankles and stands up shakily, holding onto the wall.

"Now me. Don't leave me here. Please don't leave me here." *Shelby Rae is whining, beyond undignified. I remember how she giggled as she talked on that phone in her closet, and it puts me in a right temper.*

Erin does the decent thing and frees Shelby Rae's hands without speaking. Then she and I clamber out the window beside the dead-bolted door, Shelby Rae calling after us as we fly down the stairs.

"Where's Noah?" *Erin asks me.*

Hoping she won't start yelling for Noah, I lead her to the barn. When we're within a dozen yards, I slow my approach, and she thankfully follows my cautious lead. I take her around the back to an opening I found that's well away from the main door.

After we enter the barn, Erin and I ease ourselves along the wall as far as we can. I expect Jocko to make an appearance, but the barn is eerily silent. I can see down to the end where Zach is silhouetted in the light from the big doorway. Behind me, Erin catches her breath, and I stop and look back at her. I can't have her throwing a spanner into the works now. Then she surprises me. Glancing around, she spies one of the longer bits of pipe lying about and stoops to grasp it, sliding it slowly toward her. What a grand girl she is.

Ahead, Zach bends to lift something from the ground. Gripping poor, unconscious Noah by the ankles, he pulls him along on his back. This will worry Erin, but I don't dare make eye contact with her. Not yet. Zach groans with the effort and moves stiffly. One of his blue jean legs is in shreds and dark with what must be blood. Good Jocko. But where is the dog?

When we're within a dozen feet, I stop and look back at Erin. Her face shines like that of a fair Celtic warrior. She's ready. When she meets my eyes, she raises the pipe and nods. Our feet are soundless as we cross the dusty, hay-strewn floor. Once again, I leap onto the deputy's back, but I don't stop there. Quickly, I claw my way to his front, and he hesitates a moment before he can fight me because his feet tangle over Noah's legs. We barely miss falling onto Noah. As I jump away, Erin is right there, bringing the heavy pipe down on the deputy's head.

"STAY ON THE GROUND. Don't move!" Erin's hands trembled the slightest bit where they met the pipe, but she knew she could hit Zach again if she had to. She might not have felt so brave if she couldn't hear sirens getting closer. It was almost over.

Zach slumped against a crate, intense pain evident in every small movement of his head. His voice was hoarse. "Don't worry, your boyfriend's not dead. Noah's like a son to me."

"You're sick. You're no better than his father."

"If I hadn't taken some care of him, he'd have turned out like his old man." He coughed, and tried to stand.

"Sit down!"

The sirens got louder and louder, then shut off one at a time. Erin heard tires skid to a stop on the gravel. Doors opened and slammed shut.

Zach chuckled. "Princess, I've got a gun on me. If I'd wanted you or the kid dead you'd be dead already. You have no idea."

He looked insane, laughing and bleeding, his face and neck

covered with deep cat scratches. *Where are Jocko and Trouble?* Erin was worried about the animals, but didn't want to take her eyes off of Zach.

"Zach, come on out!" Sheriff Bowen's voice boomed from a loudspeaker outside the barn. Erin's heart still pounded in her chest, but she also felt a huge wave of relief. She prayed an ambulance had come as well. Noah wasn't moving.

"She thought she could live without me, you know? But I knew she couldn't. I gave Shelby Rae *everything*. Even shot your mama so she could have your father because she wanted him so bad. It was like it was meant to be. One minute I was after that loser, Jeb Daly, and the next minute he was inches from your mother. The opportunity of a lifetime. Don't tell me anyone else could've done better for her." He gingerly started rise again, but this time she didn't stop him. "Now, move out of my way, Erin, so I can go out there."

I even shot your mother so she could have your father.

Erin couldn't speak.

"Cat got your tongue?" Zach looked serious for a moment, then began laughing at his own joke.

"You killed her. On purpose." Erin could barely get out the words, then they came in a rush. "You murdered my mother so Shelby Rae could marry my *father*?

"I said so, didn't I?"

"She put you up to it, didn't she? Of course she did." She felt her world crumbling all over again. Seven years of lies and pain and now the truth was even more painful than the lies had been.

Zach's face darkened and his words flew at her with flecks of spit. "Don't you *dare* talk about Shelby Rae like that, you stuck-up little *bitch*. I did it *for* her. She doesn't have to ask me for anything, because I know what she needs and I always have."

"She asked you to kidnap her, didn't she? You two are insane. And sick. You're murderers!"

"Stand aside, little girl. Or I'll change my mind about leaving you alive." Zach's voice was tight and controlled. "The sheriff out there has no goddamn patience and might shoot us both dead just to get it over with." He inclined his head toward Noah. "How much longer do you want him to wait?"

Later, she wouldn't remember moving aside for him or dropping the pipe, but only the barn filling with people in uniforms and a kind voice asking if she was all right.

ERIN WATCHED as the EMTs shifted Noah onto a backboard so they could transport him to the hospital. He hadn't regained consciousness, but from what she could tell from the EMTs talking to their radio, his vital signs were okay. She could hardly bear to look at his face, which was pinched with pain even though he was out cold.

Her father came to check on her and Noah, then went back outside to deal with Shelby Rae, who had been hysterical when he first arrived. Another set of EMTs was tending to her and Erin was sure that, by now, she'd been sedated. Erin learned from her father that he'd called the police the second Shelby Rae had called *him* from inside the house. She couldn't believe Shelby Rae hadn't bothered to call them herself. Then again, maybe she could.

The EMTs had Noah all ready to go, and Erin was following them out of the barn when Trouble stepped out of the shadows.

"There you are. Come here." When Erin tried to pick him

up, he dashed back into the shadows. He turned, and she saw his green eyes flicker. Jocko lay motionless on the ground at his feet.

"Oh, no." Erin rushed to the little dog, fell on her knees, and gently rested a hand on his side. *Still breathing, oh thank goodness.* "You're going to be okay, buddy. I promise you're going to be okay." She reached over and caressed Trouble. "Thank you." Then she called to the cop who was guarding the scene. "Could I get your help? My dog's been injured. Badly."

Together they shifted Jocko onto a board, much in the way the EMTs moved Noah, and carried him outside with Trouble close behind.

Erin called to her father who was standing near a blanket-wrapped Shelby Rae, looking half-angry, half-miserable. "We need to get Jocko to the vet's." Concern softened his face.

Shelby Rae wailed.

"He's breathing," Erin said.

"We'll take a look at him. Not supposed to, but what the hell. I've got dogs." The EMT with Shelby Rae walked over and took the board with Jocko on it, while Bruce held Shelby Rae's arm so she couldn't interfere. "Hey, Jamie," the EMT called.

Together the two male EMTs lifted the dog into the ambulance, where they could examine him.

Erin saw that Noah had been loaded into the second ambulance. The bands of the oxygen mask were strapped across the sides of his face, but she couldn't see much else. "Please, can I go with him?" she asked the female EMT who was about to close the door.

"You family?"

"No, but..."

Sheriff Bowen, overhearing, walked over. "Why don't you

stay here, Erin? We've called his mama, and she's on her way to the hospital. Noah's unconscious and wouldn't even know you were there. I promise you can go over later, all right?"

She was torn, but knew it made sense. Plus, she had Trouble and Jocko to watch out for. But she would get to the hospital the minute the animals were taken care of. Trouble sat at her feet. This time when she picked him up, he nuzzled into her arms.

Zach Wilkins stood against a police car, handcuffed, with another deputy and a state trooper guarding him. He was talking to a stone-faced deputy, smiling and laughing.

I even shot your mother so she could have your father. Murderer.

THREE HOURS LATER, Erin was standing at Noah's bedside. He'd just been moved from the emergency room and into a room of his own, but was still not awake. The scans had shown no serious internal damage to his brain, but his left femur was fractured because Zach had pushed him so hard against the SUV. Annette sat in a chair on the other side of the bed, holding her son's hand.

"Is Mr. Daly coming?" Erin felt shyer than she had the previous night at dinner.

Annette, who still wore her red polo shirt with the store's logo on it, shook her head. "I don't know if Noah told you—I probably shouldn't even tell you—but his father forced him to bring a package to him out at Honeysuckle Jamboree. We believe it had drugs in it."

Erin had heard of the place. In fact, her father had absolutely forbidden her going there as a teenager, even just to explore the empty grounds.

"Jeb got out of prison and from day one starting hanging

out with the wrong people again. He was carrying a gun, and you know it's against the law for him to even own one. Noah told me all about it last night after you left, and I called Sheriff Bowen this morning. They went out there to pick him up first thing. I gather the people out at the jamboree weren't happy to have the law pay them a visit."

"I'm sorry."

Annette's frown deepened. "It's no more than he deserves. I never was good at standing up to him, but he does *not* get to mess with my son. I hope they lock him up for good." She was quiet a moment, looking at Noah. They sat in silence until Annette turned, her friendly eyes resting on Erin. "What about you? You look tired, honey. And how are your dad and Shelby Rae?"

Erin felt embarrassed, and more than a little responsible for Noah's injury. If only she hadn't called him to tell him where she was going. Her father had said that Noah was simply in the wrong place at the wrong time.

"They're questioning Shelby Rae. I don't know that she did anything illegal. I mean, she got Zach to fake her kidnapping, but the ransom money was technically *her* money. It's complicated. Then Zach killed Julie Berry because he thought she told my dad that Shelby Rae and Zach were having an affair. Which apparently wasn't true. Zach was really weird about Shelby Rae, but she says they were never, you know, lovers. Honestly, I couldn't believe it when Zach really kidnapped her the second time. I mean, why would he do that?"

"It's like we never really knew Zach," Annette said, lowering her voice as though she didn't want Noah to hear. "I don't understand. He almost *killed* Noah. He was our friend. If he hadn't confessed, I never would've believed it."

"There's more, but I'm not sure I can even go into it right now. I'm sorry."

"Of course you are, sweetie." She reached over to squeeze Erin's hand. "Listen, will you sit here while I stretch my legs and grab a coffee? We can talk more when I get back, or talk tomorrow. I'm taking a few days off work."

"Sounds good." Erin tried to make her smile extra bright. None of this was Annette's fault. She and Noah had been dragged into this drama along with Erin and her father seven long years ago.

Erin moved the chair closer to Noah. He looked much more peaceful now that he was getting oxygen and lying comfortably. She wondered if it wasn't also due to his mother's presence, and the sound of her voice. Erin felt a little jealous of Noah, but reminded herself that nearly all of her memories of being with her mother and father were happy ones. She'd been so lucky.

Impulsively, she took Noah's hand. It was warm and dry.

Noah's breathing changed and became suddenly deeper. His face looked confused, and he fitfully turned his head from side to side. Finally, he relaxed some and opened his eyes. Erin knew she should run for a nurse, but she didn't want to let go of him. She waited until he figured out where he was. "Hey," she said.

Noah squeezed her hand. "It's you."

"It's me."

"How did we get here?" he asked.

Erin sighed. "It's kind of a long story. Everything's okay though. I promise. Your mom's here, and she'll be right back."

"So we're alone, like on a date. Which date would this be? Second? Third?"

"Let me see." Erin thought a minute. "Fourth, if you count

hanging out at the dock together. Fifth if you count us being together in the barn when I hit Zach over the head with a pipe so he wouldn't kill you."

"You did that?"

"Yep."

Noah closed his eyes, and his lips curved into a slight, satisfied smile. "You're one bad ass girlfriend. But maybe we could just go to a movie next time?"

oah had his arm around Erin's shoulders as they crossed the park's grassy hillside, and told himself it was only because he wanted to be close to her. The truth was that he was still a little unsteady from his head injury. Fortunately, the pain had dulled to a shadow with the help of continuous ibuprofen, because there was no way he was going to miss watching *these* fireworks with her. The Rotary Club always did a great display, and he was anxious to make new memories with Erin.

His mother followed a few steps behind. She'd been quiet throughout dinner at the house, where Noah had grilled brats and served them with sauerkraut, which Erin had never had before. There was apple pie and a Thermos of coffee in the basket his mother carried.

Noah had been stunned and proud to learn that his mother had called the sheriff and parole officer on his father. She showed the parole officer the two ounces of pot and five thousand dollars in cash her husband had stashed in the crawlspace. After he was picked up at the jamboree, he was only too eager to snitch on the prison counselor who was going to handle selling the drugs on the inside. It made Noah sick to think of what a stupid ass his father was.

"Let's put our blanket over there." Erin pointed to a small rise.

"Too bad we couldn't bring Trouble and Jocko," Noah said. "It's like half our team isn't here. But I guess you never know how animals are going to react to fireworks."

"Tammy Lynn will be back for Trouble tomorrow night. She's going to stay over, then head back home. I'd love for you both to meet her, except things are pretty weird at the house right now." Erin shook out a plaid blanket and straightened it over the grass. "Dad hired a lawyer for Shelby Rae, even though she's not charged with anything right now. Zach hasn't said she was involved in Julie's murder. My dad says he'll probably be locked up in a mental institution because he's insane."

"Your dad's a good man." Noah's mother knelt on the blanket and opened the basket. Noah had smelled the pie baking that morning and had barely been able to stay out of it as it cooled.

"I don't know what's going to happen with him and Shelby Rae. She cries a lot, but he's sleeping in a guest room and disappears to the office first thing in the morning. He may even be there right now."

Darkness fell quickly. Noah's mother set the small camp chair she'd brought a couple feet above the blanket, leaving Noah and Erin alone to watch the fireworks together.

"How's your head?" Erin gently stroked Noah's hair.

"It's good. Really good."

Erin took her hand away and smiled.

"Oh, no you don't. If you're going to stop doing that, then I'm going to tell you for the next year that it feels like hell, so you won't stop." Taking her hand, he placed it comically back on top of his head.

They both laughed. She did continue stroking his hair, and he rested his hand on her knee as though it were the most natural thing in the world.

When the fireworks began, they watched in awe as the colors exploded against the clear July sky. Noah couldn't remember ever being so happy, and he was already beginning to think what it would be like when she went back to school. He was eager to make plans to get into school himself, even if it meant working two jobs while he was there. UK had a great design and architecture school. Or maybe he could go to Cincinnati. It wasn't far from Lexington. He didn't want to be far from Erin, ever again.

Erin squeezed his hand. "Let's make sure we come back right to this spot next year. It's perfect." She rested her head on his shoulder.

It was as if she'd been reading his mind. "Definitely." He kissed the top of her head, and she looked up at him and smiled, the bright stars of fireworks stars reflected in her eyes.

Now that all is tickety-boo with Jocko after his mishap with that cretin Zach Wilkins, he's almost back to his annoying self. But his furry brow is furrowed wherever he goes. His human has closed him out of her boudoir, where she now spends most of her days and nights, weeping or moaning for someone to pay attention to her. What little dignity the woman had has fled. Her attire has gone beyond dishabille to downright demented. Nothing she puts on matches up and her hair has lost its silky blonde luster and shows a dark strip of brown at the part. If only I could tell her myself that I spotted several strands of gray yesterday when she swooped down *and picked up a startled Jocko and carried him down to the kitchen with her.*

"When is this stupid cat leaving?" *she shouted. No one answered because everyone had left the house to get away from her.*

I wonder what will happen to Shelby Rae? I can't see Erin and her father putting up with her behavior forever. Maybe they will simply find new digs and leave her behind. They would certainly be welcome in Wetumpka. Shelby Rae would not.

Today everyone is home. Erin is in the kitchen cooking up a meal of fried chicken, cornbread, and fresh asparagus. She's telling everyone it's because my beloved human, Tammy Lynn, is on her way back to fetch me, but I believe she is hoping to impress Noah, who is also invited to dinner.

Did I mention Tammy Lynn is on her way back from Italy to take me home to Wetumpka? Did I mention I'm eager to go?

As I stroll through the house, I confess to feeling a bit of nostalgia for the place: for the walks by the lake, and the excellent bits of food shared by Erin and her father. That Bruce is such a noble chap. Overhead, I can hear Jocko whining at his human's door. While I will admit to having become slightly fond of Jocko, I despair of his taste in mistresses.

Bruce is in his office. The door is open just enough for me to slip inside. Wait. How have I missed knowing Noah already arrived and is inside the office as well? Neither of them notices me as I settle beneath a table.

Noah leans forward in one of the overstuffed leather chairs. His hands are clasped together, and I sense he's nervous. "Remember that day I met my father out at Honeysuckle Jamboree, where the white supremacists were meeting?"

Bruce interrupts. "Damned shame. I hope there wasn't anyone we know there. You never think something like that will happen in your town."

"It's pretty far out of town, and to be fair there were license plates from all over. But I did see someone I knew there, besides my father. I didn't want to look too hard, you know? But as I was leaving, I saw Earl Potts about to go in. I recognized his truck, and he was behind the wheel."

"Earl?" *Bruce's voice is full of surprise, as well it might be.* "I've known Earl for years. He's never expressed any of those kinds of opinions that I know of. Are you certain? I know you weren't in the happiest frame of mind yourself."

"I'm very sure, sir." *Noah says.* "But it made me think. About Tionna Owens."

"Now, wait a minute, son. Let's be careful here."

"Mr. Walsh, I might be wrong, but it's been bugging me since that day. I checked our records on Tionna's car. Earl put Andrew on her brake job the last time it was in. Andrew's a good guy, and he went to tech school, but he doesn't have much experience working solo except doing simple oil changes and rotations."

I admire Noah's earnestness, and his sense of deduction. Obviously he's learned much from observing me in action.

"And?"

Noah lowers his voice. "What if Earl put Andrew to work on her car on purpose, because he didn't want someone who would do a good job? What if he actually turned her away the day she died because he either didn't want to help her or—"

Bruce interrupts again, sounding gobsmacked. "You think he was hoping her brakes would fail and she would die? Because of her skin color or her lifestyle? Good God, that would make him a monster."

By the time Erin comes knocking politely on the door, Bruce and Noah have come to an understanding. Bruce will investigate Earl's actions further, and make overtures to Bryn if he finds their suspicions are true. Not to mention he will make sure Earl is prosecuted if possible, and, if not, loses his job and becomes unwelcome in any garage or dealership in the country.

I follow them out of the room, glad there will be some kind of resolution for Bryn and Tionna, though they may never have real justice. No action can make up for someone we love being taken away from us.

While I would prefer to wait in the library window awaiting Tammy Lynn's arrival, I allow Erin to pick me up. She calls for Jocko, and he readily gambols down the stairs, tongue flapping, as though he hasn't spent the last two hours whining outside Shelby Rae's door. Noah joins the three of us as we traipse down the path to the dock closest to the house, not the one where I found Julie Berry. He carries two proper rods and reels. They're nothing like the collapsible bendy thingy he usually uses.

I relax in a spot of sun on the dock, watching the insects on the water or napping. Jocko dashes up and down the dock for a while, occasionally barking at nothing as though he's lost the plot, poor sod. Finally, he settles in the shade on the bank.

To my surprise, Noah and Erin catch a pair of striped bass despite engaging in plenty of kissing and cuddling as they fish. We return to the house just as Tammy Lynn pulls in the driveway, and while I pride myself on not displaying undignified demonstrations of affection, I make sure she knows I'm quite chuffed to see her.

We enjoy a delightful evening. While everyone else is on the patio having drinks, I discover Shelby Rae in the kitchen filling a plate with chicken, cornbread, and chocolate chip cookies. She snags a bottle of wine, too, to take back to her room, thus depriving us of her company. As she leaves the kitchen, she spies me in a corner observing her. Her eyes narrow and she makes a noise that's a sad cross between a meow and a hiss. I will not be provoked, and only blink. Perhaps I'll leave a special gift for her in one of her sheepskin mule slippers tonight.

Noah's mother has come for dinner, and she looks much less weary and overworked than she did the first time I saw her. Erin and Noah are rather sweet with her, and when Bruce announces that he's arranged with his accountant to pay any bills Noah incurs to earn his undergraduate degree, to thank him for all he's done, she bursts into happy tears that give her the hiccups. Everyone laughs.

Bruce does not forget my contribution. He tells Tammy Lynn he will donate five thousand dollars to the Wetumpka animal charity of her choice because of my fine detective skills. The assembled humans toast my success, but I pretend not to notice as I enjoy my fine dinner of asparagus tips and fresh grilled bass.

TROUBLE'S DOUBLE CONTEST WINNER
Black Velvet Elvis

This is Black Velvet Elvis, so named because I flippantly remarked that he was so black and velvety someone should paint a picture of Elvis on his side, and it just stuck. And the name suited him. He thought he was The King of Rock and Roll and Everything Else. He showed up one day when I was working in the yard... he didn't just wander across the lawn or out of the bushes, he came walking down the street and turned into our driveway like he lived here. Turns out he was right.

I was pulling weeds in the flower bed when I noticed a quick movement out of the corner of my eye. I looked up just in time to see a black cat trot down the street and turn in to my driveway like he belonged here. He came straight to me, wound himself around my ankles, and refused to leave.

Of course for the kids it was love at first sight, but I said, "No, don't feed him. He's so friendly he must be someone's pet. Leave him alone and he'll go home." The next day he was still on our porch so I gave him some water, not because I wanted him to stay, but because that's just the humane thing to do. Day three I caved and fed him.

When it became obvious no one was looking for him, I started casting about, asking friends if they knew anyone who wanted a cat. We already had three cats, a dog, and an assortment of fish, birds, and rabbits. Our space and budget were stretched to their limits, and I was firmly convinced that there was no more room at the inn. Unfortunately, everyone we knew who wanted another pet was looking for a kitten. No one wanted a half-grown black cat.

My next strategy was to get him vetted. I reasoned that it would be easier to find someone to take him if he was neutered, tested for diseases, and vaccinated. I dutifully schlepped him to a mobile spay/neuter clinic and got all the necessary bloodwork, shots, and procedures. When we arrived home, I intended to release him and keep an eye on him, but my husband said we couldn't possibly make him stay outside after he had surgery. "Why not?" I asked. "They do it with feral cats all the time. He'll be fine." But no, Dan insisted that we bring him in to recover indoors. Little did I know that "recover" was code for "stay forever."

It was around this time that I idly commented that he was so glossy his fur looked like velvet. He was sleek and shiny with not a speck of any color but black. "Someone should paint a picture of Elvis on his side'" I remarked, and to my everlasting regret everyone started calling him Black Velvet Elvis. He was clever, energetic, and endlessly mischievous, and spent his days alternately terrorizing and charming every member of our household.

We had no idea how long Elvis had been wandering before he found us, but as with any pet of unknown provenance, he had some definite quirks. The first and most obvious was that he clearly had no idea where his next meal was coming from, or even if there would be a next meal. He ate anything and everything he could get his paws on. He ate his food, the other cats' food, the dog's food, and anything left unguarded. Some of his more memorable meals in those early days were a baked potato, a peanut butter sandwich, and an entire chocolate Easter bunny. Once, he came within a whisker of scoring an entire steak that some inattentive person left dangling on the end of a fork, inspiring Black Velvet Elvis to launch himself across the room like a rocket. It was both impressive and scary.

Eventually his food anxiety subsided, but his dislike of men did not. This was unfortunate for Dan, who was the real cat lover among us and who was largely responsible for Elvis's permanent residency in our house. He was never overly affectionate to anyone, but he was especially leery of men.

The reasons didn't bear thinking about.

He never completely adapted to life indoors, and would watch and wait for someone to open the door a fraction too wide so he could seize his chance and bolt. He led us on many a merry chase when he heard the call of the wild.

He also hated riding in the car. Vet visits in particular were a torment for everyone involved. One year in early December on a routine trip for vaccines, as his carrier was lifted out of the car he flung himself against the inside so hard that the door broke off and Elvis bolted into the woods behind the vet's office.

The weeks that followed found us spending every free moment tramping through the woods, canvassing nearby neighborhoods, putting out hundreds of flyers, and calling every vet, rescue, and pound for miles in every direction. No sign of Black Velvet Elvis. Dan spent as much time as any of us on the search, but given Elvis's mistrust of men I doubted whether the cat would come to him even if he found him.

A few days before Christmas, with hope dwindling and a winter storm bearing down on us, Dan and our daughter decided to make one more last-ditch effort to find him. In the cold and dark they drove streets and alleys we'd driven a hundred times already. Just as they were about to pack it in, on impulse they turned down the alley behind a grocery store one more time. A kind person we'd asked about Elvis had offered that stray cats often hung around there because they could smell food in the dumpsters. As they reached the end of the alley, a shadow flitted across the road and disappeared under a parked trailer. Amanda was out of the car before it stopped moving, the headlights illuminating a crouching black outline. For a heart stopping moment she thought he was going to run, but she called his name and as soon as he heard her voice, this unaffectionate, unpredictable cat launched himself into her arms.

Elvis returned to us a changed cat. Our sleek and fit little panther was thin and bedraggled to the extent that I wouldn't have been sure it was him if he hadn't still been wearing his collar. The changes weren't just physical, though. Apparently his walk on the wild side convinced him that our house wasn't such a bad place at all. Oh, he still heard the call of the wild once in a while and had many more outdoor adventures in our neighborhood, but by and large he was much calmer and more affectionate. And our other Christmas miracle? He abruptly decided Dan was all right after all. His suspicion of men disappeared entirely and for the next nine years he entertained, tormented, and charmed everyone who entered our home.

The first sign that something was amiss was when his coat lost its black velvet luster. I immediately took him to the vet, and although she was tactful, I'm sure she thought I was overreacting. I mean, who pays for a vet visit for a cat whose only symptom is that he's not shiny enough? But over the next two weeks, in spite of a battery of tests that revealed nothing, he declined so alarmingly that by process of elimination we concluded that he was suffering from a brain tumor.

We buried Black Velvet Elvis in the flower bed, in the exact spot where I was standing when he first strutted down the driveway like he belonged here. Because, as it turned out, he did.

— KATHY JONES PILLATZKI

CPSIA information can be obtained
at www.ICGtesting.com
Printed in the USA
BVHW041515280623
666441BV00004B/962

9 780966 395471